One

"Mmmm...nurses."

Danny started to come round. First the lights and then the nurses. Lots of them. Then the pain, just one of those. He couldn't remember anything having exploded up his nose but that was what it felt like. He brought his hand up to check what had happened and winced on contact.

"I wouldn't be touching that for now" a nurse said to him, not for the first time.

"What happened to me?"

"You don't remember?"

"Well, no, not really, I was, eh, moving house and then the bath and the ceiling, the CEILING!"

It all came back. With a bang. Another one.

06:30am. Laxmi started the laborious process of escaping from his house. He had a good process now and could almost do it with his eyes shut. The chains, the bolts then the set of three locks. The ones you always saw in American apartments on TV. He opened the inner door and then repeated the process on the storm doors. Finally, he removed the bar spanning the two doors and peered anxiously through the peephole. Nothing. He put his ear to the door and listened, his shivering hand reaching for the handle. Looking back to Shazia, he gave the signal and flung himself out the door. The sound of all the locks being reapplied echoed down the close as he bounded down the stairs, his heart leaping.

Arriving at the bottom, he sped quickly out into the street, turned and sprinted the 3 yards to the shop door. Outside the shop he felt unprotected, hair standing up on the back of his neck. There was a strange tingling sensation in his arse like there was a gun aimed at it. Again, almost on automatic, he started escaping into his shop.

His heart beat loudly in his ears as he fumbled his way through the multitude of locks and bolts and then finally, with a hurried lurch, pushed open the door. He turned quickly and shut it behind him. The regular beeping echoed the pounding in his chest as he, almost frenetically, rushed to switch off the alarm, knocking over a peanut display on the way.

He went back to the door and slid across the large bolt on the inside and, with that, his heart began to slow to a healthier pace.

"Result!" he said, punching the air, "only 90 minutes to wait and then I can open up!"

He sat down behind the till and watched the sombre, early morning world trickle past the window, slightly obscured by messy, white writing telling of cheap strawberries.

*

07:55am. On the first floor above the shop, Mrs Isobel Moyes, already dressed and in her coat, picked up her handbag and turns towards the door. She opened and closed it silently and made her way downstairs. Outside Laxmi's shop a single newspaper lay on the mat. With a small wave inside, she picked it up, turned and shuffled back upstairs, her head bowed.

Back inside, she sat down at the table by the window, the paper placed squarely in front of her. The pot of tea, which she had prepared before going downstairs, is now ready and she poured a cup, no milk, no sugar. She takes a sip and begins to read.

By 08:30am she has read the entire paper, even the sport. She didn't always read the sport but she couldn't be sure, so had started. Closing the paper, she folded it gently and placed it on the pile that stood against the opposite wall.

"273" she said. Her first daily ritual complete, she picked up her bag again, walked back out into the close and headed for work. By 09:00am she will have sold her first pie and her second ritual will have begun.

*

It wasn't really ability that got Danny through life. He wasn't daft but neither was he all that clever. He bumbled through school on no wings and several prayers and carried his good fortune through a law degree at University. He was fly; he could talk. His unlikely academic success came a very close second in the surprising stakes to his success with women or "the ladies" as he would say. Not classically pretty, not rugged yet not ugly, he was most often uselessly described as "interesting looking" by those who felt it necessary to express an opinion. Most often perplexed but unashamed young ladies when responding to the question "What did you see in him?" He was certainly more Robin Williams than Marlon Brando on the looks front and as it happens, when it came to talking too. Danny was all about mouth. It got him into trouble and it got him out of it again. Repeat for beds, bras and panties. He loved the ladies

2

Scott M. Liddell

THE BEATLE MAN

▶ Closed Loop Publishing ◀

A catalogue record for this book is available from the British Library.

ISBN 978-0-9556830-0-8

www.thebeatleman.com

Thanks to:

John Bankier for the opening line.

Doug Mair for his generous help and support, without which I would never have got this far.

Stuart Douglas for his constant encouragement.

My darling wife Jeanne for her help, support and patience.

For everyone who won't be able to read this. We know who they are.

and the ladies loved him, the difference being that he didn't love them long enough to actually love them.

So many hearts were broken when we talked his way into a job in Glasgow. He had studied law only because, in his words, "did you see Al Pacino in …And Justice For All? How cool was that?" It was the only answer he ever gave. Probably because it was the only one he had, the truth. Danny didn't choose his destination; he only ever chose to leave.

Several rungs down from defending a Judge lay the job of Trainee Conveyancing Solicitor. Certainly not 'cool' but definitely in Glasgow and definitely right in the middle of 'manto central'. And he'd have money, the best manto-magnet. Therefore his joy was unsurpassed when his firm told him that he would be able to rent a flat that they dealt with back in the West End, his hunting ground, the buffalo filled plain, the pampas, student country, Mantosville, Arizona. And it wasn't at home.

He got into the car and headed for the motorway.

"Ya dancer!"

Danny's joy on the motorway didn't last as far as track 7 of Pet Sounds. His specially chosen soundtrack for the opening credits of his career was about to get interrupted. Approaching the outskirts of Glasgow, the large illuminated sign crossing the carriageway said 'Traffic Slow for 5 Miles'. Caroline No.

"Cars in Line No!" he said to himself, smirking at his cleverness. The smirk didn't last.

"Shit bugger bollocks!"

He was going to be late for work. His first day and he was going to turn up late.

"Shit kicking fanny pads!"

He contemplated a dastardly move to the Riddrie turn off and through to the City Centre.

"No will else will have thought of it" he thought and gave out a little Muttley.

By the time he reached the bottom of the hill he realised his decision was much more Captain Caveman than Prof. Pat Pending.

"Keek bum toley fart!"

He wasn't finished.

"Arse, arse, arse, arse, ARSE!!!!"

He made it to the car park at 09:30am and, sprinting like a bastard, arrived at the office only 45 minutes late.

"Hi, I'm…" Puff. Pech. "…I'm Danny McColl…I, eh start here today, I've to ask for…" Puff. Pech. "…for Mr. McWilliams."

The receptionist gave him a look that suggested he looked as sweaty as he felt. She slowly and deliberately flicked through a book on her desk. After she had let Danny suffer enough, she looked up and said "Mr. McWilliams doesn't get in until 10:00am on a Monday. Please take a seat and someone will be with you shortly."

Danny looked quizzically at first, wondering what, if any, of that information she had gleaned from her leisurely flick through the doubtless irrelevant desk diary. She sensed his bemusement.

"Please. Take a seat."

"Yeah, eh, yeah, OK"

"Stuck up cow'" thought Danny, she'd get it, not because she was good looking or anything, just because she deserved it.

11:15am. Arthur McWilliams breezed into the office like someone who had spent the weekend in a cabin cruiser on Loch Lomond attempting to shag the pants off a croupier from a City Centre Casino. It was rarely true these days, but that was always the line. He saw Danny and, like all successful men, not only instantly recognised him but also knew exactly what to do to make himself look extremely impressive.

"Danny, Danny, Danny, my boy, come with me. Ms. Hamilton, hold all my calls until 12:30, no, make it 2, Danny and I are off for a spot of lunch."

Ms. Hamilton nodded obediently and, as Arthur swept Danny briskly from the office, her professional air slipped and she was heard to let out a 'wank'.

Being the senior partner in a successful law firm had a number of major advantages. Quite apart from having several different houses to hide in when your marriage goes a bit wrong, you also had lots of time, lots of money and the requirement to do very little work.

"Don't get me wrong" he told Danny "I've worked hard, damn hard, but I think that gives me the right to a little, shall we say, leeway, in my approach. Got to leave some room for Arthur McWilliams."

Danny nodded vigorously through bleary eyes. It was too early, even for him, for beer. It was definitely too early for whisky. He would need to work hard at this lawyer lark. A large platter of shellfish appeared on the table. Danny recognised some large prawns and mussels. The rest he thought he had seen before but only with a David Attenborough voice-over or attached to the face of the Predator.

"Aaaah, langoustines, fruit de mer!" said Arthur with gusto. With a loud crack, he ripped the recently boiled animal open and devoured the flesh. A few pieces fell from his mouth and rested on his large paunch.

"Not so fast fishy, you have to go in there via the mouth!"

Arthur's laugh was as loud as it was enthusiastic. It was the kind of laugh you only ever wanted to hear from someone else's table. Danny looked around sheepishly but no one had even looked up.

"Tuck in boy, tuck in and we'll get down to business."

Danny tucked. The food had all the fiddly fun of an over-filled kebab but none of the bulk. Minutes of wrangling with some of these little shits only ever resulted a very small piece of vaguely edible stuff. By the end, the platter looked like the aftermath of a Ninja attack on Sea World. Danny was still hungry and it hadn't taken the edge of the whisky at all.

"OK, to business. Waiter, two ports, better make it large ones, oh and bring the cheeses."

4

He let out a huge burp. Again, no one looked up.

"Danny, good to have you on board, I can see it in your eyes, you've got what it takes. But, and here's the bit, prove to me you've got what it takes and one day you'll be a flatulent fat bastard like me, if you fuck up, then you'll be the one getting the cheeses. Get it?"

"Eh...yes sir."

"Sir! Don't call me Sir! Have I been knighted? No, my name is Arthur."

Danny looked up. The whisky coursed through his veins. He was Danny, Danny McColl. Time to start acting like it.

"I get it Arthur, you big, fat, flatulent bastard."

"Danny, my boy, I like your style, I think we're going to get on just fine."

Arthur told Danny about the job. He told him what he would have to do. It took a while. Danny could have summarised it all with the phrase "do exactly what the fuck I tell you". But Arthur dragged it out through a couple more ports and several more whiskies. The cheese, at least, had some bulk and took the edge a little from the alcohol. Enough for Danny to take in the bit about where he would be staying and how there was "a little trouble selling the place". But it was a "prime location" and would be available to him for a "nominal fee". This was all music to Danny ears, although the bass was starting to get a little loud.

They returned to the office. Arthur had drunk enough to floor the remaining world population of white rhinoceros. He breezed back in just as he had done earlier.

"Ms. Hamilton, give Danny the keys of the flat and phone him a taxi. Any messages?"

She gave Arthur the messages and he wandered into his office, presumably to have a sleep. The keys came from a desk drawer.

"Thanks doll face," said Danny, now lording it as the drinking partner of the boss.

"Don't mention it", she said. If Danny hadn't been so pissed he would have noticed that she said this with unexpected and apparently genuine pleasure. Not the effect he was aiming for at all.

"When the taxi comes give him this address and sign the slip when he gives it to you, it's paid on account."

"Account! Account!'" repeated Danny, gradually taking the 'o' out of the word for comic effect.

"Yes'" she interjected "you are. Can I suggest you make it here at 09:00am sharp tomorrow?"

Danny fell into the back of the taxi. Just before he left he had remembered that all his bags were in the car in the car park. Ms. Hamilton, 'Jenny, lovely, lovely Jenny' said she would arrange for them to be taxied out to the flat. He handed the driver the address and slumped back.

The taxi lurched and rolled its way through the City Centre traffic. The afternoon sun burned through Danny's eyes. The seafood danced the Highland fling as it mixed with the Islay Malts. Danny began to feel very sick. His lunch, both liquid and solid, stayed in place and the taxi pulled up and the flat. The red sandstone reflected the light like an Arizona sunset.

The taxi driver offered a slip to sign. Danny threw up all over the slip and most of the taxi driver's arm.

"Jesus fuck!" the taxi driver jumped back and almost fell into the road.

Danny muttered a sentence that allegedly contained the words "dry cleaning" and "account". The taxi driver apparently got the meaning.

"Too fuckin' right." He took off his jacket and threw it on the floor of the cab. He jumped in and sped away with as much wheel spin as his diesel engine could muster.

The puke was as much necessary as it would have been tactically essential for a 9am start. He staggered into the close, the cool air and dim light helping him to regain a few of the more vital senses.

*

Laxmi had watched the whole kerbside event from behind his shop window. At first it had been amusing. He had seen the bags arrive on their own and now the young man that was following him. He was moving in and the only empty flat was across from him.

"Oh no, not another one" he said out loud.

"Sorry?"

"Eh, sorry that's £3.95."

The customer left and remained confused right until they walked into a large puddle of sick, largely comprising parts of small, fleshy invertebrates.

*

There were two keys and two locks. It should only take, at most, three attempts to unlock both locks. As he approached double figures, Danny was starting to get slightly pissed off. After the fourth or fifth attempt the need to pee had become too great and he had decided just to wet himself. What the hell, he hadn't escaped the puke either.

The door finally gave in, opened and Danny staggered in. Only then did he notice his bags that had made it there before him. He left them at the door. He needed to prioritise. He needed to suss the place out; he needed to change. He needed to sober up. On balance, Danny decided the best thing to do was to have a sleep and sort the rest out later. He couldn't get into bed without stripping off so, to avoid this hassle, he decided to have a quick sleep in the bath.

He got in and was asleep almost instantly. The excitement of the day had clearly got to him. He dreamt crazy dreams. He dreamt of cabin cruisers and croupiers, of the playboy life and limitless success. He didn't dream of lying in a bath fully clothed in his only suit covered in, and presumably smelling of, puke and piss.

He certainly didn't dream of the ceiling coming down on his head. Luckily, the water came through first. Like a cold wave waking you on a sun-drenched beach, a waterfall of cold water crashed down on Danny from a steadily growing hole in the ceiling. He awoke instantly but had several moments of panic where he failed to answer the questions (in no particular order) Where am I? Why am I in a bath fully clothed? What is that awful smell?

He made it out of the bath just in time to avoid the large chunk of ceiling that soon collapsed into the wake of the water.

"Fuck, fuck, fuck, fuck!" He was awake now, he remembered where he was, he remembered what had happened and he remembered that no cunt drops a ceiling on Danny McColl's head without getting a flea in their ear.

He picked up his keys and marched purposefully up to the floor above. What he saw he didn't at all expect. At the top of the next set of stairs should have been a landing from where you could access the two doors of the top floor flats. Instead, the stairs terminated against a large, wooden wall, crudely painted and containing a single door, hanging loosely on its hinges. Across the wall in large letters were the words "Finches Ya Bas".

Danny approached the door and knocked. It was made of very thin plywood and his knock hardly made a sound. No one came. Already incensed and getting more irritated with each passing moment, he knocked harder. Still no answer. Eventually, he had had enough and screamed, "What cunt brought my ceiling down?"

A moment passed and suddenly the door opened.

*

"…and the next thing I remember was waking up here."

"Well, don't you worry, let's start by getting you out of these clothes. Whatever happened to you, it looks like they did a bit more than just hit you."

Danny thought about explaining. But she was a nurse, she was cute and whatever chances he had with her probably hinged on her not knowing that the puke and piss were his.

Two

The morning rain softened the edges of the crisp white footprints that led out to the graveside. A henge of dark coats stood hunched and inanimate, backs turned against the cold wind. Wiping the condensation from the car window, Danny peered through the rusting cemetery gates. He watched as the coffin slid slowly underground. After a few minutes of lifeless vigil, the bodies turned from the grave and stumbled back across the expanse of snow-covered grass and kicked-down headstones. Funnelling towards the gate, the walk got easier as they found the firmness of the path somewhere beneath their feet. The gate creaked open and was held back to let Danny's Mum leave first. Her face pale, she got in, gathering her coat as she swung her legs round. Danny started the car engine and drove off without a word, tyres spinning in the melting brown slush.

Overnight rain had washed the sick away. Laxmi had lost a number of potential customers because of it but didn't risk clearing it up himself. It was Tuesday so he expected Mrs. Moyes a little earlier. She came down on the stroke of eight and he let her into the shop.

"Good morning Mrs. Moyes."

"Thank you Laxmi, could I get an extra box of teabags this week, I've been drinking a lot recently."

Laxmi walked down the centre aisle of the shop and added the teabags to the rest of Mrs. Moyes' pre-prepared shopping.

"Did you see I have a new neighbour? Looks like another lawyer boy."

"Another one? Will they never learn?"

"Apparently not. I haven't seen him yet this morning. Then again, the state he was in when he arrived yesterday afternoon, I'm not surprised."

Mrs. Moyes picked up her shopping and busily left the shop leaving the usual money for Laxmi plus a little extra for the teabags. Upstairs she put the shopping away hurriedly and scanned the paper quickly. No tea on a Tuesday.

"274."

Laxmi scanned the street closely, as he did every Tuesday. Right on time at nine o'clock the mini bus pulled up at the door of the close. Seconds later he appeared, smartly dressed as usual, the sun catching his small round glasses. Laxmi squinted through his traffic-dirty windows.

"Mean Mr. Mustard" said Laxmi.

"I really should stop talking to myself. I could end up like him."

*

No one ever considers what happens to a square peg if you, by brute force or ignorance, manage to get it into a round hole. This occurred to Arthur as he woke up with his barrel-like frame crushed into the pint-sized bed on his boat. It was only a feat of human origami that got him into the bed at all and only a bottle of whisky that enabled him to get any sleep. It was only his fear of sleeping alone that kept him out of the much larger double bed at the stern.

The scene outside the window was painfully idyllic. A calm Loch with a clear view to Ben Lomond in the distance. The low sun reflecting off the water, shooting knitting needle-like into the back of his reddened whisky eyes.

He slowly unfolded. Every joint wailing for WD40, every sinew screaming the name of a reputable mattress manufacturer. This was the body of a broken man misrepresenting the life of a successful one. A large glass of water followed by a coffee and the suggestion of a shower and he was at the mirror a little nearer to human. And yet, the mirror was still not kind.

Three months ago, Arthur's wife had thrown him out of their house. A relationship spanning decades all but ended by the temptations of a man with a large wallet and a small, wandering penis. It had seemed like a good idea at the time, a number of times, but now, this fat, red-nosed excuse for a man had to finally wake up to where he should be waking up. Not crammed on a boat like a tramp in a doorway. But at home, with the woman he had spent his life with. If she would have him.

*

At 10:00am the next morning, Jenny Hamilton started to fear the worst. Danny may have been a loathsome little scrote but not coming into work on time could only mean one thing. She had phoned the flat and there was no answer. She couldn't leave it any longer.

"Yes Jenny?"

Arthur McWilliams sat behind a large wood and leather desk. He hadn't been able to hide the can of Irn Bru when Jenny entered.

"It's Danny, he hasn't appeared this morning."

"Hasn't appeared? What do you mean?"

"I mean, he's not here and I've phoned the flat and there is no answer."

"Shit. OK, you'd better phone the hospitals. Damn stupid bastards, they promised me, they bloody promised. Keep me informed Jenny, Thanks."

It didn't take long to track Danny down. He had been kept in over night for observation as he had a slight concussion from a 'severe blow to the nose'. He would need some clean clothes before he could be discharged as the ones he was wearing were covered in 'fluids of unknown origin'.

Jenny's face screwed up "Jesus, they've really gone to town this time."

Jenny scribbled down the ward number and headed for Arthur's office. She stopped for a drink of water from the dispenser. She put her cup underneath and it filled as a large bubble rose in the tank above. The words 'fluids of unknown origin' went through her head. She had another glass. She'd leave that bit out. He had Irn Bru; it wouldn't be fair.

She entered. Arthur was on the phone. She turned to leave but he beckoned her silently to stay.

"Look, I'm sorry, I'm sorry, how many more times to I have to say it? Look I gotta go, and if you can get me those notes by the end of the week then that would be great."

Jenny knew what Arthur was trying to hide; he didn't need the attempt to disguise the content.

"Sorry about that, so?"

"So, he's in hospital, blow to the head, concussion."

"Did they say how?"

"Well, they couldn't be sure, but it looks like a head-butt."

"Bollocks."

"They didn't mention them."

Arthur looked up with a "please, not now" kind of look.

"Do you want me to go and get him?"

"No, I'd better go. Look, send Malky round to the flat and see what the story is. Tell him no hassle and if he sees any of those Finch bastards tell them their money is in serious jeopardy."

"He's already on his way, I have a feeling that Danny might not be seeing his notes that I sent round there last night."

"Jenny, what would I do without you?"

Jenny wanted to say 'get caught with your pants down' but didn't. He wasn't a bad guy to work for. It was a shame he was such a letch. A fact that won't be lost on the nurses he was no doubt about try to impress with the old 'cabin-cruiser' routine.

*

"Arthur, sorry mate, won't be in work today. Got a bit of a bastard behind the eyes."

It wasn't visiting time but Arthur had made up a story and marched in anyway.

"Don't worry Danny; the office can wait another day for your talents. Although you're going to have to learn to handle your drink better."

"Was that Irn Bru I saw you drinking on the way in?"

10

"Very observant, cheeky little shite. So, what happened to you?"

"Haven't got a fucking clue, I was kinda hoping you could tell me?"

"Why would I know?"

"Because you're a busy man and you already told me if I fucked up I'd be getting the cheese, so if you're here being all nice then it can only be a guilt thing."

"I could be here for the nurses?"

"No chance mate, they're for young stallions like me, not flatulent old bastards."

"Danny, remind me why I hired you?"

"Because I'm a smart-arse?"

*

In the Wild West they would have terrorised innocent citizens, robbed banks and held up stagecoaches. There would be a price on their head and wanted posters on the wall of every Sheriff's office. Many a posse would have tried to track them down. But no one could have, not even Randolph Scott.

This wasn't the Wild West, it was the West End but the Finch Brothers still terrorised innocent citizens. The four brothers lived with their sole sister and Ma Finch in the two top floor flats in the close. Many years ago they had built the wall across the top of the stairs to form a corridor between the two flats. Everyone in the close and surrounding area knew of them and had had their lives affected by them.

The two eldest brothers had been in jail but since their release had been too difficult to pin down. The two younger twin brothers, who along with their sister made the rest of the family, had been frequent young offenders but since they moved into adulthood had been as difficult to incarcerate as their elders. The trouble was that if any one brother was in trouble, the others could intimidate the witnesses or, more often, the victims into withdrawing the charges.

Even when they could be caught and charged, a combination of the leniency of the courts and the work of smart-arsed lawyers meant they were a major waste of police time. So much so, that they were hardly ever bothered by the police.

The other inhabitants of the close lived in a constant state of terror. Most of them had, at some time, had their houses ransacked, their possessions stolen or occasionally their bodies grievously harmed. None of them could leave. Selling their houses was virtually impossible with the Finches around. Laxmi suffered the most; he was constantly under threat and lived like a recluse in his flat on the second floor. Strangely, his shop was never attacked. It had occasionally been daubed with graffiti but, on the whole, it had been largely untouched. This he put down to the influence of Ma Finch who often shopped there.

Although she said very little, she was the only one to have any control over the boys at all. It was likely that she had told them to leave the shop alone and they had complied.

Mrs. Moyes was an easy target too, especially now that her son wasn't around. She would often be bumped around or have her bags tipped open. She would regularly come home at night to find faeces through her letterbox. All this she took with a solemn grace. It helped that she and Laxmi had devised a system to allow her to get her paper and shopping in relative safety. They'd spot the pattern soon, they always did. But until then it continued to work reliably.

Opposite Laxmi was the flat that was most often empty. Five or so years ago it had been owned by an old man who had died. He left no will and no heirs that could be found so the flat was handed over to his lawyer. They had been trying to sell it ever since. Very few buyers came forward. Those who did were very quickly deterred by the ominous presence above. After a while, the firm took it off the market and decided to use it as an occasional accommodation for visitors or new recruits. This had worked at first until a client from London had been hospitalised during an overnight stay. The Finches caught him snorting coke in the close. The Finches, despite their otherwise total lack of morals, hated drugs and drug users. They did a real number on this guy. It was 6 months before he returned to London. There were no witnesses and the guy had no memory of ever being in Scotland.

It was at this point that Arthur McWilliams decided that enough was enough.

*

The only way to avoid the Finches was to lock yourself away and never come out. That was why, of all the people in the close, the Beatle Man was the least affected. With the exception of his regular Tuesday morning trips, he hardly ever left the house. When he did leave, people always noted that he was smartly dressed. He rarely spoke. But when he did, he only said lyrics. And only from Beatles' songs.

*

"So you paid the Finches to stop hassling the folk that lived in the flat so that you could get it sold."

"Yeah, something like that."

"And you thought you could use me as a Guinea Pig to see if they were good to their word?"

"Well, I wouldn't say Guinea Pig. I thought it was safe. They promised."

"They promised? You took the word of these notorious nutcases?"

"I was paying them money, it's the language they understand."

"Arthur, I'm very disappointed in you."

"You cheeky little shite, I should…"

"Should what? Say you're very sorry, what can I possibly do to make amends?"

"OK, OK. Look the flat's fucked for two weeks, so…"

"You expect me to go back?"

"Well, yeah, this was an unfortunate accident, I didn't know you would go to their door shouting your mouth off."

12

"Did I? Oh yeah, the ceiling, I must've. How do you know?"

"Malky spoke to them."

"Malky? No, I don't want to know."

"Anyway, they've said if you keep out of their way and I keep paying then there'll be no hassle."

"Oh well, that's my mind completely at rest."

"OK Danny, I'll give you 5% of the sale price of the flat when it sells if you can stay in it long enough to make it at least look like the Finches aren't the neighbours from hell."

"And when it sells you'll stop paying and the new tenants ass is grass?"

"Yeah, it's a tough life."

"How much are we talking about?"

"Minimum 5 grand."

"Not enough."

"And you can stay in my Penthouse Clydeside flat until the flat is sorted."

"Jacuzzi?"

"You bet."

"Done."

"I kind of think I have been."

Danny might have felt cheap but a Jacuzzi? Manto-heaven, surely.

Three

Malky Simmons lumbered out of his Ford Escort van and walked up into the close. Everything was quiet as he laboured up the stairs, his walk slowed by a heavy night of beer and arm wrestling. At the flat he paused and took a sly glance up to the top floor. Despite his bulk and his well renowned ability to handle himself, even Malky thought twice about messing with the Finches. At least in packs of more than two anyway.

He used the spare set of keys and went into the flat. Everything was pretty much as it had been the last time he was there, except, of course, for the fuck off big hole in the bathroom ceiling. He peered up into the cavity fearful of a pair of evil eyes staring back or worse a hand throwing a dart. It was dark. The water had run through the floor and collected in the ceiling. Then the ceiling had collected on the bathroom floor.

"Gonnae need a plumber n' a spark" said Malky to no one "oh aye and some cunt to fix the roof."

Malky was known for his fighting or "protection" as it was sometimes called. His only previous contributions to the building industry had involved carrying heavy things or knocking things down. There was no sign of Danny's cases and he sure as hell wasn't going up to the Finches to ask for them. He unclipped his mobile from his belt and pulled it out from beneath his substantial gut. It was an older model but looked far newer held in his bear-like paw. His over sized fingers fumbled with the tiny buttons and then he pressed it to his ear.

"Eh, it's Malky ... aye ... no ... no sign ...aye I checked ... the roof ... aw ... aye the ceiling'...aye...it's fucked man...two weeks...aye cheers."

Malky walked back out and got into his van. Miscellaneous tools and scrap metal clanged about in the back as he drove away heading for the bookies.

14

Another day's work done, another fire put out. He had already decided on his first bet.

*

Danny left the hospital at lunchtime with a disappointing total of no phone numbers. Then again, with your nose splattered all over your face, what can you expect? He did, however, get an invite to a nurse's night out at one of their regular West End haunts. Well, to Danny it was an invite; anyone else would call it eavesdropping. He had known for a while that nurses got in cheap but he had his eye on wee Shona. She was cute and looking through a gap in her buttons he had seen enough frilly lace to suggest that she might be worth getting somewhere with. He had everything he needed, the sympathy vote due to the face, the ever present McColl charm and, of course, keys to a penthouse apartment that featured stunning views of the Clyde, gch, dg and the prospect of a shag in a Jacuzzi. Although he may have to keep the last part to himself during the opening exchanges.

Arthur had told him of the sad demise of most, if not all, of his clothes. A combination of exaggeration and a good knowledge of the bollocks designer clothes market had upped the compensation to a grand. Danny could replace his suit and the other assorted rags for a couple of hundred. He might even throw in another suit. That would leave some serious cash for clothes to score in and the scoring itself. He would have to leave some money to replace his football boots, the only real loss. They had been with him for many years and had become a natural extension of his legs and feet. They were the pair that he scored the now legendary overhead kick with in a Uni game at Westerlands. He had intended donating them to the Hunterian museum when he eventually hung them up. Outside the hospital he went into a phone box and phoned his mate Charlie.

*

Not quite midday, but already the pavements were radiating the heat from the bright summer sun. Usually sun such as this meant that someone somewhere had an imminent exam, the sun Gods tempting and teasing followers away from the Gods of learning to the Gods of sloth. But not today. This was the sun of the end game, the pay off or, in Charlie's case, the sun that comes with a great weight being lifted.

He had been at the University all morning. No one could say when the degree results would be posted. Coffee and chat, nervous smiles hiding certainty for some, impending disappointment others. Everyone knew Charlie didn't have to worry and admonished him anyway. They didn't understand. Charlie didn't believe in destiny, he didn't believe in other people's assertions. He needed the black and white: that simple line of the paper that said "1". Nothing to celebrate, no reason for a party, just the delivery of what had been expected, what he was always meant to, born to do. Whilst others waited in hope of celebration, Charlie only wanted relief.

The son of two lawyers, grew up with the law, destined for the law and, above all, always expected to excel at the law, Charlie First Class Honours

15

degree was not a wish it was just the next inevitable stage in his progression. Anything else, well, anything else simply hadn't been discussed.

So when the hubbub started and the exodus to the results boards began, Charlie was an odd mix of emotions. Belief in himself, blended seamlessly with a fear of an outcome that was beyond anything he had ever known.

He walked the gentle rise up University Avenue at a steady pace. His heart compelled him to walk faster; his brain insisted that he not appear eager. Rounding the corner through the large metal gates he prepared himself for the nervous hunt for his name. And then, all at once, 21 years of weight and wait lifted.

"Charlie! Don't look so worried, you got a first."

Someone he didn't really know that well broke the news. Taken aback, he was unable to reply and brushed past to search the boards himself. It didn't take long. Finally, there it was in black and white. No joy, no celebration, just relief. He allowed himself a smile as those around him congratulated him and he them. But he wasn't all that happy; he had just avoided being sad. So when everyone else headed to the pub, he headed home, it was just the next phase.

Back out the gates, he started to head across the road and down to the underground station. On a wall on the opposite side of the street, a figure sat on the wall, curved back, head resting on its knees, legs bent in front of it. A Henry Moore in student khaki.

"Danny?"

The figure didn't move. But Charlie knew who it was.

"Danny, what…"

"What am I doing here?"

"Well, yeah."

"I'm asking myself the same question."

After Danny's Dad died, his final year had fallen apart. He stopped attending lectures, tutorials, stopped studying. On Charlie's advice, he had delayed his final year so he could do it again the year after. He wasn't getting any degree today.

"Good to see you anyway"

"Yeah."

"What, I mean, why did…"

"It's a nice day, the girls have got their big ones on."

It was a Danny phrase but not a Danny delivery. He was there simply to reflect on things. But it wasn't Danny's way to admit that.

"How about I buy you a beer?"

"I think I should be buying you one, you're the one with something to celebrate."

"Celebrate?"

"Yeah, you know, your first."

"How did you…"

"Charlie, the bookies stopped taking bets on that one when you were five."

If only someone had told Charlie.

16

*

"Peachy, my good man, ca va?"

When Danny spoke to Charlie the vocabulary and the accent were equally affected. One night they had watched The Man Who Would Be King. The fact that one of the characters was called Danny was enough, the both decided they would be king.

"Daniel, you cad. Damn fine to hear from you. How are you?"

"Had a bit of bother, you know, in the nose department."

"The nose department, been visiting the body parts superstore again have we?"

"Oh bravo, Peachy bravo, no I'll tell all later, for now, how about a small beverage and then on to the Queen of The Nile tonight?"

"I'd be delighted Daniel."

"In the Uisge for 8 then? And Peachy, don't bring a lady, we go in search of fair Eastern maidens."

*

Charlie had been in Danny's year at Uni. He was always the smart cookie of the class and had walked straight out of Uni straight into one of the top law firms in Glasgow. While he hated Danny's attitude towards law, he always admired his style and often let himself get carried along in his wake. It was his only route to a good time. Shy and unassuming, sandy hair with thin round silver glasses, he was not the world greatest icebreaker. He had noticed right away that Danny was Russian and probably nuclear powered and could drive you to the North Pole without upsetting your house of cards.

It didn't bother him too much that he always ended up with the less attractive friend of one of Danny's conquests. It was better than nothing and took so little effort. He thought he was handsome but this had only ever been confirmed by his Gran and, what with her cataracts and all, couldn't be relied up as the best judge.

He had his standards though and would never consider one of Danny's ex's. He nearly made an exception for Delores Finnegan, a flame-haired Irish girl who had captivated him through most of his first two years and Uni. They got talking at a party and things were going well. At the back of Charlie's mind was the fact that Danny had told him that she had said that Danny was the best shag she had ever had. In the end, this proved an impenetrable barrier and he wandered off silently to the punch bowl. It was only after graduation that Danny told Charlie about the lie. He laughed, but only just.

He usually looked forward to a night at Clatty Pat's. This time he wasn't so sure. A Danny second wasn't good enough any more. He knew whom he wanted.

*

"Peachy, now we move on to the Isle of Islay…"

17

Danny was half way through his whisky tour of Scotland. An expensive and, to Charlie's mind, entirely pointless and dangerous drinking binge that usually formed the starting point Danny's nights out.

"... and then we sail bonny boat like a bird on a wing..."

Charlie didn't join in the song. It would appear that, unlike Danny, he had to go to work in the morning so was trying very hard to keep his intake down to a few pints. And his job wasn't just about selling houses, it was proper law and needed a damn sight less of a hangover than what you could get away with if you only had to tell people that the house they have just bought was built on an abandoned mine and, while it may collapse any minute, Scooby and the gang had already been and unmasked the ghost that lived there. Charlie laughed at the image.

"... that's the spirit Peachy, now drink up, the maidens await!"

They wandered off onto Park Road and then left into Great Western Road. On Kelvinbridge the paused for a while as Danny tried, and failed, to persuade some first year Chemistry students that 'they could test ma' tubes out' if they wanted. They walked away disgusted.

"... fuckin' dykes" said Danny, the effects of whisky salving the disappointment.

They arrived at Clatty's after only just avoiding the temptation on the 3 in 1. The pakora could wait. Danny had a nurse called Shona on his mind and she was "hotter than chilli sauce".

They entered and headed straight for the bar.

"Two bottles of water". It was a familiar tactic.

"You see Peachy, boys like to be drunk but the girls don't like the drunk boys, so we must walk a fine line."

Although presumably not a straight fine line. Standing at the bar Danny surveyed the throng, standing, sitting and dancing. So did Charlie. Danny's eyes rested on a group of girls. They let out a huge whoop as the DJ spun the perennial floor-filler Dancing Queen. Four of the girls and turned to the fifth and shouted, "you're terrible Muriel" in Unison. The girl gave an "oh no, not again" look and carried on dancing. They all laughed.

"Is she here?" Charlie was getting jumpy. The sooner Danny met up and took her home for a shag the sooner he could get home himself.

"Oh yes Peachy, 1 o'clock, green satin dress, slinky as fuck."

Charlie turned his head. He didn't see the satin dress; he didn't see the group of frolicking nurses. He couldn't hear the music and fairly soon he might not be able to feel his legs. Through the crowds on the dance floor, all he could see he was very familiar with. The back of a head that he had stared at for hours. The blonde hair that he had tried so hard to smell or touch. The person he adored. She was here. And so was Danny. Room 101.

"Aye, I see her Danny, she's a babe, fire in there mate." His plea was as heart-felt as it was hesitant.

"Patience Peachy, the Dan plan requires that I get clocked first. See anyone that might be of interest to your good self?"

"Eh...no...well... aye, place is very well populated, why don't we get a seat?"

"A seat? No, no, we need to be in full view of the lovely ladies."

The first thing Charlie saw the day he started his job was now the last thing he thought about every night. Behind the desk at reception sat Kelly. She greeted him on arrival and laughed politely when he forgot his own name. Kelly had the blondest of blonde hair. It was done in a 40's style that made her look like an image from a cigarette card that so entertained the boys in the forces. This image was perfectly matched by her curves and those never-ending Betty Grable legs. She was a throw back from a past time and it only served to make her all the more beautiful in the present.

Charlie stammered a hello every morning. Strained to hear her conversations over coffee. She would occasionally talk of a boyfriend but they were always short-lived. Most of the time it seemed to Charlie she was on her own. It didn't make sense. Neither did introducing her to Danny, which was what he was just about to do. She had walked through the crowd towards them. He didn't need to look round, he heard Danny's jaw drop. He watched it drop further when she said hello to Charlie.

"Hi Kelly, this is, eh...my mate...eh...Danny."

"Danny McColl, pleased to meet you, can I buy you a drink?"

It had begun; the nightmare had begun. The one where everything Charlie had ever worked for and dreamed about was stolen from him by his talentless gobshite pal.

"No, its OK, I'm in a round. See you tomorrow Charlie."

"Aye, OK."

She walked off. Neither Charlie nor Danny spoke until the rhythmic sway of her hips had disappeared out of sight.

"Peachy, my boy, you've been keeping her quiet."

"She's just someone from work."

"Just someone from work! There's no just there. She's an angel Charlie. Ha! Charlie's Angel!"

"Well, I wouldn't bother Danny, I think she has a boyfriend." The lie wasn't worth it; it hadn't stopped Danny before.

"Maybe Peachy, maybe, tonight is Shona's night, the lovely Kelly can keep."

The arrogant fuck. Charlie was relieved that he was not already leaving with her but fumed at the way he spoke about her.

"Hiya dollface." Danny was speaking to Shona who had just appeared at the bar.

"Hiya fucked face. Shouldn't you be at home resting?"

"What? When I could have come here and saw you? You must be joking!"

It was starting, Charlie left for the toilet. On his way back he saw Danny miming the effects of sitting in a Jacuzzi and then dangling keys. The writing was on the wall. True if destroyed. He decided to leave; he'd make an excuse later. On his way out he turned to look at Kelly. She was sitting with a couple of friends looking slightly forlorn. She looked up so Charlie raised a hand and mouthed "see you tomorrow". She raised her glass and smiled a thin smile.

The bouncer held the door open and said goodnight. When Charlie was outside he said "no, not really" to no one in particular.

Four

Laxmi was on a roll this week. He had made it to Wednesday with virtually no contact with the Finches at all. He had even risked a trip out at night for a visit to a friend with Shazia and had ghosted in and out successfully. As a result, he sat behind the till in what was, for him, a fairly buoyant mood. That made the shock of seeing the Beatle Man even greater.

As he appeared at the door of the shop, Laxmi decided that now was the time to find out if the stories were true. He had always liked to think they were but surely no one can only speak in lyrics. It's absurd. Anyway, he had nothing to lose; the guy came into his shop once in a blue moon.

"Blue moon" Laxmi chuckled.

The Beatle Man walked in through door to the accompanying chime. Laxmi struggled to make eye contact but to no avail. His small eyes, hidden behind the small round specs, remained fixed on the end of the shop. He walked down the far away aisle and out of sight.

He reappeared carrying a packet of fabric cleaner. The type that bleached things white again. As he approached the till, Laxmi felt the time was right.

"Hello."

"Good morning, good morning."

'Lovely weather we're having'

"Good day sunshine."

"Eh…that'll be 89p, please."

He handed over the exact money.

"Thank you."

"Thank you."

This wasn't conclusive because it wasn't a conversation. Laxmi had to push it further.

"Remember if there's ever anything else you need…"

"I'll always be here if you should need me…Goodbye."

Before Laxmi could reply he left with another musical chime.

"I'll always be here if you should need me…mmmm…if it isn't a lyric it's a strange thing to say."

Laxmi stood and thought of as many Beatles' songs he could remember. It didn't ring any bells. Just to be sure he scribbled the line down on the back of a paper bag for later. He surveyed the empty shop still puzzled by the mysterious presence.

"I look at the floor and I see that it needs sweeping…"

He chuckled and sang as he cleaned tiled floor of the shop.

*

"275."

Upstairs Mrs Moyes had not gone to work. Wednesday was half day so at least she wasn't letting anyone down for a whole day. She didn't feel up to it. The photo albums lay where she had been reading them the night before. The scrapbook lay open displaying the headline 'Young actor stars in Amateur Production'.

She flicked back through a few pages and the tears welled again in her eyes. At the window, the dirty orange buses sped past. People walked up and down. Across the street, a young boy ran out into the road but was caught by his mother. She hit him and he cried.

"Where are you?" cried Mrs. Moyes. Collapsing on the floor, fists tightly clenched round a handkerchief. The tears ran down her face making trails of dark mascara as they fell.

After a few minutes her sobs became a whimper. She looked up to the sideboard and saw the whisky. There was a loud crash out in the close. Maybe now would be a good time.

*

"Police brutality."

"Sorry Sarge?"

"Police fuckin brutality!"

Sergeant Derek Murdoch was not a happy man.

"You see Constable; people define Police Brutality as something that we do to them. No one ever considers the possibility that they can be brutal to us."

Immediately, the Constable knew the problem and knew he had to change the subject. It was the bane of every policeman or woman working in Maryhill Police station. Someone would appear at the desk and say, "Can I see Chief Inspector Taggart?" before laughing uproariously before either running away or telling their real business. It affected the sergeant more than others.

"They think it's funny don't they. That bunch of shit-stabbers in Cowcaddens think they can make TV programmes and it won't effect anyone. BUT IT EFFECTS ME! GODDAMIT! Then, it gets worse, that poor sod McManus dies and they don't stop the bleedin' thing or even change the title…!"

A young man interrupted his rant. He was wearing what appeared to be brand new designer gear. A broad smile stretched across his face but was somewhat let down by a nose that did the same. His timing couldn't have been worse.

"Hi, my name is Daniel McColl, could I speak to Chief Inspector Taggart please?"

*

Danny had woken up feeling very chirpy. Drinking water in the club had worked as usual and there was only the faintest trace of a hangover, a slight fog in his head that told him that there had been drink but not enough to suggest that there had also been sick.

The rest of his body told him other things. His legs ached and the muscles across his chest and down his arm were tight. It felt like someone had rammed a mincer down his boxers. All over, his skin felt dry and chapped. The tips of his fingers looked like prunes.

"Jesus, I thought nurses were meant to cure the sick."

With a wry smile, it all came back. He was chatting to Shona, getting nowhere fast, about to give up. Then her mate, what was her name, Muriel, comes over and gives him the "fire right in, big man" face. Soon after they were leaving to a chorus of "you're terrible". The wry smile turned to a look of concern.

Danny was now going to have to seriously reappraise his life. Not so long ago he had said that as soon as he had shagged a nurse in a Jacuzzi then his life would be complete. He was going to have to set his sights higher now.

He wandered out of the room expecting to see Muriel smiling politely. There was no one there. The flat had many rooms, most of which he was yet to explore. She could be anywhere. Then he saw a note lying at the side of the Jacuzzi.

"Nice Jacuzzi, shame about the fuck."

Catchy, Danny thought. She really was terrible. Not to worry, with suitable McColl embellishment the story will still stand up in a court of law. Anyway, now that he remembered better, she was a bit of a porker.

He picked up the note and put it next to the one that accompanied the money that he was to use to replace his clothes and, of course, his boots. He wandered over to the Jacuzzi and flicked the switch. The bubbles built up slowly. He poured a brandy from the conveniently placed decanter and climbed in. This was the life. How many Stenhousemuir fans do this on a Wednesday morning?

The bubbles made his body feel light, the warmth made him sleepy again. Tipping his head back, he drifted off into a waking dream.

Al Pacino was there, but it wasn't Al Pacino, it was Danny. He was in court. Summing up, the final speech. His chance to impress. To his right sat the jury, 12 nurses in underwear, hanging on his every word. In the dock sat a man. He didn't recognise him but he was sure as hell gonna send him down. Strutting round the room, he had victory in his sights.

"Are we as a nation going to sit idly by while men like this get away with brutal attacks on innocent victims? These people need you."

He walked up to the defendant and stared him in the face. The face. The face. Suddenly, Danny woke up.

It was him. His drunken subconscious had stored the image and now it had come back to him in glorious Jacuzzi vision.

"These people need you?"

Words he had heard before. Danny had agreed to sit on the flat. He had agreed to take the money. His boss was in the palm of his hand but yet he hadn't agreed to not uphold his rights as a citizen. Al Pacino wouldn't let it lie. And now he had a face. And a surname. Of a, no doubt, well known criminal. It was more than enough for the police to go on. He wasn't going to ignore the pleas again.

"I'm coming right down there to have his ass."

Danny mimed slamming the phone and caused a plume of water to splash over the floor.

"Right after I get myself some new threads."

Sure, maybe he was turning into Huggy Bear. But it wasn't half fun.

*

"Yes sir, how can I help you?"

This wasn't good. The Sarge had gone from mad to pleasant far too quickly. Where had all the anger gone? It couldn't have dissipated. It was still in there, waiting to come out. This didn't bode well.

"I have been assaulted."

Danny spoke clearly and indignantly as yet unaware of his inadvertent police brutality.

"I can see that sir, but we can't do anything for fashion nowadays can we?"

"What?"

The constable tried to slope off but was caught by a glare from the Sarge.

"Am I to surmise that you would like to report an assault on your person?"

"Yes, look at my face."

"I didn't like to presume sir; it can be so unfair to those less fortunate than ourselves. Constable Pearce, take this young man into interview room two. I'll be there shortly."

Danny wandered off with the officer. When he was out of sight old Murdoch laughed and laughed. This was going to be fun.

"So, you say you were assaulted."

"I don't just say it, I was assaulted, head-butted, in fact."

"Aaaah, I see, head-butted, Pearce make a note of that, butted with a head, head-butted. And when did this happen."

"Well, it was two days ago, on Monday."

"Any particular reason you waited until now."

"I was in hospital."

"And you were released today…?"

"No, yesterday."

24

"Pearce, make a note, yesterday, Tuesday, a day ago."

Danny didn't really know what was going on. He was a victim. Now twice over.

"So, what can you tell me about this incident?"

Danny told him the story. He wasn't strutting round the courtroom but he spoke as if he was. Clear and lucid, he would leave no doubt that he knew what he was about; making sure to mention that he was a lawyer.

"Mmmm …a lawyer eh? Make a note, Pearce, a lawyer, like Petrocelli, although it appears that his home is only slightly damaged and not half-built."

"Look…" Danny eyes flicked to the Sarge's arm "…sergeant, I get the feeling that you are not treating this assault with the gravity that I believe it deserves. I was assaulted and I know who did it."

"I was wandering when you would come to that."

"I was assaulted by a man named Finch."

The lead on PC Pearce's pencil snapped. If there had been a bell it would have tolled. Any pigeons in the area would have scarpered en masse. It was one of those moments. The Sarge's demeanour changed.

"Finch, which one?"

"I don't know which one, but I know his face, if you can supply me with the mug shots I'm sure you have I'll pick him out for you."

"Look, Mr.." he paused and looked at Pearce, who added "McColl".

"Mr. McColl, I can see that you have had a bit of a bump but I don't really see what I can do?"

"You can arrest this Finch?"

"Which one?"

"The one in the photo that I am going to pick out for you."

"Danny, can I call you Danny? Go home and stay away from the Finches then maybe you won't get a bloody nose and I won't go wasting my time."

"Wasting your time? I'm coming to you with a report of a vicious assault and I can identify the assailant."

"No, you can't."

"Yes, I can."

"Were you drunk Danny?"

The pause was all the Sarge needed to know.

"I had had a drink, yes."

"How can you be so sure of the face?"

Danny almost said that he saw it in a dream but changed his mind in time.

"I know the face. I'm a lawyer, we're trained for this kind of thing."

The Sarge only just avoided laughing.

"OK then lawyer boy, then you'll be familiar with the term identical twins

"Eh … yeah."

"Well, I make it my business to know that the two older Finches are out of town, so that only leaves the other brothers, who just happen to be identical twins. Unless he had a name badge on, I'm afraid you won't be identifying him in a hurry."

"But…"

"Danny, let's not waste any more of your time or mine. I'm not going to arrest any Finches and you're going to stay out of their way. And if you EVER come in here and mention Taggart again, I'll kick your arse from here to Dumbarton Rock. Is that clear?"

*

That night Laxmi sat with the scrap of paper in his hand and started to go through his Beatles records. It was as good an excuse as any to listen to them all again. Shazia soon got bored and went to bed to read a book.

By 2am, he still hadn't found the song and was sure that he had proved that the rumours weren't true. No one could memorise all the lyrics to the extent that that was all they ever said. It just wasn't possible.

Then, at 02:15, just as he was getting up to turn the stereo off…

"I'll always be here if you need me…"

The second verse of Step Inside Love.

"Fuck me." said Laxmi and wandered off to his bed, tired, bemused but still a little impressed.

Five

It is statistically certain that coincidences will happen. Given the number of people in the world and the numbers of things that happen to them it is beyond doubt that something wildly improbable is happening to someone somewhere. Sometimes it's a pleasant surprise, others bring an eerie foreboding. The worst are those that arrive laden with a cold irony. Such a coincidence arrived at the bottom of the garden one morning in the hands of a man carrying a large bag on his shoulder and looking like the most sullen thing imaginable. His sullenness was in no way related to dull thud of coincidental pain he was about deliver, he was just like that, occupational hazard or pre-requisite, the difference wasn't immediately apparent or important.

He lifted the heavily sprung metal flap and dropped in two letters, recoiling theatrically as the letter box snapped shut like, to his under-stimulated mind at least, the jaws of a Nile crocodile.

The letters lay on the carpet below, two confirmations, one for the father, and one for the son. Both were expected but their impact and consequences remained undiscussed. So, when they were finally picked up but a nervous Mary McColl, their mutual fates were sealed as they were unsealed.

In the first letter, merely written confirmation of what they had long known. His job was gone. 57 and unemployed with only a minimal redundancy payment. They had always known how it would be. But until it arrived on paper it had never seemed real, never worth discussing. Things had been how they were for so long, they didn't even know the words to discuss anything different.

The second letter should have brought celebration. Danny had been offered an unconditional place a Glasgow University.

Her arthritic hands struggling with the opener, she laid them out on the table next to each other. She understood what each said, but together they couldn't be fathomed. The cold irony coincidence. One doors closes and another one opens? Or do they both get shut.

She was too ill too work, he'd be too stubborn to get a job. He wouldn't get a job just to help them survive, not any job and certainly not anything that was beneath him. And that meant no job would be good enough. But no job wasn't good enough. So where did that leave them? Where did it leave Danny? She clutched the worn beads round her neck and prayed. Not for guidance or hope of resolution but simply that Danny would come home first.

"You'll just have to get a job."

"I'm going to University."

"And leave us here with nothing? You will not. You'll get a job, get earning for this family."

Danny got back second. Long before his return his Dad had made a decision.

"I'm going to University."

"Look son, wake up, I've got no job, and we've got no money. How could you go gadding about University?"

"I'll get a grant."

"A grant? How can me and your Mum live off a grant?"

"You don't, I do."

"You selfish little shit."

"I'm selfish?"

"What's that meant to mean?"

Sensing the rising tension, the tea maker tried to turn peacemaker by making tea.

"Now, its not meant to mean anything, now lets have a cup of…"

"No Mum, I don't want tea, I want to go to University and I will go to University."

"Over my dead body."

Danny took his letter from the table and left the room, his Dad's words still ringing in his ears. And those words still ring in his ears.

*

The excitement in the house could be heard in all their voices. The cases had been packed for over a week now. The flight bag was been packed and repacked. The tickets and passport had been put in all the available pockets at least twice. Finally they had decided to carry them in the inside pocket of a jacket with a zip. It was safe. More accessible. Didn't risk the juice or sweets coating them with something that would make them unusable. Anyway, you could check them more often if they were in a jacket. Saved opening and shutting the bag endlessly.

It was the culmination of two years of saving and planning. Money set aside, corners cut. Sacrifices made. All for a holiday. But not any holiday. A holiday on a plane. They would be the first ones in the street to do it. They booked the family taxi to the airport early to make sure everyone saw them go, the luggage tags displayed prominently.

A furrow was being ploughed in the carpet. In turn, each of them walked to the window to see if the taxi had arrived. Each time they would turn with a sigh and sit back down, resetting the spring on the chair.

The excitement had carried them this far with no fear. Now, close to departure, they had starting to think about flying. No one they knew had ever flown. Pioneers. The kids didn't care; they flew round the room on arm-like wings; whooshing and making high-pitched engine noises.

"Prepare for take off Captain!"

Their eyes met and their faces paled. She picked up the brochure. The beach. The sun. The happy faces. The excitement returned. The baby's nappy needed changed. Passed some time. Add one more nappy to the flight bag. And wait some more. Sometimes you can be too ready.

*

Sometimes you can be too cocky.

Charlie recognised the voice, his stomach plunging almost instantaneously. The bastard had done it deliberately. He phoned, found out what time he was going for lunch, what time he would be back and then turned up early. This was typical Danny behaviour. He had known from the moment Danny saw Kelly in Clatty's that he wouldn't let it lie. He didn't even let it lie a day.

Before reaching the top of the stairs, he slowed to listen to what particular brand of McColl patter was being pedalled today.

"…so I got the old lady's handbag back but, as it flew out of the idiot's hand, it caught me in the nose. Did she not have £30 in 2 pences in the bottom of the bag? Made a bit of a mess as you can see. But still…"

Jesus. This was grade A shite. Charlie couldn't bear any more and lurched for the door before Kelly had a chance to reply.

"Danny! You're early…"

Danny turned round and his face replied, "so are you ya shit, I was moving in for the kill there."

"Just passing the time telling Kelly here about the old snoz, you know, with the handbag and everything?"

He raised and eyebrow to punctuate the deceit.

"Yes, the nose, of course. I'm sure Kelly has work to do so we better get on."

This wasn't the plan. Danny should have had a phone number by now.

"Aye, OK then, maybe see you around Kelly?"

She was quiet. Too quiet for Charlie's liking. Just quiet enough for Danny. It was as good a sign for one as it was bad for the other. As they walked off towards Charlie's desk, Danny turned round and mimed a yawn pointing in Charlie's direction. Kelly laughed and gave a dismissive wave. Maybe the hastily improvised plan B had been good enough.

"Danny, don't even try to come up with a half-decent reason why you are here."

"Oh, like that is it? Well, maybe I won't invite round to the pad then?"

Charlie shook his head. The pad? Sheesh.

"So you couldn't do that on the phone?"

"It wouldn't do the place justice. I need to wave my arms to describe the splendour."

"Fuck off Danny."

"Right now?"

"Yes."

"... and how shall I fuck off?"

"Quickly."

*

Michael and Martin Finch were identical. They looked the same, they acted the same and they were both objectionable little shites. Like most twins, they shared a bond. In their case, a bond that made them equally mischievous, equally clever and equally nasty.

They had not yet progressed into the more serious crimes perpetrated by their elders and still contented themselves with being a nuisance and generally upsetting as many people as they could. The elder Finch brothers found this kind of stuff a bit trivial these days and usually frowned upon the activities of the twins, as it would invariably attract attention that could threaten some of their other 'interests'.

So, time was running out. The elder Finches would be back from their "business" soon and the opportunities for mischief would all but end.

To achieve maximum effect, they had started what had now become their usual ploy. A few days of quiet. Enough to let everyone in the close relax. And then strike.

After a lot of thought and not inconsiderable planning they had decided to strike at Mrs. Moyes. Like all their victims, she was innocent and she was an easy target. Like all their attacks it would be meaningless and they would get away with it. Laxmi was off limits and anyway he wasn't enough fun any more and his shop too well defended.

At 08:00 every morning the bakery takes delivery of a range of cakes and pastries. The van pulls up outside the shop and the cakes are carried on plastic pallets into the shop. The twins had followed Mrs. Moyes to work. They waited outside the shop all morning smoking stolen cigarettes and spitting profusely, hoods up to complete the image.

The van was only a few minutes late. They crossed the road behind the van so they would not be seen. Crouching behind the van they waited while the driver opened the back. Mrs. Moyes came out as the driver brought out the first pallet. He handed it over. The sign for Michael to strike. As Mrs. Moyes turned to head for the shop Michael appeared suddenly from behind the van, sprinted across the pavement, ducked under the palette held in outstretched arms. Pushing up, he sent the contents of the palette spinning. He then sprinted off down the street.

The cakes looped in the air and came down on Mrs. Moyes covering her in cream and icing. The driver sprinted off after Michael leaving the distraught Mrs. Moyes sitting on the pavement. Meanwhile Martin, unseen nipped round

30

to the back of the van, grabbed another palette and strolled quietly back across the road.

The other people in the shop came out to attend to the now crying Mrs. Moyes. The driver returned puffing and barely able to speak.

"Bloody....'tards..."

They tried to get Mrs. Moyes to go home. She had been ill; she should go back and rest. But she had seen the face. She knew it was a Finch. One of them. What was the point in going home? It would only be leaving the frying pan.

"Did you see who did it?"

"No, it was too fast."

The driver came back into the shop.

"The wee shites stole a palette. Looks like that was what they were after all along."

Mrs. Moyes knew different.

*

Sometimes being too cocky worked. For some people. Well, for Danny.

"Hi Kelly?"

"Eh... yeah..."

This had thrown her well-practised receptionist manner.

"Hi, it's Danny McColl, Charlie's friend, we spoke earlier..."

Pause for reaction.

"Yeah ... hi Danny."

Good enough.

"Look, I know this is maybe a bit, well, y' know..."

That's enough shyness.

"... I was wondering if you fancied, maybe, going out some time?"

Despite her looks or maybe because of them Kelly didn't get asked out very often. People who knew her, of course, stayed well away. When she did go out with people, it invariably didn't last long. Danny wasn't pretty but he was game and he seemed quite funny. When you don't get many offers?

"Yeah, OK."

Ya dancer.

"How about I pick you up from work and go for food?"

Don't give her time to chance her mind.

"Yeah, OK, about half five."

"See you then."

*

The Finch twins didn't have to spend hours devising plans of extreme mental cruelty. It just came naturally. Most of the time they had no realisation of the kinds of torture they were performing. They saw the prank and that was all. Blind to their own brutality, the didn't have the decency to recognise their own evil.

They could have stolen the cakes at any time of the day. There would have been other deliveries. But they chose to do it early in the morning. Why? Well, why not? Because their victim would know that they doubtlessly planned

31

something else and would therefore have the whole day to worry about it. No. Not deliberately, but actually. Naturals.

Mrs. Moyes was very quiet for the rest day, even quieter than normal. She knew that stealing cakes was not enough for the Finches. She knew that the only way to perhaps stop anything was to go back home. The only way to get caught in the middle of it was to do exactly the same. Caught in the middle of the mental dilemma, she suffered the most destructive of tortures. Alone with her thoughts of a pain that not even those inflicting knew about.

*

Danny breezed into the office like he owned the place.

"Hi Jenny."

Jenny looked up ready to be disdainful but, seeing Danny's nose and remembering what Arthur had told her she decided to at least try to be pleasant.

"Daniel, how's the nose?"

"I'm starting to quite like it, a big hit with the ladies."

Danny winked. Jenny forced a smile.

"Is the big man about?"

"I presume you mean Mr. McWilliams. He is with a client, I'm afraid."

"No probs…could you just let him know that the flat is fab and that Danny is good with the deal and will be paying a friendly visit just to kick things off. He'll know what I mean."

"I'm sure he will."

"Cheers doll."

Despite everything else. Jenny did rather like being called "doll".

*

Danny had decided not to think too much about what he was just about to do. Thoughts of Lion's dens, frying pans and fire flitted through his mind but were shooed away by others that involved Penthouse flats, five grand and lots and lots of nurses.

He had worked it out. These Finch boys no doubt thought they were a bit tasty. So, would not be expecting him back in a hurry. Therefore, by going back he would display a certain amount of bottle and may, as a result, get some kind of hoodlum respect.

In short, he thought he was Jimmy Cagney in Angels With Dirty faces. Nothing that giving these kids a clip round the ear wouldn't solve. By going back to the flat right away they would know that he wouldn't squeal on the chair. Wouldn't they? And anyway, he couldn't let these people down.

*

In the end Mrs. Moyes couldn't take any more waiting. Everyone knew she was out of sorts and so, after much cajoling, she agreed to go home "to get over the shock".

She walked staccato fashion back home. Sometimes hurrying to get it all over with. Other times slowing to postpone the inevitable. Eventually she entered the close and climbed the stairs staring fixedly upwards. She turned the corner and, from the landing, saw that her worst fears were realised. The storm door to her flat sat slightly ajar. What before had been the way back to her refuge had now become the Entrance to Hades. She made it as far the storm doors.

Looking inside she could see that the walls of the vestibule had been splattered with the contents of numerous cakes. Chocolate éclairs. It was a sweet dirty protest. Some of it was so high up she knew she could never reach to clean it. They didn't know that. They were just naturals.

The prospect of what lay inside was too much. Stepping back out of the door, ashen white, Mrs. Moyes fainted. She started to topple towards the stairs.

A young man climbing the stairs saw her about to fall. Sprinting up the top few steps he managed to catch most of her weight. Unfortunately, as she fell, her head flipped back and hit the young man on the nose. Which would have been bad enough even if his nose hadn't already been broken.

*

Inside Danny was delighted to find that a) the stuff on the walls wasn't shite (although he still wasn't brave enough to taste it to be sure) b) there appeared to be no other obvious signs of ransacking and c) everything he needed to make a cup of tea was laid out neatly on the table, so he wouldn't have to do any ransacking of his own.

He managed to get Mrs. Moyes into the flat and onto the settee where, after a short while, she came round. Initially she screamed because there was a strange man in her flat and she appeared to be covered in blood. After another brief lapse into unconsciousness she came round again and Danny had a cup of tea prepared.

"Hi. I'm Danny. I just moved in upstairs."

"..."

Mrs. Moyes held up a bloody hand in front of her face. Through the fingers she could see Danny's face. It was starting to make four.

"Eh, sorry about the blood, you fell outside on the landing and we had a wee bump."

"Oh..."

"Don't worry, this wasn't all you, it was already fairly smashed up. Are you OK?"

"Eh...well...a cup of tea might help."

Mrs. Moyes was never sarcastic. Danny was never any good at comforting.

"Oh sorry, here, I made this, milk, no sugar."

Danny handed it over and stood back proudly waiting on the inevitable "How did you know that?" He hastily prepared his response in which he described how is intuitive mind derived from the precise layout of tea making equipment that the person responsible was very particular about their tea. So particular that, if they had taken sugar, there was sure to be sugar there. It's all part of a lawyer's well honed powers of observation and deduction. Let me take you back to the night of the tea making...

"Thanks son."

The question was not forthcoming. Danny fell off the high horse of High Court haughtiness.

"So, what happened here Mrs Moyes?" Remounting, unsteadily.

A bit easier, involving reading the nameplate on the door. Your witness.

"The Finch twins. They stole cakes this morning and broke in and…"

"Yes, I saw. They don't seem to have done anything else though?"

"No, it seems OK."

Danny noticed the cup emptying quickly. He was also slightly intrigued by the fuck-off big pile of newspapers stacked neatly against one wall.

"More tea?"

"It's OK, I'll get it son."

Mrs. Moyes walked over to the table and poured more tea. Halfway though pouring she stopped and sat down weeping on the chair.

"What's wrong?"

Danny saw her eyes resting on a A4 sized jotter sitting on the table, covered in cake.

"Why this? Anything else but not this."

They were naturals.

"What is it?"

"It's…my scrapbook."

"A scrapbook?"

Danny finished pouring the tea and Mrs. Moyes drank. He found some tissues and cleaned up the book. After a while she settled down and started to talk. It seemed like she was talking more than she ever had.

"My son is an actor. Not a famous one, y'know, but he was…is…good; He's getting there. I kept all his cuttings, everything. Even the bad ones, I always said that was important, made you better."

"Has he been on telly?"

"Only bit parts and walk-ons, y'know…"

"Still, he'll be getting bigger parts soon, eh?"

"Well…"

Danny sensed her mood changed. Talking about her son she had become extremely animated. Now the melancholy of before returned.

"I don't know, he's…gone away…"

"Away…?"

"Two hundred and… nearly a year ago. He left for an audition and no one has seen him since."

"I'm sorry."

"Don't be, he'll be back, I know he will. I look for him every day."

"Are the police not looking for him?"

"Well, aye, you know, I mentioned it to them, but they say he was a grown man, people leave places. They said they were looking mind."

Danny saw her glimpse at the papers.

"I'm sure he will be back, maybe he's just gone to collect an Oscar?"

Mrs. Moyes smiled.

"Thanks son, y'know, for everything."

"No problem."

"You'd better go and get that nose seen to. It's still bleeding."

"OK, but could you do me a favour?"

"Aye, sure…"

"Could you write me a note? I have a feeling they're not going to believe me at the hospital."

Six

Danny sat waiting in the hospital for the second time in under a week reflecting on the wonders of life. Not so long ago he had jumped in the car and headed for his new career. As yet, he was still to do a single days work and had, instead, shuttled between Penthouses and pavements covered in sick and then onto hospitals in an orgy of blood and foaming baths. This, as the saying goes, was the life. All he needed now was to get out of the hospital in time to meet Kelly and for her to be clothes-removingly impressed by his further tales of heroism. Or, failing that, the faithful old Jacuzzi.

In a weak moment, he had caught himself thinking differently about Kelly. Sure, getting her kit of was still top priority but there was something about her. Something that could maybe let him take a couple of dates. Danny didn't know what made her different. To anyone looking at the two of them together it would have been obvious. She was way out of Danny's league.

*

Charlie watched Kelly leave like she was going off to war. If he could have followed her down the platform he would have. He smiled a sad smile knowing that she may never return. Even if she did she would be changed forever, shellshock. He decided to work late, stay all night if necessary. It was going to be tortuous and if his evening was going to be ruined he could at least vent his anger on sealing the fate of a hapless defendant.

*

"Hi Danny."

"..."

It had finally happened, like a forgetful Best Man, Danny was, probably for the first time since the age of 2, speechless.

"Sorry, I'm a bit late…I…oh what happened to you face?"

36

"Eh…well…"

The truth is an often under-utilised ploy in the game of love. Progressing only just enough past speechless to allow him to talk, Danny couldn't manage even the faintest of lies. He did, however, only tell part of the truth. Something that, even afterwards, he was never really sure if he regretted.

"It's…nothing…a woman fainted in the close, I ran up the stairs to catch her, her head hit my nose as she fell."

"That's…"

"Unlucky, I know…never mind eh…let's eat."

Kelly looked truly amazing. Jazz mag amazing, only without the airbrushing. Or the staples. Even fully clothed she would easily be the best wank Danny could imagine. That alone was enough to reduce the usual McColl banter to ruins, but what really did it was that Danny knew instantly that he would not be taking her back to the pad for a shag. Not because she might not want to but because Danny was scared.

Laxmi locked up early for the night. Things were a bit slow in the shop; a few more hours locked away safely at home seemed an attractive proposition. On his way up the stairs, he saw Mrs. Moyes inside her storm door on a ladder.

"Bit of decorating?"

"Eh…no…sort of the opposite really."

"What happened?"

"Eh…"

Her eyes darted about nervously.

"Oh, how about you make me a cup of tea and tell me?"

"OK son."

Once inside they locked the storm doors securely. Laxmi saw the remaining cake on the wall.

"The Finches?"

"Who else?"

"We really are going to have to do something about them."

*

He held open the door.
She ordered sweetly.
He ate politely and cleanly.
She smiled.
He told funny stories.
She laughed at all the right bits.
He told sad stories.
She frowned.
She told stories.
He listened and proved he was listening.
She walked to the toilet, wiggling and jiggling.
He watched intently, breathless and longing.
She drank wine, sipping gently.

37

He drank orange, driver.

Half way through the meal, his nose gushed blood.

His medium steak became rare.

She mopped.

He tipped his head back.

She was concerned.

He finished the meal with a napkin up each nostril.

She finished the meal still smiling.

He apologised.

She refused the apology.

He paid, nonchalantly, signing the slip with great difficulty, head still pointing to the sky.

A lift home?

No, it's…

No really, please, my nose is fine now.

They got into the car.

"So, where to?"

"West End…if that's not out of your way."

"No, that's ideal, that's where I am."

This was not a Jacuzzi night. Kelly was not a Jacuzzi girl. He'd be back in the West End flat soon, so that was where he stayed. They headed along towards Charing Cross and onto Woodlands Road. The busy motorway buzzed underneath. Danny's head buzzed with pain and lust. Or was it love?

"Where to…?"

Kelly didn't want Danny to know where she stayed exactly. She hoped that Danny would think that she was just being cautious.

"Just drop me at Kelvinbridge underground, that'll be fine."

It suited Danny fine. He decided to crash out at the flat and drove round the corner and parked. It was a still a bit early and it had been quite a night, so before heading home he popped in for a quick double in The Doublet.

Once again, this decision would be one that Danny would not really know whether to regret or not. If he had gone straight home then he may have ended his relationship with Kelly prematurely. When she left they had agreed to go out again. He was going out with Kelly. The beautiful, funny, kind, adorable, utterly shaggable, manto of the millennium that was Kelly. Kelly. Danny's Kelly. My Kelly. Danny McColl and Kelly.

Danny McColl and Kelly Finch.

*

Danny slept fitfully between blonde dreams and bloody nightmares. In the morning, he awoke a different person. He didn't realise it yet but somewhere deep beneath the still fully functional McColl exterior a heart had been awoken. Of course, he realised that ending a date without a shag was a bit out of the ordinary. He also realised that perhaps not wanting to end the date with a shag was a bit different for him. He was, however, unaware of how he had changed, how his view on life would be different from now on and how much mortal danger he was now in as a result of his new love. The first change happened that very morning.

*

It came to Danny in a dream. A voice he knew said, "These people need your help." A lone horseman. Black shirt. Big hat perched on a bald head, approaches the village. The villagers need help. The brooding hero (and his six pals). Only they can save the day.

When Danny woke up he had all but made up his mind. Sure, staying in the flat was a means to an end. He'd make some cash. Some poor sap would buy the flat and end up living with the Finches. But why not, while he was there, try to change things for the better? These villagers deserved a better life. Danny had nothing to lose. His nose was already broken beyond recognition. They were good people; all they needed was a spark of resistance, someone to make the unifying speech and to stand strong in the hail of bullets. What they needed was Yul Brynner. And Danny was here to play the part. Only this time with a quiff.

"Hi, Mrs. Moyes, it's Danny, we met yesterday?"

Danny had knocked on the door but got no reply. Shuffling footsteps approached the door like the stealthy menace of Danny's first ever act of compassion.

"Aye son, aye, thanks again."

"Can I come in?"

Mrs. Moyes gave the look of the permanently concerned. Then, remembering whom this was and that he had helped yesterday, her face softened and the thought of some company opened the door beyond that crack at which it now set. Evil is seldom that narrow.

"Come in son, aye, come in, have a cup of tea."

Danny entered. He tried not to look but Mrs. Moyes caught his eye observing the slowly curdling cream cake high up on the wall.

"Still some to clean off', she seemed apologetic.

They sat down for tea. Everything was as it had been; the pot had been ready to pour. There was enough tea for two. She seemed in a permanent state of readiness for an unexpected visitor or calamity. Def Con 2.

"So, these Finches are quite a bad lot then?"

"Aye, I've known them all since they were wee. Always been trouble, one of the elder ones went to school with my Gary. Nothing but bother the lot o' them. Although, the daughter seems a nice lassie. Keeps herself to herself. I suppose you would living with that lot."

"So, do the parents never keep them under control?"

"No son, no. I don't know the whole story mind you; they were here when I moved here with ma Frank. Ma Finch hardly ever goes out. When she does she says hello, seems nice enough."

"And the Dad?"

"Dunno son, never been any sign o' him all the time I've been here. S'pose that's what it is, no discipline in their life. So, you seem very interested in them?"

"Aye, well, you know what they say, know your enemy."

"Well, son, you keep well away. They already spoiled your looks enough. And I've no helped much either, mind you, but anyway, they're trouble and it'll not do you any good sticking you nose anywhere near their business."

"The state it's in now it won't do it any good sticking it anywhere!"

Mrs. Moyes laughed. It was the first time Danny had seen her smile.

"So, what about the other folk in the close? Do they get hassle too?"

"Aye, poor Laxmi, you know, the shop down stairs. Always getting some kind of abuse or something. He lives in fear."

"Aye, I noticed he has more locks than Goldie."

"Eh?"

"Never mind, so what about across the hall here. Who lives there?"

"Well, there's a story. Dunno his name. He moved in not long after us. Hardly ever goes out. Very smartly dressed. Obsessed with the Beatles, folks call him the Beatle Man. You know, after the Beatles."

"The Beatles?"

"Aye, seemingly he only ever says the words from their songs. I dunno, he's only ever said Good Morning to me, seems a funny thing to say if it's from a song.2

Danny sat perplexed for a moment. These were no ordinary villagers. It was going to take more than a few minutes basic handgun training to turn them into an effective fighting force.

Seven

The car came five minutes early. In their excitement the kids piled in. The boys crushed in the back. Baby was carried. The cases were squeezed into the boot and it was forced shut. Mum got in the back with the twins, Dad got in the front, checking for tickets and passport almost as he walked. Inadvertently inventing body-popping years ahead of time.

Uncle Dennis dropped the clutch in his taxi and made an aeroplane noise as he pulled away. Everyone cheered. The tumult continued most of the way to the airport. Every mile or so Uncle Dennis turned and asked "Are you sure you've got everything?" In the end, Dad got so flustered that Mum had to issue a one-word reprimand "Dennis!" That was all it took.

At the airport, Uncle Dennis parked near the door blocking the taxi rank. Fists were waved. Expletives were returned. When Dad got out with the baby everything calmed down. Dennis threw the cases onto the pavement and with one final "tickets and passport?" he winked, wished them all a good time and sped off. Presumably making more aeroplane noises.

Trolley. Walk. Check-in. "Passports please?"

"Eh? Yeah, they're here somewhere."

Mum looked incredulous, thinking "he's only checked them once every five minutes for the last two hours."

"Ah, here they are."

"This is a bus pass sir."

"Eh, aye, sorry…here they are…"

Mum tutted. The boys whizzed round the wide-open check-in area shooting each other down with imaginary machine guns "ya-ta-tat-tat. Ya-ta-tat-tat".

Tickets. Baggage checked in. Only three hours until the flight.

"I could murder that Dennis for his cheek."

41

"I could murder a cup o' tea."

*

"I could murder them sometimes y'know"

"I bet you could."

"Not that I would of course."

The thought of Mrs. Moyes trying to harm anything made Danny smile. It was an Akira Kurasawa kind of smile.

"Have you ever thought how they would react if you fought back?"

"Fight back? Son, that bump on your head must've effected your senses."

"Just made them sharper."

Danny was getting a bit carried away. He was nearly ending his sentences with "ma'am".

"Obviously, we can't go head to head, mano-a-mano. But they don't strike me as being all that clever, perhaps we just need to outwit rather than out punch?"

"Son, you're not dealing with something that you can outwit, they're just evil, and anyway, even if you did and they found out it was you, they wouldn't leave you with much wit when they got to you."

"They won't know it was me."

"You're very sure of yourself?"

"I'm a lawyer Mrs. Moyes, I have to be."

If she had known, she would have rolled her eyes.

"I've the beginnings of a plan. We're going to trap them. But first we're going to need some bait. Do you think Laxmi would help?"

"I dunno son, he gets enough bother."

"Don't worry, no one will know, no one will remember."

*

As plans went, it had far more bones than flesh but Danny felt sure that he'd think of something. He knew he couldn't go head to head with nutters. The only way you could do that was to understand that you had to be prepared to go as far as they would, be just as extreme. In the case of the Finches this was much further than Danny was likely to entertain. No, this would take subtlety and guile. For a while Danny decided to set aside Pacino in favour of Henry Gondorf. It was the Finches that would be stung. The excitement was carrying Danny far further then he realised, far further than was sensible.

The plan emerged by accident but with a little inspiration from the local constabulary. The next day, Danny was walking back from the 3 in 1 with chicken pakora when big Malky emerged from a pub with a slightly lolloping gait.

"Malky!"

"Eh...?"

"Danny."

"Oh aye, Danny, aye..."

Danny thought quickly. It was during the day. Malky was quite clearly jaked. In his pocket, Danny saw some papers that looked like Malky should

42

have delivered them a while ago. Danny also noticed that Malky was a big bastard. A useful ally when you are planning to defend a village or sting an Irish American hoodlum.

"So, does Mr. McWilliams know you hang about in pubs when you should be delivering court papers?"

"Hey, look, don't get smart…"

Malky's brain lurched into gear only to find the body it controlled over a barrel.

"Does he know you drive about on his business over the limit?"

"Look, I…"

"Never mind, I'm not looking to cause trouble, but maybe you could do me a favour?"

"Eh…aye…whatever."

In that moment the plan set firm in its mould. Danny took Malky back into the pub and told him what he required in return for his silence.

"Rohipnol? No! I'm not getting involved in any rapes…"

"Malky, I can assure you, no one is getting raped. Pillaged maybe…"

"You sure?"

"Listen, no one is getting raped, ye folla?"

"Aye, well…"

"Can you get me any or not? Or should I be popping into the office for a wee chat?"

"No, no, it's OK, I know a guy, and he'll sort you out."

"No, he'll sort you out; you get the stuff and drop it off at the flat. Ye folla?"

"I'll need some cash…"

"How much?"

"75, maybe a 100…"

"Malky, does this face look stupid to you?"

It did.

"Here's 50. You can keep the change if you can tell me the name of a disreputable tattoo artist."

"Eh?"

"A name…please?"

*

To Danny, life was like sitting on a swing. You could rock gently back and forth but things didn't really get good until you got to the extremes that sent your stomach contents flying wildly about your body. The point at the zenith of the swing that was as unsettling as it was exciting, that was what Danny lived for, the top of the swing, the final whoosh, the fringes of common senses. Adrenalin turning to dopamine.

And this was that extreme. Drugs deals, stings, Jacuzzis, nurses and Kelly.

"I love you Glasgow."

Danny skipped back to the flat. Before going upstairs he popped in to see Laxmi.

43

"Can I help you?"

"Hi, I'm Danny just moved in upstairs?"

"Ah, yes, Mrs. Moyes told me about you. Terrible business with these cakes. Thank you for helping her."

"No problem. Evil little shits those Finches."

"Yes, but, eh... keep your voice down, y'know..."

"Aye, sorry. So, you ever felt like getting them back?"

"What? You're joking?"

"'Me? No, not at all. Why not?"

"Because, short of wiping them off the face of the planet, I don't see how you wouldn't come off worse."

"Well, how about if I told you that I knew of a way to get them back, help the police lock them up and maybe make them scared to leave their house? And..."

"I'd tell you that you were either mad or stupid."

"Or both?"

"Probably."

"I can do it, but I'll need your help."

"Me? No, keep me out of it. I've got enough trouble."

"No problem, you won't be involved. All I need is some information and maybe a little stock."

"Look, I have customers and this is not the kind of thing that it is wise to discuss, y'know."

"OK, how about I tell you what I have in mind later? Come to Mrs. Moyes' flat at 8pm. OK?"

"No."

"All you have to do is listen. If you don't like it then I'll say no more and leave you alone."

"OK, 8 o'clock."

"Great." Danny turned to leave.

"Danny?"

"Aye."

"Why are you doing this?"

"The village needs help."

If he was being racist, it was the most pathetic attempt Laxmi had ever heard.

*

It didn't seem fair not to allow everyone in the close their pound of flesh, so, on the way up the stairs to the flat, Danny stopped at the door of the Beatle Man to see if he wanted in on the action. From what he had heard he fully expected that he wouldn't want to not join in but it gave him an excuse to exercise his curiosity.

After two firm knocks Danny waited for an eternity before the door swung briskly open.

"Hello, hello."

44

Before him stood a man in a bright white suit. He was very neatly turned out; round glasses perched on the end of his nose. Looking back through the lenses Danny couldn't notice any discernible prescription.

"Hi, my name is Danny, I just moved in upstairs."

"Yesterday."

"No, I've been here for a few days now."

Danny smiled; maybe the story about the lyrics things was true.

"What makes you think you're something special when you smile?"

Maybe not, but it was already becoming obvious that a sensible conversation would not be found on this doorstep. Giving up, Danny chose instead to try and catch a glimpse behind him into the flat. The Beatle Man closed the door slightly in response. Danny resorted to plan A.

"Do you ever get any trouble from the Finches?"

"I know nobody can do me no harm."

"Eh...aye...well, they leave you alone then?"

"We're all alone and there's nobody else."

This guy is a nutter.

"OK, well, I'll be off then."

"You might not know it now but when the pain cuts through you're going to know and how."

A shiver ran up Danny's spine as he entered the flat playing back his words in his head.

"When the pain cuts through...? He's off his fuckin' chump."

*

"Hi Kelly, it's Danny."

"Danny, hi!"

Her sudden and unexpected enthusiasm just about stopped Danny's heart bursting through his ribs.

"I..."

"Did..."

They both started to speak at the same time. One answering the question the other was about to ask. After some fumbled apologies they determined that they both had had a good time.

"I was wondering if you fancied going to the pictures?"

"Aye sure."

"What do you fancy seeing?"

"There's that new one with Jim Carrey."

This was a major set back but not something that couldn't be overcome. Danny had been hoping for something from the Scorsese season at the GFT. He was a big enough film buff for the both of them.

"Yeah, that'll be great." Danny tried not to be too obvious spitting out the words; he instantly had plans for a hip flask to get him through it.

They set the date and time. Danny said he'd book in advance "his films are quite popular." An internal monologue added, "fuck knows why."

All that remained now was to phone Charlie and be completely obvious about not mentioning Kelly.

"Peachy!"

"Hi Danny." Charlie responded flatly and without the required accent.

"Oh, like that is it."

"Look Danny, is this about anything important, I'm a bit busy just now."

"Oooh sorry, I won't keep you. One quick question."

"OK, shoot."

"What makes you think you're something special when you smile?"

"The Beatles, Hey Bulldog."

"Quick as ever Peachy, just checking."

"Just checking what?"

"That your still a smart-arse."

"Pot. Kettle."

Danny said goodbye and hung up.

"Hey Bulldog? Never heard of it. Weird bastard."

*

Defying recent convention, Danny lay back in a bath of water rather than the now, more normal, sick, piss and plaster. He gazed up into the soon to be repaired hole and chuckled to himself.

"It's been a funny old week."

He never had been one for much deep reflection but now he wondered if there was some great scheme at work. When things get this weird, he surmised, it can only be because there is something driving events, some prepared end game for this bizarre opening. A Queen sacrifice that leads to mate in 4 moves.

"Mate. Mmmmm…forbidden donuts."

His mind drifted off and thought of Kelly. The rest of his body did the same and before long there was more than his shoulders breaking the surface of the water.

Maybe it was all a game. Maybe to win the girl he had to help the villagers. It seemed that everyone he had met recently had some role in play. Apart from that weird Beatle guy, but every game has its joker.

His next move was planned; he would get Laxmi's help and take revenge on the Finch boys. It was an aggressive, attacking strategy but that was how he liked to play.

"Get your late tackles in early."

The tension of the battle was mounting.

"Nothing that a quick wank won't sort out."

Danny was convinced that George C Scott as General Patten would have done the same.

"Sherman tank! Ha!"

*

Just before 8 Danny got to Mrs. Moyes door. As he raised his hand to knock he realised that he had failed to organise this with her. This was quite

46

clearly a rather sizeable oversight and one that might put pay to his planning session for this evening.

"Shit."

Scratching his head for inspiration, he noticed that the inside door was open. The last time he had seen it left like this was after the Finch boys had been about their business. Ever the caring opportunist, Danny leaned inside.

"Hello, Mrs. Moyes?"

Nothing. This isn't good. He called again. No reply.

He couldn't leave, she may be hurt or she may be out and left her door open. Whatever the possible scenario, going inside seemed the best option.

The light from the living room illuminated the threadbare carpet that covered the centre of the hall floor. A border of polished wood ran all the way round. A small hall table sat to one side. A picture of a young man sat at an angle on the wall above.

Danny tiptoed further into the hall, then, realising that his sudden, silent appearance may cause a bit of a shock, he called out again.

"Hello, Mrs. Moyes, your door was open, I…"

He could hear a quiet whimper coming from the living room. The door opened with an ever-increasing screech. Doors only ever make noise when you are trying to be quiet. He could have opened it quickly and silently.

Mrs. Moyes sat next to her teapot crying. She didn't look up. In her hand she had crushed a single A5 sheet of paper. It looked like a flyer. Today's paper, usually neatly stacked on the pile by now, was strewn all over the floor.

"Mrs. Moyes…"

"Aye son, aye…"

Danny walked over the kettle, filled it and flicked the switch, the little red light looking like her bloodshot eyes. Situations like this were one of the main reasons that Danny considered conveyancing to be his likely career course. Family law was all very well and good but you usually had to deal with people in distress. Danny preferred the option where he got to help people make large sums of money selling their house or buying their dream home. Now he was in the kind of situation he had chosen to avoid and all because he had chosen to make a large sum of money from selling a home (but probably not one that appeared in many peoples dreams, have you met your neighbours the Manson's?). In for a penny…

"Let's have a nice cup of tea" opened Danny "it always does the trick in Eastenders."

It was upbeat but not offensive, broke the ice without tipping the igloo into the water.

Mrs. Moyes started to wail uncontrollably. Oops. His head now in a spin and a career in Family Law now completely out of the question Danny tried to work out what the hell he had said. He needed clues. The newspaper.

Looking at the floor the headline "West End Stage to East End Pub for Glasgow Actor" shrieked out "Shut the Fuck Up with the Eastenders references, OK dimwit?"

The wailing continued and Danny stared blankly about the room, in a trance of futility and inaction. It was broken by the click of the kettle.

Danny made the tea and handed Mrs. Moyes the mug. She took it and dropped the flyer to the table. Her hand shaking, she took a few sips and begun to settle. The headline on the flyer read "A new production of Catcher in the Rye comes to Glasgow".

"It was his part you know."

"Part in…"

"In this play, Catcher in the Rye, he was going to audition for it. He never got there. He would've got it. Instead some other laddie gets it and now he's away to Eastenders."

To Danny, this suddenly felt like finishing all the sky in a jigsaw. He still wasn't confident about the thatched roof though so let the talking be its own cure.

"I've got nothing against this laddie, it's not his fault, but that should've been my laddie, off to London, famous, in the papers."

"He will be."

"Aye, well, sometimes I wonder, y'know."

A conversation broke out and Danny was relieved that maybe he could talk his way out, without further wailing.

"It's only Eastenders, it's the token Jock role, they put them in and then wheech them back out when folk complain about the accent on Points Of View. What's that Ruth one doing now?"

"Even so, it would have been nice…"

"No, your boy is made for better things, Hollywood, Ewan Macgregor…"

"Who?"

"Sean Connery?"

"Aye. That would be good, although I don't think he's the James Bond type."

It was lucky that everyone had heard of Sean Connery, Danny's list of successful Scottish Hollywood actors was virtually exhausted. Virtually in an actually sort of way. It's the accent. Gerard Kelly was mildly amusing as a supposed gangster in Brookside but as a trainee Jedi knight? You needed screen presence to carry off being a Russian sub commander with a Scottish accent, something sadly lacking in say, Gregor Fisher. Elaine C. Smith might've done OK though. Danny chose not to share this observation at this juncture. He was starting to get the hang of this counselling thing. Note to self, no unrelated TV or movie related references, keep it simple and never, ever mention Gerard Kelly. Then again, that applies in so many situations.

There was a knock at the door.

"That'll be Laxmi." said Danny, apologetically.

"Laxmi?"

"Aye, I'll just go and see him."

In the hall, Danny saw Laxmi enter slowly, much as he had done himself.

"She's a bit upset. Maybe we can calm her down and go and chat in my flat?"

"OK, but come down to mine, I've got a crate of beer to test from a supplier."

Danny gave the surprised look that Laxmi had become accustomed too. He didn't wait for the question.

"Yes, I do drink. And I'm quite good at it too."

Danny blanched and decided to forgo an apology.

"Well, I'm not too shabby myself and although not a Hindu, I can claim to be quite a cheeky shi-ite."

Laxmi appreciated the cheek, all he wanted was to be treated like anyone else and if that involved getting the piss ripped from time to time, so much the better.

They got Mrs. Moyes settled down and she promised that if she got upset again she would come down to get them. There was a moment when the sad old woman, the Indian shopkeeper and the pisshead, gobshite, soon-to-be-a solicitor felt something that none of them expected. They didn't know what it was exactly. Togetherness? Mutual appreciation? Anyway, whatever it was, it was fuck off unlikely and in their own way they knew it.

Danny and Laxmi turned to leave. On the way up the hall, Danny pointed at the picture of the young man.

"She said he went missing the day of the audition for Catcher In The Rye. I wonder if he had the script with him?"

"I know he did, he showed it to me just after he got it."

Eight

It looked as familiar as it did alien. At one end, the bar still spanned the width of the room, its bustling light now the quiet grey of a metal shutter. The tables, usually alive with bodies and glass, stood exposed, their frail legs and peeling tops exposed by the lunchtime light leaking in through the nicotine stained glass. No noise. No disco. No bingo callers or karaoke singers. This was the club that had been the teenage chore, the family treat, the purgatory of coke and crisps, beer breath and drunken Uncles. The dark and smoky atmosphere of those nights replaced by the colourless silence of recent death, shuffling feet and muffled sandwiches.

Danny remembered the last night he had been here. The night he had tried to drag his Dad away, away from the liquid that was slowly killing him. The night that, to him, his Dad died, not now in this phantom show of grief. The sad faces that knew he was ill but still told him to "Get away", "Let your Dad enjoy himself". They were all here, no contrition, no admission. They had been saved. They had been spared the blame because every face in the room, every set of eyes now turned to Danny as he entered the wake and unanimously voted him the villain of the piece. No one said anything. They didn't have to. Even if he hadn't did what he did, it would still have been his fault. He was the one that went away when his Dad needed him, when he should have been bringing in a wage instead of this ridiculous "trying to better himself", "ideas above his station". A closed community full of closed minds. Trying to be different is crime enough.

Going no further than the door, he waited until he was seen. Deek and Rab, his only friends from school, nodded as much as they could without getting noticed. Deek started to move towards him but a glance from his Dad and he was stationary again. He nodded an apologetic and confused face at Danny and shrunk back into the corner. A few whispers and his Mum was told he was there. She got up slowly and after an interminable tour of thanks and condolences she shuffled towards the door without looking up. As they headed for the outside door the familiar noise of the metal shutter rising above the bar signalled that it was time for first orders. The club was due another wake.

*

The thoughts had run through Danny's head like an open sewer. It had taken practically all night for them to run dry. With each twist of his body in bed, the screw turned tighter, his head spun faster, the constant whirl of pain and anger running round the inside of his skull like a bike on a Wall Of Death.

The image of the man that they had buried. The memories of the life that had been destroyed, the knowledge of that the lives that he had destroyed. Had he saved them? Really?

Behind even the cheeriest smile or the cheekiest face you can often find pain. Danny thought he was different, that was what he told himself and everyone else. What he did, he had to do. One too many black eyes, one too many piles of vomit. He threw him out, he beat him up, and he made sure he never came back. He was going to die anyway.

*

Laxmi handed Danny a can and, like most first drinks, he accepted it with steely determination rather than honest thanks. The crack would never be allowed to show. It was beer; he had grown to love it despite everything. For once this was not about the top of the swing, this was holding on tightly to the chains.

"Cheers, what the hell is that?"

"Hungarian lager."

"What?"

"Yeah, I know, the distributor told me it would be the next big thing after Czech lager."

"And it wasn't?"

"Taste it for yourself, hope you like it, I've got 4 cases to get through…before the end of last year."

Danny took a long draw from the can and, with an exaggerated wince, swallowed.

"I've tasted worse."

"You have?"

"Yeah, I was a student remember, you have to be on your guard or you can end up drinking a glass of piss."

"You didn't?"

"It's an episode in my life I'd rather not go into…at least this is cold."

Laxmi's face looked like someone had just pished on his best rug.

"Who's piss was it?"

"You know, I never did ask and I couldn't really tell from the taste…might have been an Australian."

"Eh…?"

"Slightly oaky…"

51

Danny basked in the glow of what was, as far as he could remember, his first ever combined piss and wine gag. He presumed that there was probably a good one in there about turning piss into wine but couldn't quite get his head round it and, as it would probably involve some sort of religious reference, he decided against it. He was having enough trouble getting his head round Hungarian beer drinking Hindus. In for a penny…

"So, you're not a Hindu then?"

"Lapsed."

"Lapsed?"

"Yes, I'm a lapsed Hindu, just don't tell my Mum."

"Why, does she think you're a lapsed Catholic?"

"Yes, my name is Laxmi Joseph John Paul Bernadette Mehta."

It was one of those situations that don't work on paper. Then again, the paper wouldn't have had any Hungarian beer. It would simply read "Take one Trainee Conveyancing Solicitor and one Indian shopkeeper, place together in a room. Then throw in a cunning plan."

"Let me get this straight, you want me to leave a case of spiked booze outside my shop in order to trap the people who make my life a living hell?"

"Absolutely."

"Fuck off."

"Now, I'm sure another beer will help you see it in a better light."

"Double plus fuck off."

"OK, let me run through it again. All I need you to do is to donate a little bit of al-kee-hol. I do the spiking. I do the trapping. You don't need to do anything."

"But they'll know it came from my shop. They'll take it out on me."

"I'll wait a while before doing anything, they'll never put two and two together."

"This is still not sounding like a good idea."

"Did you see what they did to Mrs. Moyes flat?"

"You don't need to tell me what they can do; you're new round here. I could tell you a lot more."

"Exactly."

Danny always expected people to be as gung ho as him. He wasn't made to convince, he wasn't made to cajole. He expected everyone to follow him to the castle brandishing all the torches they could light.

"Answer one question?" Laxmi brandished the beer bottle in the way you can only do when you're getting a wee bit pissed.

"Shoot."

"Why?"

"Because they're evil little bastards."

"No, why you? Why do you care? Are you Shiva?"

"Who?"

"Shiva, the destroyer of evil."

"Eh…no. I'm just me."

Danny wanted to tell him the truth. Well, his truth. He wanted to tell him that he was Yul Brynner, he was Al Pacino, he was the one that was honour bound to defend the weak against the oppressor. He was the one the people needed. Somehow he didn't think that it would work with Laxmi. He tried a different approach.

"I'm John McLane."

"Who?"

"You know, Die Hard. Yippekayay Mother Fucker?"

It took a wee while and a whole lot of Hungarian lager before Laxmi finally agreed. Danny took his now cooperative nature to prise a few key facts out of Laxmi. The best time to catch the Finches passing the shop, when to leave the alcopops out. Their regular movements; where they would take them. Danny stayed just sober enough to remember the information. It was a technique he had learnt during a great number of drunken conquests. What was the point of picking up and ultimately shagging a girl, if you couldn't remember a thing about it? Why have a scalp if you can't hang it on your totem? He remembered them and with any luck they wouldn't remember him. A butterfly collector.

The plan was falling into place. The villagers had the guns and could just about point and shoot in vaguely the right direction. Now it was time to start digging the trenches.

*

"Fucks sake Danny, it fuckin' 3 in the morning"

"I'm terribly sorry Malcolm my good man but as you can no doubt tell I am trousered."

"Aye, well, fuck off, you've already woken up the missus."

"Big hugs from me, look where's my rohipnol?"

"Eh…what the fuck are you talking about? Fuck off."

Malky hung up. Danny did the only thing he could in this situation. He turned the receiver to his face and stared into the earpiece. A Paddington hard stare. That'll show him. The age of the mass-market videophone still sadly a few years away.

"Ah fuck it."

And with that and a graceful, synchronised relaxing of all leg muscles (henceforth known as a 'Hungarian') Danny swan dived onto the settee. And he slept, instantly and deeply.

In the tenement all around him the night passed. Laxmi crept to bed and didn't wake anyone. Mrs, Moyes lay awake, images of her son as a child filled her head. The whole family was there, her husband too. A sunny day in Weymss Bay getting on the ferry to Rothesay. The putting and the palm trees. Palm trees! How they laughed. Palm trees in Scotland? Much of the camera film went in creating Rodeo Drive like pictures of their pale bodies on holiday next to the palm trees. One of the pictures sat next to her bed. The three of them. The family. One dead. One missing. She looked up and the sodium orange glow through the window lit up the face of the young boy with the ice cream. Pale and innocent, waiting for his life to happen. Waiting to be.

She turned the picture face down to the cabinet. Her fist clenched tighter on a hanky and she sobbed knowing that in the morning she'd feel the undeserved guilt of the eternally hopeful.

Others were awake too. Another picture was turned down to a cabinet. Another sob could be heard. Elsewhere singing could be heard.

"...take these broken wings and learn to fly..."

*

The same border of white flowers still poured through the rusting wire fence, the pale leaves looking green and frost covered behind. He never did find out what they were called. Behind the flowers the same five brick high wall held back the earth and kept the tiny postage stamp lawn flat. A green square of mostly clover, moss and daisies.

The sprung metal gate creaked as he pressed his hand against the flaking painted surface. He leapt up the three stairs in one like he always did and walked up the ageing flagstone path. He dragged his shoes against the grass and moss protruding from between the cracks like a small boy returning home for his tea.

Two rusted screws held the number 45 firmly against the dirty pebble dashed wall. He forced his key into the weathered Yale lock, the shiny brass surface long since worn away. The paint too was starting to expose that which is was supposed to protect and as his hand pressed the door open a few more flakes fell to the ground. The familiar smell, the tortoise-shell carpet the incongruous collection of pictures in the hall.

You do what you can to escape. Danny's world was his bedroom with the self-installed bolt, slide it, hide it. There was a bed, a wardrobe and a small table with a old alarm clock on it. It had been his Uncle Danny's; he got it when he died. The clapper rang between two large bells on top. It had blu-tac on it now.

The walls were his escape. Every square inch was covered by a poster, favourite bands, favourite people but mainly favourite movies. The student standard Betty Blue, Pacino as Scarface and his pride and joy, the original 1975 Jaws poster. His world away from the streets, the broken glass, the mince on the table, the mince in their heads. Lying on his bed and staring at the scenes around him was all he could do to try and be somewhere else. But now he had been somewhere else and they just looked faded and sad. He left the room and went back to the living room. His Mum was much the same. The living room door was open and he entered slowly standing at the door for a while. After a few seconds he spoke.

"Trickle, seven letters, beat that Stilgoe."

"Hiya Danny son!"

"Hi Mum, still got the touch."

It was almost their only point of connection. Despite the certificates and graduation photos displayed proudly against the woodchip, it was only through outwitting the boys in Dictionary corner that Danny's Mum truly understood the abilities of her only son. It was the thing that could be bragged about at the bingo, discussed in the street.

"That's my laddie got the conundrum three days in a row now" scores far higher then any law degree ever could in the streets of Falkirk. But the streets of Falkirk had their uses and that was why Danny had come home.

"Staying for tea son?"

"Aye, if you've got anything…"

Danny knew she would, she still cooked for three every single night, she didn't know any other way.

"Aye, mince and tatties, yer favourite."

*

Danny had woken up on the settee feeling, as his name suggests, not peachy. The Hungarians may not know a lot about brewing beer but they seemed to be ante-post favourites for the World Hangover Championships. It took at least an hour to get from waking to being able to keep his eyes open reliably and without thoughts of a brain embolism. Sitting up proved problematic for what seemed like most of the day but with a heroic lurch he managed to haul his torso the right way up. Pain, nausea, aching, pain squared, nausea, extreme bladder pressure. Danny took what remained of what seemed like a very short life in his hands and headed for the loo.

The pee lasted about 15 minutes. All thought was concentrating on standing and not throwing up. Hungarian beer. Hindus. Pished.

"Buddha-pished!"

Danny laughed but had to stop as it hurt too much. There wasn't much in the flat but he was very, very glad that he had remembered to buy the emergency Irn Bru. He took a long drink from the cool orange bottle and life started to come back to his body. The pale yellow of his face combined with the unnatural orange of the juice to produce a reasonable representation of healthy red. Then his brain woke up.

"Shit, shit, shit, shit!"

He had remembered the late night conversation with Malky and had the associated realisation that he had given fifty quid to a drunken bear that had absolutely no recollection of the conversation. He then had to admonish himself for even thinking about getting Malky involved. Arthur didn't have him in his employ for his strategic thinking or his knowledge of precedent. He must know about the rough edges on his already rough exterior. It is plain folly to blackmail the uncaring oaf; it is super supreme folly with cheese to try to do this when that same oaf is out of his box. It was a rookie mistake and not befitting a law professional of Al Pacino-like standing. Malky wouldn't even hesitate to accidentally mention this in front of Arthur and then Mr. Slick-Tongue would have to go to explaining town.

Still, on the positive side, it was always good to be reminded of one's fallibility and to get away with it, even if it did come on top of the mother fucking sheep shagger of all hangovers, Hungarian style. Danny could only presume that the Hungarian's laid down such a rich base of potatoes and cabbage that the beer had less effect.

By the time the whole bottle of Irn Bru was gone (and after the obligatory loud and consistently entertaining burp) Danny felt almost human again. His ability to think returned and it brought with it a slightly revised plan. His conversation with Malky (and the £50) had at least yielded the name he needed. All that was missing were the drugs and it wasn't as if he was short of possibilities there. It would mean a trip back home but it had been a wee while and his nose was now sufficiently healed it wouldn't freak the old girl too much. It would also mean running the gauntlet of the nutter-druggy-waster collective that passed for his boyhood friends. A dangerous thing at the best of times but, on the positive side, he would always know where to find them.

Before he danced again with the darker side of life, a few things had to be ticked off the revised agenda.

*

Item 1.

"Hi Kelly."

"Danny hi."

They started with frightening symmetry.

"You like seafood?"

"What, like fish and stuff?"

"Yeah, fish, prawns, oysters, y'know, whatever."

The smoothness of Loyd Grossman subtlety blended with the fey lark-about good fun of Charles Hawtrey.

"I suppose."

"Well how about I take you for a meal?"

"Well I can't go tonight but I'm free on Friday."

"Friday it is then. Pick you up at…"

"…my work, pick me up at the office, that'll be easier, we can get some half-price cocktails round the corner first?"

"Done, see you then."

Item 2.

Danny emerged slowly from the front door of the close and covered his eyes with his hand. Turning to his left he peered into the window of Laxmi's shop. Shazia sat patiently at the till; Laxmi was nowhere to be seen. Danny opened the door; the ringing of the bell seemed to take place inside his head.

"Laxmi about?"

"No he isn't."

The answer was firm and conveyed all the 'no he isn't because he is currently ill after drinking mental beer all night with a certain waster standing in front of me against the express wishes of his faith and, more importantly, his wife, that it was supposed to.

"Tell him I said hi."

Danny backed out quietly before the smirk that was rapidly forming on his face turned into a full-blown laugh that would certainly receive an even frostier response. On closing the door behind him, he let out a loud celebratory guffaw.

This was just enough to keep his guard down and he let the sun pierce into his head like that Hellraiser guy putting on a helmet.

Item 3.

Danny, eyes well shielded, walked to his car and, after a good 5 minutes raking, blew the fluff of his well-worn Ray-Bans and placed them delicately on his nose. Safe from the glare, but probably not from the breathalyser, he pulled into the street pausing only briefly to turn the radio down a bit and open a window.

*

The Hungarians must eat mince and tatties too. It made all the difference and, given the drinking he'd have to do to achieve his goal, was a bit of a Godsend.

"OK if I stay here tonight Mum?"

"Course son, course, this is yer home, it'll always be your home."

He made a point of leaving his car keys, wallet, jacket and anything else that was valuable and not attached to his body in his room. He blew a kiss, as he always did. His Mum sat and watched one of the men her life leaving for the pub. As she always had.

Nine

The day after the letters arrived, Danny walked up the hill to his Uncle's house as he had done every week since he had been out of hospital. Uncle Dennis was dying. He took him some shopping, some videos, some books, whatever he needed. It was the least he could do.

The house didn't smell like it hadn't been cleaned in months. It hadn't. What passed for Social Services turned up often enough to make sure he was still alive and shuffled off. When you have relatives nearby there isn't much to do.

Danny let himself in out of the rain with the spare key and shouted to announce his arrival.

"Dennis, its Danny."

There was no answer. This was normal. The cancer had all but taken Dennis' voice away. He found him sitting in his usual chair under the usual cloud of smoke. There was no point stopping now. The Doctors didn't agree but "what do they know?"

"Brought you a few videos, tea?"

Dennis nodded assent and shuffled uncomfortably on his chair. Searching for a bit of buttock not yet asleep. Danny brought the tea and sat down, handing Dennis his letter.

"What's this son?"

Dennis' voice was weak. A ghost before its time.

"I got into Uni, I start in August."

"Aye, aye, yer Mum told me."

"Oh, did she phone?"

Danny had hoped to get to Dennis first. He was the older brother. If he could convince him them maybe his Dad would listen.

"Good news, eh?"

"What about your Dad son?"

"My Dad? He'll get a job. Don't you worry."

Dennis looked worried. He knew his brother.

"Son, its no' that…"

"Dennis, if I can get to Uni, get a degree, I can help them then. I'll have a good job, good money. It will be easy."

"But…"

"But until then, we'll just have to get by. I'm not giving up this chance."

"Danny, your Dad will…"

Dennis started to cough. It was a very painful, full body cough that took a lot out of him. Danny picked up the mug of tea and helped Dennis take a few shaky sips. His voice was all but gone now. He motioned to say that he couldn't really speak.

"It's OK, I understand. Look, I know it's a tough one, but they've got to let me do this. You'll help me, won't you?"

Dennis sat up as best he could and beckoned Danny closer.

"Danny, I'll not be here to help, these people need you."

*

"Roofies? What the fuck are you wantin' roofies for? You usually have no bother gettin' yer hole man?" Deek was, as ever, direct.

"It's not like that man, y'know? It's for… well, these twats fucked with me, y'know? It's a wee bit o' revenge."

As was required on these occasions, it paid to be as far from perfect vocabulary and diction as was possible.

"These wee cunts are askin' for it, right? But their big brothers are a wee bit tasty, so I'm not too happy with gettin' caught, y'know?"

"Danny! Man, what are you doin'? I thought you wiz a big shot lawyer? What are ye doing fuckin' about with these wee cunts for?"

He had a point. Luckily, Danny had left it far enough into the night to start the acquisition process so the several pints stopped him being reasoned with. However unlikely the source of the reason may be.

*

He had arrived in the pub to a mainly frosty reception. Having got there a bit early he chastised himself for not realising how far it was from Giro day. He sat tight and prayed that a well-known face would show. The faces he did recognise, recognised him and, glowering over their pints, made an instant, if erroneous cognitive leap, between trainee lawyer and dole snoop. Danny found himself staring at all the nasty looking mongrels collected around the room to make sure they were tied up enough to give him a chance to run. The mongrels that weren't tied up also seemed to provide enough danger for now.

Danny knew that any attempt to blend in without someone 'vouching' for him was about as much use as the attempt Gene Wilder and Richard Pryor made to be 'cool' in the jail in Stir Crazy. All he could do was to be normal but without forcing it. He drank beer and donated money freely to the fruit machine, nudging away from wins and only holding shite. Then, a couple of

59

unlikely saviours appeared. Deek and Rab were not upstanding pillars of the community. They were rarely upstanding and only when leaning against pillars.

They were both in Danny's year at school, well, according to the official documentation anyway. It's not that they were bad, they were more feckless than evil. An endless stream of suspensions and, in Deek's case, a wee while banged up, put pay to any thoughts of an academic career, not that they were having those thoughts.

Trouble came to them very easily. But unlike most offenders of their type, they were almost entirely lacking in intent. Their misdemeanours came about through a continual need to explore and understand the world. Like small babies, they tested things out, finding out what was hot, what was cold, ouch that's sharp, jobbies taste bad. And with the same childlike innocence they had little or no interest in or understanding of any consequences. Take this inquisitive innocence and add almost Neanderthal-like stupidly and you have yourself a recipe for disaster. So, when Rab asked the question "can you play basketball if the ball is on fire?" most people would reply "you can't" or "don't be so stupid". Not Deek. Before you could say "oh no, we'd better phone the fire brigade", Deek was already finding out. Most people would still have a gym hall. Not Deek and Rab.

Danny probably should have thought twice about trying to use that pair of reprobates to score drugs but the fact was that, despite their shortcomings, they were strangely honest, loyal and, above all, rarely believed. Just to be sure, Danny waited until a few pints had been sunk before bringing the subject up. This, of course, would make his presence there less suspicious but would probably take away some of their memory and all of their credibility in any future court proceedings. The downside being, of course, that before too long they would start to talk pish.

"So, you see on the news, right? Loadsa stuff, y'know?" started Rab, current affairs a là Paxman.

"You don't watch no fuckin' news" retorted Deek, now standing at an angle against the bar.

"Too right I do, it's on all night, sometimes I gets a bit zoomed, y'know?"

"Aye, aye." Deek spoke into his pint glass.

"Well, there is somethin' they're no tellin' us, somethin' much worser than anything."

"Are they stoppin' giros? Don't joke aboot that."

"This is no fuckin' joke man."

Danny watched the interaction between the two intellectual colossi wondering where all this was going.

"Prawns."

"Wit?"

"Fuckin' prawns."

"Wit, like they wee shrimp bastards?"

"Aye, they poor wee pink bogie bastards."

Danny, just managing to avoid choking on his pint, was suddenly intrigued.

"I had this job in Iceland y'know?"

Danny choked into his pint at the thought of Rab having a job but Rab was, by now, too far into his flow to notice.

"I used to fill freezers, like, when they were empty, I put stuff in. So, I had these bags o' prawns, right?"

Deek nodded, listening intently although it was unclear if it was interest or incredulity.

"How many prawns do ye think are in each bag?"

"Hundreds?"

"Aye, hundreds. How many bags did I put in?"

"Hundreds?"

"Aye, hundreds, every fuckin' day, thousands o' the wee pink fuckers. And how many shops sell them?"

"Thousands?"

"Aye, hundreds o' prawns, in hundreds o' bags, in thousands o' shops. How many now?"

"Fuckin' millions man, millions."

"Aye, an' every single day, y'know? Ask yourself a question…where the fuck do they all come from?"

"Aye, man, aye. Jeez, yer right, that's fuckin' weird man."

Danny thought about joining in but suspecting that more entertainment would come from just listening.

"Not just that, millions every fuckin' day, we're wipin' the wee bastards of the face o' the planet? Germocide, fuckin' germocide…it's a disgrace."

"Aye, aye." Deek nodded sagely, paused for a second and then the weight of the situation dawned on him.

"What am I gonnae have in ma fuckin' curries? Fuck. Fuck it."

Danny had had enough.

"Don't worry Deek, they have farms for them, they'll not run out."

"Farms? Farms? You're fuckin' off yer head!"

It was right about then that Danny decided that there was a chase and it was time that it was cut to.

*

"Looks guys, these wee cunts are nae bother. You know they've been messin' with some folks, it needs to get sorted, y'know, like the prawns, y'know?"

"Aye. Needs to get sorted man, needs to get sorted."

At the mention of the prawns a sudden solemnity came back to Rab.

"See that big cunt over there? Baldy, in the 'Gers top?"

Danny looked over and hoped that the huge bald bear blocking most of the wall opposite was not the one.

"Him?"

"Aye, name's Troll."

"Troll, as in big hairy Troll."

"Naw, Troll as in trolley, like off his…"

Stomach now sunk lower than his now very worried gonads, Danny looked to the seafood crusaders for some assistance.

"Cool, any chance of an intro?"

"To Troll? Fuck man…"

"Guys, come on, think o' the prawns man?"

"Aye man, the prawns, aye, come on then…"

The Troll didn't look like what Danny expected a drug dealer to look like. He was expecting a small, ghost of a person that sniffed a lot and was in need of a feed. Instead he got the side of a house in a Rangers strip. Rab followed Danny across the pub and could feel the noise lower with every step. By the time Rab stood in front of Troll, he was virtually the only one speaking.

"Troll man?"

"What the fuck do you want cunt?"

Most people would have been put off with this but in these parts it was more of a "hello, how are you doing?" Rab knew not to be put off.

"Looking for some stuff, y'know?"

"Stuff? Dunno what ye mean. Why don't you and yer dole snoop pal fuck off?"

"Eh…."

Rab paused and Danny realised that his negotiating skills were all but exhausted. He puffed up his chest and thought of Clint Eastwood.

"Look pal, who the fuck are you callin' a dole snoop?"

It was now totally silent. Rab took a few shuffling steps back.

"I'm no pal of yours."

"Fair enough, but I'm no fuckin' dole snoop right?"

The Troll looked somewhat surprised. People weren't supposed to speak to him like that. Everyone knew that. If this guy didn't know that he was either daft or…well, someone.

Danny saw the look on his face and seized the moment.

"My mates here tell me you're the man that folks round here need to be speaking to."

He was aware that this sentence made no sense but was guessing that this kind of negotiation usually started vague and got vaguer. The pub began to sense that a fight was now slightly less likely and low murmurings started up again.

"Aye, that's true."

"Let's get something clear, I'm no snoop, I'm a fuckin' lawyer, that's no fuckin' crime and if you think that talkin' to me is a problem then it's not as big a problem as I would have if people knew I was doin' it, right?"

Troll looked deep in thought, the semantics being worked out. Treacle running down an abacus. His entourage began whispering and nudging. Danny heard words "lawyer" "handy" and "wedged". At the end of the impromptu sidebar, Troll seemed happy to talk, objection overruled.

"OK, lawyer boy, what can I do for ye?"

"Roofies."

"Roofies? A good lookin' laddie like you?"

"Very fuckin' funny, they're not for me, but ask no questions, right?"

Rab was somewhat non-plussed by Danny's performance and was starting to shuffle closer again. Deek had wandered off and was peering up the reels to see if there was anything worth nudging.

"Normally, they're a fiver a shot but since I don't know you from fuckin' Adam, they'll be a tenner a pop to you."

The temptation to haggle was great. There was no way Harry Callaghan would have bought them for that price but then again he'd probably had all the luck that this punk was going to get.

"OK, gives ten."

Danny thrust a bundle of notes forward cupped inside his hand. Troll turned to one of his devotees who produced the pills and handed them to Danny. Troll never had them nor did he touch them.

"Hang on, there's 200 notes here.2

"Aye, the ton is to make sure you've never seen me, OK?"

He didn't wait for an answer, turning on his heels he winked at Rab and headed for the door. Before he had even reached the door speculation had already started about which minor celebrity had sent a lawyer to buy stuff.

Outside the pub, Danny walked away as quickly as he could with a sensation that there was a gun trained on his arse. In this part of town, there probably was. This made him walk in an awkward pelvis-first motion. Once out of sight he stopped abruptly and was copiously sick. With each wretch he laughed more until the sick became mere punctuation in the tumult of amusement. The joy overcoming the fear in the battle to be the most prominent emotion.

*

It had taken a while but his Mum eventually agreed to let him take her for her shopping. He knew she'd never let him pay. She shuffled round her usual route through the aisles picking up the same things as she always did. Special offers and aisle-end promotions were not meant for the likes of her.

The gentle meander round the supermarket gave Danny the time to reflect on the events of the night before. He had got away with murder but, for once, he knew it. As the night went on he had found it harder and harder to stay in character. Every now and then his vocabulary would get too rich for the local tastes and in these kind of places quizzical looks could quickly turn to hassle. He'd thought that going home would be easy. He now realised that he hadn't gone home, he'd gone back. Only now did he know the difference.

In his mind, where he grew up was somewhere where he fitted in, where he would always fit in. Now he was the outsider, the punishment for abandonment, for daring to move on, to try to do better. He had got away with it this time but he probably wouldn't the next.

Driving away from the house later that morning he knew he had a new home now, all he had to do was find it.

Ten

It was now more than obvious to anyone that Danny was already too far into this to stop to think about what he was about to do. It was certainly obvious to Laxmi when he finally handed over a tray of alcopops. Much as he liked the idea of getting back at the Finches, he remembered enough about his Hindu upbringing to understand the true meaning of Karma. He thought about this as he bent down to select a tray of drink in the storeroom.

Hindu legend has it that demons and deities churned the Sea of Milk and 14 jewels surfaced. One of them was filled with a poison whose fumes threatened to devastate everything on the planet. To save the world, Lord Shiva drank the poison. As he did so, his wife Parvati put her hands around his neck and held his throat tightly. The poison stayed in his neck and turned his throat blue.

Perhaps it was irony; perhaps it was a last attempt to protect himself from the repercussions of what was to come but, for whatever reason, it seemed appropriate to Laxmi to choose the blue coloured alcopop to give to Danny. For the first time in many years Laxmi thought of his grandfather, the scary, wizened old man who had scared him with ancient tales and the promise of Karmic debt always being repaid.

A better form of protection came with the insistence that Danny leave the laced booze 'as far from his shop as was humanly possible'. Danny got the idea. Not that that meant he would use the idea to any good effect.

*

It was only when he had all the parts in place (the tattooist, the booze and the drugs) did Danny realise that it was about as much use as an author with no metaphors. It was very two dimensional, it worked well on paper. It would need the other dimensions to ensure that all the ingredients came together not only in the same place but also at the same time.

He was thinking about this as he drove back to Glasgow and he decided that, like all great thinkers, he needed the right atmosphere. Even Sherlock Holmes would have ditched the violin had the Jacuzzi been invented.

Lying back so his eyes were just about the water, he watched the bubbles appear on the surface hoping that, as each one burst, it would bring with it the ideas he needed to put the plan together. The basic building blocks were simple enough. He got the washable kitchen note board and sat back down in the Jacuzzi and wrote out the seven deadly steps.

Get the drugs into the booze.

Leave the booze where they can find it.

Follow them until they drink it.

When they get woozy, grab them.

Take them to the tattooist.

Get them tattooed.

Take them back and get the fuck away before they wake up.

As all the water drained through his skin into the Jacuzzi, it got more and more difficult to come up with the necessary safe and sure plan. He got out and introduced the brandy decanter to his dilemma and, like so many naked and lost souls, was saved by the warming liquid. And he didn't even have to put up with the smelly, slavering dog to get it.

By the bottom of the decanter the plan was complete and scribbled in an increasingly wayward hand on the small note board. It was perfect, it was going to work and if it wasn't he'd now had more than enough brandy not to care.

Finally getting out of the Jacuzzi, he slipped and staggered his way to the loo and pissed out what fluid remained in his prunish, wrinkled body. Looking down he was simultaneously amused and disgusted with the thought that he might look like the Queen Mother having a slash standing up. Well, it might be easier; toilet seats might have been tough on the hips.

He came back from his regal ablutions and had one final review of the plan. It was going to take cunning, daring and a dash of panache. He'd need style, groovy style and a car that just won't stop. He'd need a hell of a lot of luck and if he wasn't in jail by the same time the next day it would be a bloody miracle.

*

Running along the street at full pelt his lungs complained violently. They'd asked for 'lounging sloth' not Sebastian Fucking Coe. It wasn't a good time to stop for a rest. It was all going according to plan. Well, it might be, but some twat left the plan next to a bubbling Jacuzzi and the plan ran off onto the tiles. It was all according to what he could remember of the plan but if he didn't get a taxi soon it would all be completely fucked.

"If this was a film set in New York I would just have to think about needing a cab and I'd get one" the only part of his brain that wasn't involved in running and breathing was suggesting. It was roundly ignored as irrelevant and not helpful just now, thank you.

Turning the corner onto a bigger road he hoped to increase his chances in a more taxi rich environment. It was now dark and the same idle part of his brain was now guffawing at the misfortune that made streetlights the same colour as the elusive glow of an available taxi.

"Isn't that funny", it opined "the light reflecting off the top of every car looks like a taxi with it's light on, ha!". Deep inside everyone, however well it is hidden, is the worst kind of wanker.

Finally, and with much flapping of lactic soaked arms, a taxi was stopped and the wheezing body was launched into the back.

This part of the plan called for wit, charm and a good degree of faultless acting. It required that a story be told to the taxi driver about how he had to find his brothers. They'd just had their tea but there might be a chance that the baby "you know how kids are" had maybe spilled the poison into the sugar bowl. Or something like that, he was never really happy with this part. As it turned out, the power of speech had been temporarily removed from his armoury and, after throwing up in the back, so was the taxi.

Sitting on the kerb, far enough away from the remains of his dinner, that he had wretched up after thrusting a tenner into the paw of the irate driver, he swore and swore and swore. Somewhere in Glasgow there was a pair of drugged twins about to collapse and he wouldn't be there to collect them, transport them and tattoo them.

In the cold light of day and in the cool of the night, with the rain drenched pavement soaking into his arse, he realised that he had maybe gone a bit too far. This was a fucking stupid idea. What had these boys done to him? One of them nothing. Did he really owe the other people this amount of risk? Was his intended punishment really fitting of the crime? Was this really the price of redemption? No, this wasn't right at all. He should go home, get changed, go out, get pissed. Get thinking about Kelly again. Anything instead of this daft crusade. Anyway, he'd proved he could have done it. He got the drugs and crushed them up. Very carefully he had removed the lids from the bottles of carbonated alcohol (as was recommended for this kind of thing). The drugs had gone in. The bottles had been resealed well enough. Laxmi had told him how there was a whole industry in India that refilled and resealed water bottles for reselling. It would take a while for the arse to fall out of that market. He had followed Laxmi's advice and it worked. He'd worked out where to leave the bottles and they'd taken the bait, albeit after a long tortuous wait and the occasional shooing away of an invalid target or two. Maybe just drugging them was enough. They could be in Kelvingrove Park now getting butt-fucked by delirious happy gay men thanking the God of all things Gay for such wondrous bounty. Who can say? Not being able to get a taxi and, worse still, throwing up in the one he did get was enough of a sign, not that he believed in signs.

With a new resolve and a new belief in signs he picked himself up.

"Hey pal...fucksake man...fucksake."

It was a sign. It was a big, fuck off sign; a sign that said in 30 foot high illuminated writing, "This is a sign". In fact it was two signs. Two identical signs. Both wazzed out their cups.

Danny looked at his watch. 23 minutes since he saw them drinking the blue poison. If the stuff he'd read on the Internet was right, in 7 minutes they would be sleeping like babies. This, however, would be of no use to him if they saw him beforehand. He had to be sure that they were already too far-gone to have any chance of remembering him. It had to be a sure fire test. Remembering his recent thoughts, but conveniently forgetting the ones relating to giving up, he decided on his opening gambit.

"Hey lads, any chance of a fuck, ah've no had it up me in ages."

The thinking was that if they were awake they would react violently to this but if they did they'd still be too scoobied to catch him.

"...fucksake man...fucksake..." This seemed to be all that either of them could say. Then again, this could still be normal.

"What is your name poof?"

"...fucksake man...f...s..."

"Yer maw, Mrs. Fuckwit Finch, she's a fuckin' man, your maws got baws."

"...ffffffffffffffffffff..."

The proof seemed irrefutable. They had not reacted to any of his jibes, it wasn't clear if they were even reacting to light and it seemed that all they could do now was exhale and dribble. If he was going to do it he'd have to move fast. The taxi idea was fucked so he'd have to get there on foot, which meant doing it in the next five minutes while the two dribbling babies could still perambulate.

Slinging an arm under each one arm he waddled off in the direction of the tattooist. To avoid any unnecessary attention he started a small song about nothing in particular in no discernible language at the top of his voice. This kind of swaggering songmanship was usual for that time of night in those parts.

He had to stop every few yards to reset his kidnapping crucifix pose and get a better grip on his charges. But not on the situation. Reticence and remorse now consigned to the gutter alongside his dinner, he marched on slowly and surely. This was the big gunfight moment. Only a few bullets left and the baddies closing in on the village womenfolk. It was time to strike, quickly and decisively. It wasn't time to think about a sequel.

Waiting at the final pedestrian crossing seemed like an eternity. Normally he'd take a couple of swift looks and bound across the road scoffing at the red man. Dragging two youths with you makes you wait diligently for the green one. Even though he wouldn't mind if they both got run over, he had no particular desire to be trapped between them at the time. And he wasn't even sure of the cleanliness of his underwear.

The light changed to green and the 'hurry up or you'll die' beeps seemed more useful than Danny had previously realised. He just made it to the other side as the large Orange hulk of a bus pulled away noisily behind him. The people on the bus didn't even take their eyes off their own personal boredom for an instant.

The plan had been to phone ahead to the tattooist when he was on his way. This was part of the same plan that had him in a taxi chatting away about "the misguided youth of today" and how he'd "better get them home" and "we live above a tattoo shop ye know". Thank fuck he didn't have to try to get away with that nonsense. Then again, he didn't know how Alf was going to react to not getting a call. It had taken quite some time, coercion, a smidge of Malky supplied blackmail and a not-inconsiderable wedge to get him to agree to do it at all. Malky was right, he was disreputable but he was still, in his words "not all that interested in getting in bother with the law". Strangely enough, all these potential ills were cured by £250 up front, £250 after it was done.

He didn't have to wait long at the door to find out Alf's reaction.

"Fuck off."

"But…"

"You were supposed to phone."

"But…"

"Fuck off…"

"Look, there's no one in the shop, it's not…"

"Fuck off…"

"How about I just leave them here?"

"How about I tell them all about you when they wake up?"

"How about I give you another hundred and I get in out the cold?"

"Two hundred."

"Fuck off…"

"Bye."

The door closed and the bright, garish images of dragons, mystical beasts and meaningless body graffiti taunted Danny from within. He knocked again with his head making sure not to hit his nose like he did the first time. Alf made him wait. The red neon sign in the window looked like it would never turn to green. The twins were now out and proving impossible to keep upright. This was all taking a new shape and that shape was shit. After a quick glance around to see that the coast was relatively clear, the twins were dropped to the floor and pushed up against the window. Both hands were now free for some serious knocking and hey, why not, some shouting.

"Alf ya fat fucker…"

Nothing.

"OK, another £150…"

Nothing, not even a flicker on the tasteful dragon curtain that separated the front of the shop from whatever evil lurked behind. Maybe a kettle and a Calor gas fire. This was not a good negotiating position and Danny knew it. They had made a deal and had agreed terms and arrangements. Danny had changed that. He now had two drugged psychos on his hands and, although Alf didn't know his name, he was fairly sure Alf could identify him to them. Dark hair, average height, average build, nose smeared all over his face. Even the

68

most dense of halfwits could join the events together, especially those honed for revenge and retribution. And there were two of them, so that makes a whole one. In this situation it was now clear that his arse was hanging well out of his trousers and unless he got some cash out quickly it was very likely it would get spanked.

"OK Alf, £200 but I've only got the £250 with me tonight."

After another long pause the curtain started to move and was thrown back. Alf approached looking very annoyed and not displaying the sunny demeanour you would expect from a so-called 'artist'. The door opened and Alf stuck his fat head out. Not having much of a neck, his shoulders came too.

"What did you call me?"

"Nothing."

"OK, £450 tonight or no deal."

"But I've only…"

"Don't worry, I take Switch."

Danny didn't have time to reflect on this but was instantly impressed not only by the effective negotiating techniques but also the convenient range of payment methods. Disreputability had come a long way. Before you know it kidnappers will be getting paid online.

"Get them inside before we both get rumbled."

Danny looked up expecting some help but Alf had already entered via the dragon. As he dragged them both in, the lights in the front of the shop started to go down. Shrill nerve-jangling whine started up behind the curtain as Alf prepared his weapons of torture. Had the twins been awake they would probably be shitting themselves except that they wouldn't be, they'd be wrecking the shop and killing Danny. So, all in all, being unconscious was best for everyone.

"Come on then, not got all fucking night."

"Right then" Danny replied like a child being hurried along against his will.

The first twin was taken into the back room and placed on the chair. There was a kettle.

"So, what are we doing here?"

"I'd like a word on each forehead please."

"You didn't say it would be the forehead?"

"You didn't ask. Look we are tattooing someone against his will it hardly matters what we do does it?"

"Well, fuck it, what am I doing?"

Danny didn't like to admit it, but he had drawn inspiration from Jim Carrey.

"Dumb on him, Dumber on him."

"Wit?"

"The word 'dumb' on his head and 'dumber' on his."

"S'pose that's not too bad, I was expectin' somethin' more like cocksucker."

"Now that would be out of order." Danny smiled wryly.

"Any particular font?"

"What?"

"Font? Typeface? Y'know, for the word."

"Eh?"

"Look, this is no amateur scribble shop, y'know."

"It's not as if you'll be able to refer to this work in advertising is it?"

"No, that's not the point."

Alf was definitely some kind of fucked up enigma that Danny would never understand. A gangster with artistic sensibilities with whom you could pay for illegal activities by debit card.

"You choose. I don't care. Something quick would be good."

"OK then, an uncial I think."

"Fair enough, off we go."

The bone-chilling whine started up again and Danny decided that waiting in the front shop would be less likely to freak him totally. Brushing the curtain aside with a flourish, he stepped out into the dull street lit front shop. The walls were completely covered in all form of weird shapes, animals, symbols, cartoon characters and band names. It was the final evolution of the cave painting human. Within this cave, the images daubed in ink on the rough walls could be transferred to the body as a sign of strength or tribal allegiance. My name is Metallica from the Garfield tribe, I come from Scotland and I love my mother. Respect me for I have undergone the ceremony of the ritual marking.

He cast his eye over the many strange images before him and, by the time the curtain opened to the overacted announcement of "Next!", Danny was almost convincing himself he could maybe get Alf to do him one now. Then, as he went in to collect the first completed twin he instantly changed his mind as he was faced with a red, scabby, bloody mess.

"I said write 'dumb', not burn him with acid."

"Give that a week, it'll be a work of genius."

"Aye, aye, better do the next one a bit quicker, they'll be waking up fairly soon."

"And what would for like on the other one?"

"Dumber."

"They look like they are identical twins, it would be a shame to spoil it, no?"

"That's the whole point."

"Whatever, I don't want to know."

Danny dragged the completed work through and brought the other one in. He dragged a leg too.

"You're next victim master."

"Very fuckin' funny, make yersel useful and put the kettle on Egor."

In 15 minutes it was done and all that remained was to get them out and far away.

"Sign here sir."

Alf kept up some kind of weird pretence of this being a legitimate transaction. He even checked the signature.

Danny shook his head but didn't speak. It was time to leave, pronto. Then something occurred to him.

"Alf, this fancy Uncial font thingy."

"Aye."

"Can anyone else in Glasgow do it like you?"

"Nope." Alf replied proudly.

"So these guys will know it was you?"

"Do I look fuckin' daft?" He looked at the signature again.

"There's more chance of them thinking it was you. No one will even think it was a professional that did it."

Danny dragged the first body out, looked about quickly and hauled him up onto his back fireman style. This was the part of the plan that he never really had worked out before the brandy took over. He lumbered round the corner and into the lane. Running as fast as he could he took the sleeping Finch to the end of the lane and set him in the dark out of the street light creeping round the corner. He then ran back and did the same with the other boy.

Alf closed up behind him.

He returned to the end of the lane and found them still out. They'd be coming round in under half an hour. They weren't far from the tattooist but there was no way of getting them much further. Hopefully they would be too disoriented to remember where the woke up.

Danny ran back to the other end of the lane. The tattoo shop was already dark and silent, the cave now deserted, Danny's money already on the way to the pub without him.

It was now time to get as far away as possible as quickly as possible. Still no taxis about. He started walking and came back upon the spot where he had thrown up before and decided that he had ran, walked, dragged and maimed enough tonight. The taxi could come to him.

He looked down at the sick in the gutter and wondered where the revulsion came from. It was just food. If it was a kebab lying in the gutter you might laugh at the misfortune of the drunk without his supper but you wouldn't be disgusted. If it was a big shite, you'd be disgusted. If you knew it was human you'd be truly appalled. What the big deal? In the end, it's all the same stuff. You eat food. After a while food turns to sick. A little later, sick turns to shite. Food. Sick. Shite. In the end, it all turns to shite

Eleven

That night Danny slept peacefully, free from all thoughts of plans, schemes, drugs and, inexplicably, worries. At this stage of the proceedings any normal human would be acutely concerned with thoughts of unmasking and retribution. Danny rarely looked beyond his current rouse. He was never any good at chess. Obsessed with his own clever attacks he never considered the consequences of leaving himself exposed. At the point where he saw his own route to certain victory he'd leave the back door open. Mate in 5. Goodnight.

Most people, certainly those that lived in their vicinity, always understood the consequences of an attack on the Finches. Because of this they went relatively unscathed. Everyone feared the retaliation but no one knew in what form it would come.

If Danny had taken the time to consider this, there may have been a slight possibility that he may have desisted. The argument for not getting involved would have been very strong.

In the 18th century and philosopher and social reformer called Jeremy Bentham proposed a way of helping Danny in situation such as this. He called it the felicific calculus and it was a simple way of working out the consequences of doing something, of balancing the good and the bad, the pleasure and the pain. You just needed to look at all the factors for the pleasure and pain such as intensity, duration, certainty and extent.

It was clear that the pleasure of his recent actions was not great and would not be long-lived. The figure on that side of the equation was bound to be low. On the pain side: it could be intense; could last a while; was almost certain; the source lives in the same building and could affect any number of people. It didn't look good. Based on this complex philosophical equation Danny should have stayed at home. It just wasn't worth it. But, of course, Danny was neither complex nor philosophical. Then again, he got about as near to being a pure hedonist as modern society permitted.

*

Moira Johnson new all about Bentham and the finer points of utilitarian philosophy. As well as being a well-respected psychologist, she gave lectures in it as part of a General Philosophy course at Glasgow University. This provided her with a good living and a neat and structured way of deciding that she no longer wanted to be with her husband. Of course, this led to accusations of cold calculation and lack of emotion. This further confirmed to her his lack of understanding. All of this let them both avoid the real problems but that was fine with them. With blame suitably apportioned they could each move forward with all the bitterness they needed to survive. This didn't fully explain why she was thinking of taking Arthur back but not everything is covered in the annals of philosophy.

Even her best friend Laura didn't understand why she would contemplate taking "that philandering fat oaf" back. Moira thought it best to meet her to talk it through. Just in case she had a point.

She had been coming here for many years and had always enjoyed the art deco splendour, the relaxed ostentation and, of course, the seafood.

"Why take him back?"

"You know, I'm not really sure, it's well…"

"You've got the house, money, his fat arse over a barrel, you're made."

"Made?"

"Yeah, life is good, go out there and enjoy like he did. Let him drink and shag himself into oblivion."

"Life is good? I go home, I stare at a wall, I don't cook, I rattle around in a huge house talking to myself and my ever increasing collection of vibrating objects."

"But that's now, its early days, you'll be fine soon."

"Will I? I'm not so sure. I think you get institutionalised y'know? Like being in jail. I don't know how to live any other life."

"Sure you do."

"I don't."

"So, its better to go and suffer?"

"No, its better to go back and make him suffer. If you think I don't know how to live any way, Arthur is much worse."

"Do you love him?"

"Love him? What does that mean?"

"Oh do come over all philosophical with me…"

Moira wasn't listening; she was listening to the conversation behind her. Leaning over the table, Moira was becoming increasingly animated.

"You won't believe what he just said?"

"What." Laura replied desperately trying to appear interested.

"He says that he feels different being with her."

"So?"

"So! It's such a cheap line. He doesn't mean that."

"How do you know?"

"How do I know? How do I know?" Moira's original whisper was getting louder "Isn't it obvious?"

Laura realised that in light of their current conversation it was perhaps a stupid question. Just one of those things your mouth blurts out before your brain catches up.

"Obvious, why?"

"Because he's just trying to get into her pants?"

Laura had to pause and think about this for a while. She wasn't sure which side of which fence she was meant to represent. Was she the supportive "of course you should to back to him" type or was she firmly on the "men are bastards" float at the fair?

"Isn't he? Isn't he?" implored Moira.

"Isn't that the point at that age?" Laura replied eventually unable to see why this was a major problem.

"The point? THE POINT?"

Laura glanced at the now empty bottle of wine and realised where the volume was coming from.

"Sssshhh...you're..."

"Don't tell me to shoosh. Why do people always tell me to be quiet? Why am I the only one that sees?"

"Sees what?"

"It's all a sham, it's a bloody sham. It's so bloody obvious."

It was obvious. Laura could see that the bitterness was still there. The lingering mistrust and anger towards men of the recently separated. She got up to go to the toilet. Moira might stop shouting if she had no one to shout at.

Moira sat silently for a while listening to the young man behind her. She recognised the signs. The words that told the tale of invented love, of implied love. The trap being set. The trap they could never get out of, because you didn't want to, because you didn't know how. It was all such a cliché. Hackneyed rubbish. Why did Nancy put up with Bill Sykes? As long as he needs me?

They had been young like that once. She loved Arthur then, she loved him now. He did need her and, despite everything, she needed him too. But she wasn't going to make it easy for him. Things would change. She'd already done enough for him. Some of it she knew she shouldn't have and won't do again.

She listened for a good while longer before noticing that Laura had come back and then ordered another bottle of wine.

"Oops."

*

"Oops."

"What?"

Danny leaned forward.

"A bit of a tiff I think."

He pointed a finger through his chest behind him. This far across the table he could smell Kelly's smell and was intoxicated. He'd need to whisper a little more.

"You know what else?" his voice got quieter, drawing Kelly forward.

"Lesbians."

"No!"

"Yes, no doubt about it."

"How do you know?"

"On the way in they were both checking you out. Now, I'm not saying I'm gorgeous but come on, I deserve at least a quick glance." It's called Fly Fishing by J.R. Hartley.

"Oh, I suppose you do." Now to land it.

"Now you, I could look at you for days and never get bored."

Cheesy.

"Well, at least until I had to go to the loo anyway."

Cheeky. Perfect balance.

Despite the reservations of the lecturer to the rear, Danny did feel very different when he was with Kelly. For most of his life variety had been the spice of his life. His motivation had always been exploration and discovery. Why shag this woman? Because she is there. And when he did? Well, it was always interesting to see how each one reacted differently: the noises they made; how they squirmed; those that screamed; some that scratched. The excitement was the newness of it all. His performance was virtually irrelevant. He got on top, his hips went up and down and he thought about a dog having a shit. It was observation, not participation. Sometimes, most of the time, he succeeded, they seemed happy. On occasions, he failed; they left with their pants in their bag and a disparaging look. Danny didn't care, they was frigid anyway. He just did what he always did. Up, down, up, down, in, out, ad lib to fade. If she didn't enjoy it, it was her fault.

If Kelly didn't enjoy it would be his fault. This is why he felt different. Of course, Danny being Danny, his reasons for it being different where themselves somewhat different. Kelly was an angel. The most delicate, the most precious, and the most he had ever wanted. This meant taking his time. Meals and movies were the beginning. Maybe they'd see a show, have a day away up North, a boat trip on Loch Lomond, anything that would pay respect to her and the feelings he had for her. Anything that would postpone his failure.

"So, what kind of music do you like?"

"Don't know really, chart stuff, whatever, stuff you can dance to.2

Well, never mind, she was hardly going to say The Wedding Present, now was she? Which reminded him, that was now his favourite dress by far. And he hadn't even taken it off yet. Underneath he was sure to find his favourite bra too and, well, all the other treasures that lay within.

"What about you?"

"Eh, sorry." come on Danny; keep the mind on the job.

"Music, what do you like?"

"Oh, eh, everything I suppose." This could be tricky. Then again she probably wouldn't like that kind of music either.

"You can't like everything."

"You can, it's a mood thing."

"What do you mean?"

"Well, if I'm on holiday abroad, I'll push pineapple shake a tree, if I'm at home at night and it's quiet, I'll hum along to Madame Butterfly."

Fun and sensitive in equal and measure, the boy is a genius. His favourite band, Rage Against The Machine could wait for now. Fuck you, I'll do anything that you tell me.

"Madame Butterfly?"

"Yeah, the opera."

"You like opera?"

The tone in her voice was surprise and perhaps a hint of disapproval.

"Well, a wee bit, not all that often. And just that one.2

Danny needed to stay off music. There was going to be a distinct mismatch. That wasn't a problem. Other than the fact that he'd need a new love tape. A few years ago he'd made a tape that he always tried to play when on the job. In keeping with his direct approach it started with Firestarter and only after a few tracks did the pace calm down to Reel Around The Fountain. Later on the pace picked up again with Love Shack but he'd never made it that far. Well, apart from the time he forgot to rewind the tape.

He started to think about what this love tape might require but he couldn't conceive of shagging along to Elton John or Peter Cetera, so decided not to think about it. This kind of thinking, however, reminded him that it had got to that time. The special time. The time in the launch sequence where everything gets fuelled up and the plugs get pulled from the launch tower. T minus 3 hours and counting. The rocket is ready for launch. Well, that is what would normally happen.

At this stage of a night out with a young lady Danny would be having his final go/no-go checks as to whether or not he was going to pork her. This was almost always a 'go' but it was prudent to leave yourself an out. As soon as the 'go' has been issued, he would start doing the groundwork. The charm would be turned up, the innuendo sharpened, the conversation swayed in a carnal direction. He then would assess the giggles, eye contact and body language and then decide how long he'd have to leave it before pushing the launch button. The final question that would send him on his inexorable journey upwards into the darkness of a space.

But tonight, as with previous nights with Kelly, the go/no-go mechanism was a tad confused. Propulsion and launch control were reporting a big go. Guidance wasn't too sure. It said that a go would be nice but it wasn't all that clear on the direction that the conversation would need to take. It recommended that all systems wait for her to make the first move. 'Poof!' screamed the boys from propulsion. But Danny just didn't know how to cross the Rubicon. He wasn't entirely sure what a Rubicon was.

So, he stayed with the charm, he stayed safe. Above all, he avoided anything that would give offence. He also avoided failure.

As he took her to the taxi rank ('no, I'll get myself back') he thought of himself as noble. He believed that this was how real, true love began. He'd have to get inside her mind before getting inside her pants.

It's funny how easy to it is to fool yourself.

Twelve

"Don't tell me, you've twatted the roof in my flat now?"

Arthur didn't look well and the can of Irn Bru, clenched shakily in one fist, explained why.

"No, but I have exhausted your rather poor supply of condoms."

"What con...oh never mind, why are you here?"

"I work here, don't I?"

"Not so far."

"Very funny. Thought I'd better start."

"Sure you're up to it?"

"There's only one way to find out."

'Fair enough, Jenny will get you to your desk, get yourself some pens and annoy Wendy for some work to do. She likes that."

"Wendy?" Danny replied barely hiding the anticipation of working with another possible conquest. This was more than obvious to Arthur and, although it would be fun to let it run to it's natural conclusion, he already seen enough of Danny's blood all over the shop.

"No Danny, not this time."

"What do you mean?"

"Wendy is...5' 11", blonde, with legs up to her arm pits..."

"Intere..."

"Let me finish ... and if you as much as suggest the possibility that you might come on to her, even in writing, she'll will dismember you."

"Sounds as if that's spoken from experience."

"Nullem crimen sine lege."

"Aaaahh, nuff said." Danny didn't have a clue what this meant but thought it prudent to make it look like he did. This was the man that was employing him as a lawyer after all.

78

"Contra bonos mores?" If in doubt, guess.

"Fuck off to your desk smart arse and get Jenny to send me in more Irn Bru."

*

Charlie arrived at work with the usual trepidation that accompanied days he knew Kelly had been out with Danny the night before. He was fearful of the day when he would see that it was too late. The look on her face that would tell him she was hooked and that she would inevitably be hurt by him. Until now he had not seen it. This was as much perplexing as it was encouraging. But while she was still going out with him. It would not be encouragement enough.

He got to his desk and looked around the empty office. Preferring to come in very early, he always had a few blissful moments when there was no noise or distraction. No phone calls to interrupt him, no stupid emails with jokes or requests for deposits for Christmas parties. This was usually his time. But on this particular morning it was torture. He'd have to wait until Kelly arrived, just before nine, before he would find out if his worst fears had been realised.

Until about 8:45 he managed to get some work done but beyond that he was checking the clock a couple of times every minute. Work became impossible. At 8:55 he went to the loo hoping to pass the final few moments before she arrived suitably occupied and, on coming out, would see her big smile beaming from behind the reception desk. Making an extra special effort to wash his hands, he bounded out of the swing door of the toilet and was instantly deflated. The desk remained empty and the newly delivered enormous heap of mail sat on the sign-in book causing consternation to a client trying to sign-in.

Donald, the senior partner, appeared and blustered his way through an apology and made some excuse based on "those damned agency receptionists". Offended, Charlie helped move the mail and said that he was sure she'd be in soon. Deep inside him, the bottom of his stomach and sunk to his knees and the ache in his legs that always accompanied such stress had started. When he was young he was told it was growing pains. Now he never spoke about it so no other erroneous diagnoses had been proffered.

Back at his desk, Charlie was really beginning to panic. He had done it. He'd shagged her. That was it, all over. Where is she? Where was she? Charlie hated Danny. Hated himself for being so slow and so scared. For wanting to be more like Danny, everything he didn't want to be. He hated the fact that he felt like this. Sick and frightened. Charlie, the young, dynamic, flawless litigator. Someone who oozed capability, confidence and security. He could stand in front of a busy court and tie people in knots with superb oration and flawless reason. Here he was, sick to the stomach, shaking and unable to even hear people talking to him.

"Yes, what?"

'Cup of tea?'

"No, no, I…em…need to go to the loo"

79

"You've just been."

"Eh...yeah, whatever."

Charlie went to the loo again and his bowels let go. He sank his head into his hands and couldn't believed what was happening to him. This made no sense. How did his body know? How could it react so quickly? His fear was quickly flushed out of him and the stinging acidity lingered to remind him that this problem was not gone. He had made a loud and obvious whooshing noise and the sound of someone else in the toilet kept him rooted to the seat. The person would doubtless have heard. While he stayed locked behind the door his embarrassment was protected by anonymity.

He waited for the person to leave and eventually got up and left. At the door, he heard Kelly's voice and he instantly felt better. Yet the worry remained. He stood behind the door and listened to Kelly tell Donald of "some trouble at home" and that she was "terribly sorry".

Charlie was immediately delighted. It wasn't Danny. Everything was OK now. Then he was forced to chastise himself for being so selfish and went through the door to see what the problem was only just missing Donald flying into the toilet like he owned the place. Well, he did.

Charlie was shocked to see the reddened puffy face of someone recently stopped crying and who looked ready to start again. There was only one pointless question that could be asked in this situation.

"Are you OK?"

"Oh Charlie..."

And with someone showing even the minutist amount of compassion the tears came again. Just like a small boy who falls and only cries when his Mum asks him if it hurt.

Taking her by the arm, they walked slowly to one of the sparsely decorated interview rooms and, before shutting the door, Charlie flicked over the sign to say the room was occupied.

"Can I get you a drink or something?"

"No, no, I'll be OK, I am OK..."

"Well, sorry but, you don't seem OK."

"I suppose not."

The small paper hanky she was using to stem the flow of tears was all but destroyed. Luckily, the caring legal profession provides tissues for clients in these rooms. Presumably for when they get the bill.

"Look, you don't have to tell me anything but if it would help to talk..."

"Thanks, I'll be OK..."

"OK then, but if you need to speak to someone."

Objection, badgering the witness. Charlie knew he was doing this for himself and not her. More importantly, he was sure it was about time he didn't give a fuck about that kind of nonsense any more. Objection overruled.

"Do you want me to speak to Donald and let you go home?"

"No, I'll be...well, I'd rather stay here."

She looked up and Charlie begged for her to say "with you". She didn't. Although he was sure there was something in her eyes. She sniffed for a while and then decided to unburden herself.

"You see, yesterday, I left early for work and I didn't know and no one phoned so I couldn't and then I got home and then it was…"

"Slowly now, slowly…" Charlie edged his seat round and put a hand on her shoulder.

"It's the twins, they've been…"

She burst out crying again and the hand on the shoulder went around into a reassuring cuddle. Charlie felt concern, guilt and arousal in equal measures.

"Someone has tattooed them."

'What?"

"Tattooed them, y'know, drawn on them…"

Charlie was aware what tattooing was but didn't feel the need to point this out.

"Lots of people get tattooed, especially young people, but it's not the end of the world."

"No, you don't understand."

No, he didn't understand. Why did people feel the need to get stupid and get permanent markings on their body? It had never appealed to him but it didn't seem like it was the biggest of disasters.

"So, you don't like the tattoos then?"

"No, they didn't want them, they didn't ask for them, we think someone did it."

At this stage in a trial Charlie would normally cease questioning as the witness had lost all credibility with the jury. He decided to play along and ask the obvious, yet foolish question.

"Sorry, I'm not with you, are you saying they were tattooed against their will?"

"Yes, we think they were drugged."

"Do they normally take drugs?"

"No, someone drugged them!"

"Woah, oh, right, ok. Are you saying that you think that someone drugged your brothers and took them against their will and tattooed them?"

Spelling it out this clearly was too much for Kelly and the crying increased from a background whimper to the full inconsolable wail. This was going to take a while. He'd better make some excuses. He told Kelly he'd be back right away and left the room on silent tiptoes, gently closing the door behind him. Back at his desk, he forwarded his phone to voicemail, stuck his head into Donald's office and asked his PA to get another temp for the day. He left before any questions could be asked. All of a sudden he was dealing with the situation, he was back of top of things and only a faint residual stinging arse reminded him that he might not be all he appeared.

Creeping back into the room he handed Kelly as glass of water. She seemed to have calmed down and started again with a little more composure.

"They went out. They said they found some drinks but after that they remember nothing until they woke up lying in the street feeling not very well. They came home and went to bed. I had already left for work yesterday when they woke up and I went out straight from work last night so I didn't hear anything about it until last night."

"Did no one phone?"

"No, I forgot my mobile and my Mum won't phone work."

"Why not? Oh never mind, carry on…"

"Well, that's all really."

"Have you phoned the police?"

"No, no, Ma…eh, my Mum won't let us."

"But this is a very serious crime" Charlie missed out the "if what you say is true" part.

"Where are the tattoos?"

"On their forehead."

"Their forehead? Ah, I see."

"And what is…"

"Dumb and…"

Kelly couldn't get the next word out. She didn't have to. He knew what it would be.

"What?" Charlie shouted louder than he meant to. Kelly sat back slightly startled.

"Eh, sorry…"

"Yeah, on their forehead"

Click, click, whirr. Charlie's brain kicked into place and he didn't like the deductions he was making. He needed to get Kelly away before he started the shouting and screaming.

"Look, I think you should go home…"

"No, but, I…"

"Don't worry, I'll sort everything out, really, there is nothing to worry about."

"OK."

"And try to get your Mum to call the police. They can get rid of tattoos you know and if you go to the police you can probably get money from the Criminal Injuries people to help pay for the removal."

"OK, thanks, Charlie."

She got up clutching a large ball of used tissues in her hand. Heading for the door, she stopped and gave Charlie a peck on his increasingly reddening cheek.

"I really appreciate your help."

"Eh…no problem. Give us a phone later but only come in tomorrow if everything is OK. OK?"

"OK."

She smiled a sweet smile and left. Charlie didn't notice. As soon as he heard her leave the office he let loose.

"Fuck, fuck, Danny Fucking McColl, you total fucking idiot."
He was making a lot of noise. Colin stuck his head into the room.
"You OK?"
"Never been fucking better, cheers"

*

It was the sickening crack of her cheekbone breaking against the wall that finally did it.

"Get the fuck away from her you bastard!"
He looked up as much in disbelief as anything else.

"Don't you dare talk to your father like that."
He struggled to correct the slurred diction brought on by another long day on the bottle.

"Get away from her!"
He walked over, his face started to contort with more pointless anger.
"Don't you..."

Before he could finish the sentence Danny hit him as hard as he could. He went down holding his surprised and bleeding face. Then the anger again.

"I'll fuckin' kill ye, ya..."

As he got up Danny kicked him in the head. His Mum let out a yelp and the chair was thrown back by the force of the body hitting it. She cowered in the corner, unable to speak. Blood from his face was now running out onto the polyester sheepskin. Dazed, he got back up and was put back down again by a boot to the head. Grabbing his feet, Danny dragged him toward the door. A trail of blood ran from the fake sheep and across the carpet, the real blood giving it its first appearance of having resulted from a slaughter. In the hall, he started to come round a bit and his kicking legs made him harder to move. Dropping his legs, Danny kicked him in the stomach where he knew he would hurt his already painful liver and he was subdued again. The front door was opened and the tired, bloody body was dragged out onto the steps.

"Don't you ever come back to this house again."

Danny stepped back into the house and, as he closed the door, looked at the face of his father, covered in blood, worn by alcoholism and showing, for the first time Danny could remember, fear.

It had all begun a few years before, immediately after he had lost his job. He had nothing to do and the pub was at least somewhere to go every day. The usual pattern was followed, start with the beer, but you can never drink enough. So you move on to vodka or whatever else was handy. Then he got handy. It started with the occasional slap and then started punching and burning her. Usually Danny wasn't around. He was away at University, or "that place" as his Dad called it. He only saw the results, the bruises and the scars, physical and emotional. His Mum had been such a bubbly wee woman but, in a short space of time, the beatings hollowed her out to a shell of her former self. All of her humanity was gone, all that remained was the body, not the person, the robotic routine that went to the shops, cooked the food and went to bingo once a week.

Even now, after he was gone, this same routine remained, all the way down to the amounts of mince she bought and cooked.

He didn't come back after Danny threw him out. Two days later Danny returned home from late lectures in the dark of a winter night. The gate opened with its usual creak but stopped against a lifeless body at the side of the path. Even in the sodium glow of the streetlight the pure skin was white except where the blood and bruises stood out to identify the body. His face looked exactly the same as it had done when Danny had closed the door on him as if he had gone nowhere. But he had. He had either been in the pub or with a bottle for every minute since getting thrown out. It was only some strange primal instinct that had told him to get home. When it was too late. When he was already dying. Like an elephant heading for the graveyard, his subconscious detected the final and fatal failure of his liver and directed him home.

The next day the police arrested Danny. The physical evidence was obvious and they had a duty to investigate. The post-mortem results came quickly and were conclusive, death from massive liver failure. The bruising was a few days old and, anyway, Danny had told the police all about it and why he did it. They didn't seem to mind. In fact, their faces condoned it even if their words couldn't.

His Mum never blamed him either, although it was hard to tell. For a year she very rarely spoke, unable to cope with the removal of her aggressor and her structure in one go. Danny often thought about why he had finally done it and why he had let it go for so long. He was proud of his strength but ashamed of the weakness that proceeded it. He was particularly proud of the line "Get the fuck away from her you bastard!" It wasn't until he watched it again that he realised he had been paraphrasing Ripley's line to the Alien Queen in Aliens. He watched it over and over again.

At that time, while he was guilt ridden, weak and confused, the link between film and real life planted itself into Danny's mind.

*

There was a delay. They didn't say why but it seemed obvious that there wasn't a plane parked outside to get on so that might be something to do with it. The kids were getting very fractious. He had already arsed the half bottle of whisky from duty free and had fallen asleep in a ridiculously uncomfortable position. He'd wake up with a pain; serve him right. Another walk round the duty free shop, bags already stuffed with fags. Back to the discomfort of the moulded plastic chairs; another bag of crisps for the kids; another round of toilet trips. Then the bing-bong.

"Ladies and gentleman, we are pleased to announce the departure of our flight to Malaga today. Could you please have your boarding cards ready and make your way to Gate 7 where the plane is now ready for departure. Once again, we apologise for the late departure of this flight which was due to the late arrival of the inbound aircraft."

The bing-bong had woken him up.

"Told you, no plane."

"Get up you, get those bags and get in that queue."

She was nervous; she didn't need him flaking out on her. Not now.

"Aye hen, aye."

He always called her "hen" when he was being conciliatory, a sure sign that he already had the hangover he deserved.

They got up, clutching their collection of bags and children in all available arms. They shuffled into the queue, boarding cards already sweaty from being tightly clutched in nervous palms. The girl at the door smiled broadly through bright red lips, she took the boarding cards and indicated, without speaking, how cute she thought the twins were. Through the door and out into the cold.

"Glad we're leaving this behind"

He didn't disagree but at that moment the cool air was necessarily refreshing. The plane sat on the wide grey expanse of tarmac. Steps led up front and back, funny little trucks sat at one side and buzzed all around.

"It's like Thunderbirds out here, eh?"

Through the window at the front you could just make out the pilots, staring intently at a clipboard. Up the stairs and onto the plane.

"Good afternoon."

Another broad smile.

"May I see your boarding passes?"

"Aye, eh, I showed them to the lassie back..."

"For your seat number?"

"Oh aye, sorry, row 19."

In their haste and wonder, they had got on the front steps instead of the back. After what seemed like an hour of pausing and excuse me's, they finally got to their seats. Bags were thrown roughly into the wee cupboard above and everyone got strapped in ready for take off. It's what the wee card said you should do.

Thirteen

It was clear that the firemen were starting to get annoyed. It was curry night; the bell had rung just as they had taken the first few lids of the hot metal cartons. It was now getting colder by the second. Hot food is never good cold.

"Do you know who might have done this?"

"Yes."

"No."

Laxmi and Shazia spoke in simultaneous contradiction. They both knew who had smashed up the front of their shop and set the fire at the door. Exasperated, Shazia wanted to tell someone in authority, she had had enough. Laxmi, concerned about further retribution and someone finding out his part in the probable cause, would rather say nothing.

"Well, what we mean is…" he looked at Shazia hoping that she would let him wriggle out of it, "…that we might know who it was, but, you know how it is, nothing we can prove."

The fireman gave up the questioning, it wasn't his job and anyway, a panda had just pulled up. A large, overweight policeman emerged, straining as he hauled himself out of the passenger seat. Sergeant Derek Murdoch was not a happy man. He had brief discussion with the fireman in charge and they headed back to the disappointment of a reheated Biryani.

He surveyed the damage. Both of the large windows on either side of the door had been smashed. Something small enough to get through the mesh had been used. This gave the hint of some pre-meditation. Across the remaining glass and mesh the word "Psycho" had been sprayed in a bold red. Where the can had lingered longest, the red paint had run in narrow lines under the letters. Hitchcock meets Kubrick in Glasgow Ned revenge attack.

The fire has been started in the door recess; it wasn't a large fire, not really a huge threat and it looked like a bit of an afterthought, which suggested randomness. Like the Mehtas, Sergeant Murdoch knew who had done it. Also like them, he also knew that there wasn't all that much he could do about it. This seemed a little beyond their usual pranks, the sudden escalation of their attacks was a cause for concern.

"Why don't you do something?" Shazia was getting increasingly upset.

"Don't worry, we will investigate this fully." Even he wouldn't have believed his lie.

"Why? You know who did it. Lock them up, just lock them up."

"I'm sure the policeman will do all he can." Laxmi joined with Sergeant Murdoch in an unspoken collusion. He looked at the floor as he spoke, too ashamed to lie to his wife's face, to scared to give away any guilt to the police.

Sergeant Murdoch was pleased to get the support but couldn't bring himself to duck the issue entirely.

"Mrs. Mehta, I'm sure you understand that this is a very difficult situation. To do anything about it we will need evidence and witnesses. Do you know if anyone saw what happened?"

"No, it was very early in the morning."

"OK. Well, I'll ask around, see if anyone saw, maybe there was someone across the street or passing on a bus. We'll see…"

It was all a big game. These were just words of placation and denial. There was nothing he could do, even if someone had seen the Finches do it, no one would give a statement.

"Well, one thing you won't see is us round here much longer!" Shazia spun on her heels and headed for the flat, her sudden outburst taking Laxmi by surprise. With her gone, some of the pretence could now be dropped. Both men relaxed a little.

"Any idea what set them off this time?"

"No, no, none, they're just…well, you know…"

"Oh aye, I know alright but I'm surprised. They're no angels but if never seen them be like this before. Setting a fire on their own doorstep? It's just not…well…"

This discussion was making Laxmi very uncomfortable; the one that was awaiting him upstairs would probably be no better.

*

It seemed appropriate on his first real day in the office for Danny to uphold the hunter-gatherer tradition by making a daylight raid on the stationary cabinet. Not being entirely sure what he would have to do in the weeks to come, it seemed sensible to take at least one of everything. Like an ancient hunter, he would find some use for every part of his kill, even those little rubber things you put on the end of your finger for some reason. He couldn't find a stapler so settled for two boxes on staples in its stead.

Struggling back to his desk with his bounty still warm in his arms, he was forced to drop it all noisily in his desk. Heads popped up from desks like Meerkats on seeing a rattlesnake. Wendy was on the phone and stabbed him repeatedly with a 12" hunting knife stare. He apologised in hand mime and regretted it with an equivalent sphincter version. Arthur was right; it seemed dangerous to even imagine her legs draped round your neck. Rosa Kleb with the wee knives installed in expensive looking Ravel court shoes.

The phone in Danny's flat rang; he didn't hear it. He was arranging his hanging folders 5 miles away. He then put little labels on them and gave them all names. He started a notebook and wrote his name in the inside cover and the date at the top of the first page.

"Why don't you write, 'This book belongs to…' in the inside cover too?"

Concentrating on the neatness of his handwriting, he didn't see the Wendy walk over behind him. Silent as well as deadly.

"Well…I…eh…just…eh."

"Never mind schoolboy, how about you get these searches done for me, OK?"

When rhetorical becomes an order: modern man management, par excellence. Danny understood that the attitude displayed on first encounter was the most important. It sets the tone of a relationship, established a place on the squash ladder of life. You could save yourself a lot of climbing by getting a good starting position.

"Ma'am", he tipped an imaginary cowboy hat and spoke with a Southern drawl.

She didn't react and walked away without as much as a glance. Well, at least he didn't get punched; it was a start.

Danny's mobile rang on silent in his jacket pocket, which was hanging on a stand behind him.

He'd better get these searches done but before he did that he had to get logged in and tell the world he had arrived. It took a while for the clunky old machine to boot up and Danny scoffed loudly through the tortuous wait for the disk to rattle its way to completion. Looking round the office he saw a far better array of hardware and realised that he was suffering from new boy shite hardware syndrome. Eventually it wheezed its way to popping up the login box and he was amazed to find the username and password, handed to him on a Post It by the awkward, uncommunicative IT monkey, worked first time.

"Fucked up geek but efficient, pretty much all you need."

He was also pleasantly surprised to find that his email software worked first time too and he started composing the email that would announced his start of work to all his email-enabled friends.

"To all those that bask in the shadow of Daniel James McColl,

I have arrived. I have a desk, a computer and an unrivalled law career ahead of me. Do not be afraid but prepare yourself for being extremely impressed.

Beer anyone?

Dan The Man"

He clicked send. The searches sat on his desk. He'd better get them sorted, there was no point being cheeky and incompetent.

"Ah, fuck it…"

Putting the searches back down again, he fired up the PC again and got his new email address on the Stenhousemuir mailing list. He then emailed the guys to say he was back in the online world. A flurry of "Welcome Back" messages arrived from his fellow Warriors. He read the first few and then noticed a slightly different looking email that had arrived in the middle.

"Aaahh...Mr. Charles Agnew I presume…"

The message had no content and the subject line simply said "Do Not Leave The Office"

"Weird fucker."

Danny carried on reading the recent tales from Ochilview.

*

On receiving the email, the adrenalin built up by the frustration of the phone search was immediately channelled into preparing Charlie for what was to come. He switched his phone to voicemail, set his email to "out of office" and told reception that he would be out for most of the afternoon. Intending to get a taxi, none appeared immediately and this gave him time to think that walking over might allow him to prepare for what he intended to say or do. Anyway, he could never be sure that Danny would hang about in the office for any time at all. Usually giving Danny a direct instruction would result in him doing exactly the opposite.

He stepped out in the middle of one of those rare Glasgow pauses in the rain. A wide gap had opened in the clouds and bright sun streamed out and made the wet streets shine. It was one of those precious times in Glasgow when you didn't have to stare glumly at the pavement. You can look up and see the hidden detail in the buildings above and the faces of the people walking by. In all these faces, around every corner, Charlie could see Kelly. Small glimpses of blonde through the crowds made him walk faster until he could see it wasn't her. He could still smell her and feel her on his hand. Was his need to confront Danny about upholding a fundamental moral? Was he just giving his friend wise counsel? Or was he just exacting some melodramatic defence of the family of the woman he loved? In short, was he just being like Danny, everything he didn't want to be? In the end, his motive wasn't all that important. He had to do something. He put the less pleasing of his motives to the back of his mind and pushed the large gold coloured handle on the large glass door that led into the arena.

"Danny McColl please."

"I'm sorry sir, I don't believe we have anyone here of that name."

"You do, he started today, conveyancing department?"

"I'll just...eh…"

"He's got a bit of a sore looking nose?"

"Ahhh, yes, I know who you mean now, please take a seat."

Charlie sat down and flicked through a newspaper without his eyes ever resting on a word. He got to the end and started the same process in reverse. The door opened and he sat up sharply. The large figure of Arthur McWilliams ambled through the doorway.

"Charles, to what do we owe the pleasure? Mooching for a job?"

This was all he needed.

"No Arthur but you'll be the first to know when my current meteoric rise for some inexplicable reason takes a down turn."

"Touché. I hear we are making some in-roads into that firm of yours."

"Really?"

"Yes, I believe young Danny has conquered that ice queen of a receptionist of yours."

"I don't know what you mean. Look Arthur this isn't Eastenders and I'm sure you've got better things to be doing."

Despite popular ideas to the contrary, you don't get to partner in a law firm with a complete lack of social understanding. Even Arthur knew that Charlie was in no mood to chat. With a hurrumph of a goodbye he strode into the street en route to his licensed annex.

Charlie had intended to remain calm for as long as possible but the encounter with Arthur and, in particular, his reference to Kelly meant that the Kofi Annan approach was no longer possible. The sanctions wouldn't do any more; it was time for Desert Storm. So, when Danny finally wandered slowly through the door…

"What the fuck have you been playing at?"

"Eh?"

"What…the…fuck…have…you…been…playing…at?"

The building anger made Charlie talk slower and louder in a manner suggesting "how do I have to speak to get it into your thick skull"

"Hey, hey, calm down, calm down, lets get outside and see what's lit the banger up your arse."

The walked silently out the door and a few yards up the street.

"You."

"Me, what?"

"You've lit the banger up my arse."

"A neat trick but I didn't realise we were that friendly."

"Stop fucking about Danny, I've spent the whole morning with Kelly in tears."

"Woah, woah, back up there horsey. This boy is a gentleman and a scholar. I don't know what was wrong with Kelly but it's nothing to do with me…OK? I never did anything…"

"I'm not talking about Kelly. I'm talking about what you did to her brothers."

"What? Are you on fucking drugs? I don't know Kelly's brothers. I didn't even know she had brothers. This is…"

"What? This is what? Don't give me your fucking lies. You don't go out with someone and live in the same close as them and not know they have brothers."

It was too much to assimilate in one go. If she lives…then they must be…then I must have…cognitive overload…reset.

"Get to fuck."

They stopped at a pedestrian crossing and the people thronged around them stopped the conversation for a while. It gave Danny time to gather some thoughts and attempt to discard most of them. At the other side of the street Charlie broke the silence.

"Look, I know this isn't the best time but are we just going to walk about?"

"What? Eh...no...we'll go in here for a coffee."

Danny sat down and Charlie came to the table with two large Mochas with cream.

"Are you telling me you didn't know you lived in the same close as Kelly?"

"Yes. She always asked me to drop her off quite a bit away. I thought she lived there."

"So, you didn't even know her surname?"

Danny was embarrassed to admit that it had never crossed his mind to ask.

"No, I didn't..."

"Know she is a Finch?"

"No."

This was bad. Very, very bad. He was in love with a woman whose brothers he had just had mutilated. It's not going to down well in his wedding speech. "Not long after I met Kelly I had such good fun with today's lovely Ushers". Well, it was recoverable. No one knew it was him.

"So why did you do it?"

"Do what?"

"Was it because one of them head-butted you?"

"Eh? What, oh yeah, why would I go out with Kelly because her brothers head-butted me?"

"I'm talking about the recently acquired tattoos on their foreheads."

It was important for Charlie not to notice his arse dropping off and his legs flopping helplessly to the floor.

"Eh...eh? But...what tattoos? What does them...what do those...what do the tattoos have to do with me? People get tattooed all the time."

"Not like this. Not against their will."

"Look, I don't really know these lads but they don't seem like the sharpest tools in the box. Who knows what they get up to? There could be hundreds of reasons why the ended up tattooed."

After a shaky start Danny was starting to put up a decent defence. Sadly this was about as good as it got. It was the moment in the Bruno V Tyson fight when Harry Carpenter blurted out "he's hurt Tyson". Let the pummelling begin.

"People don't ask to get the words "dumb" or "dumber" tattooed on their forehead."

"Maybe they have designs on a career in the judiciary?"

The joke was as weak as the case for the defence. Charlie took a long drink from his oversized mug and sat back into his self-coloured pseudo-sixties armchair.

"Danny, don't...fucking...lie...to...me."

The angry staccato had returned. The effect was somewhat diminished by the blob of cream on Charlie's nose. Danny decided it wasn't a good time to point this out.

"I'm...not...fucking...lying...to...you."

"Don't waste your breath Danny, I know it was you."

"Oh, do you now lawyer boy? Pretty circumstantial evidence you've got there."

"OK, have it your way. I'll give you evidence. Motive, they attacked you, therefore there is reason for revenge. They were tattooed with "Dumb and Dumber". You saw that film with Kelly a few nights ago. It's all good evidence...aw, fuck this Danny, it was you."

"You call that evidence?"

"I don't need evidence Danny, I know it was you."

"Your some kind of idiot savant now, are you?"

"No, but I am fairly savant about idiots."

"Very fucking clever."

"Unlike you, what the fuck were you thinking about?"

"Hold on there Sherlock, I don't remember me admitting to thinking about anything."

"Right Danny, for the last fucking time, I know it was you."

Danny took a sip from his coffee. He looked out the window and the world walked by the way it usually did. People going places, doing things, late for this, early for that, same old pish.

"Same old pish."

"What?"

"Oh nothing, you've got cream on your nose."

Charlie wiped it off and looked Danny in the eye. Danny looked back. He could see clearly that Charlie was in no doubt. Charlie finally knew for sure that Danny had done it.

"How was I supposed to know?"

"Know what?"

"That they were her brothers?"

"What? So if they weren't her brothers it would have been OK?"

Charlie moved on beyond the admission without a flinch.

"They're shite Charlie, it's not just me they attacked you know, they've got everyone in that close terrified."

"So? When was that you're job? We have police for stuff like that."

"I went to the police! For all the fucking good it did me. Just told me to piss off."

"What did they do that made it OK for them to be marked for life?"

"You should have seen what they did to this poor old woman."

92

"Danny, let's not kid ourselves here."

"I'm not kidding, I did it, OK, are you happy?"

"Happy? My friend is a felon and someone that I care…well, how can I be happy?"

"I don't know you cared, no wait, I get it, you were talking about Kelly weren't you?"

"No."

"Now who's lying?"

"OK, so I like Kelly. Big deal. Unlike you, I haven't committed a crime."

"Maybe not, but it certainly explains why you're so het up about it. You wouldn't think twice about banging up those little scrotes for as long as you could persuade the judge into."

"Don't compare what I do within the bounds of the law to what you did. Any feelings I have for Kelly are irrelevant, you broke the law and not with any trivial misdemeanour either."

"Keep your fucking voice down."

"OK, let's get out of here."

"Where to?"

"Oh, I dunno, let's walk down the river."

"Oooh, how romantic. We are in the mood for love."

"Shut your fucking mouth or I'll hand you into the first policeman I see."

"Oooh, love and hate, the full gamut of emotions."

Charlie was at a loss. He had Danny over a barrel and yet it seemed like it was some kind of vibrating orthopaedic barrel and Danny was still managing to enjoy it. The sun was still shining as they walked past the heaving shops and bus queues down towards the Clyde. Most people were too concerned with the thin plastic of bag handles cutting off their fingers like cheese wire to notice the heated discussion wandering by.

"I know why you did it, y'know."

"I know. I was motivated by revenge, blah-de-blah."

"No, I'm not talking about that."

"What now? What is it now? Deep-seated homosexuality?"

"No, it was because of your Dad."

"What? Fuckin' hell, Charlie, you are one weird mother. What the fuck are you talking about?"

"You have never grieved for your Dad."

"No fucking wonder, he was cunt."

"My point exactly."

"Sorry Charlie, you may be a good lawyer but you make no sense as some half arsed psychoanalyst."

"I don't expect you to understand but it's true."

"What's true? That he was a cunt? I know that."

"No, it's true that you never grieved for him and that is at the root of your problem."

"Problem? Sounds as if you're the one with the problem Sigmund."

"Look, Danny, I know it can't be easy for you to talk about or maybe even think about but your Dad dying had a big effect on you. "

"No shit, I got to stop watching him beat up my Mum and piss all her money up a wall."

"Will you let me finish?"

"Who's paying for this session?"

"Right now, me, I've got clients I should be seeing."

"Don't let me stop you."

"Look, you threw your Dad out and he died soon after. You connected the two, part of you thinks you killed him. To hide the guilt you have to hate him. He has to be evil and you have to be a hero. If you're not a hero then you're a murderer. You choose to live with the easier of the two."

"Go back to your fucking client, this is just shite."

"Let me finish, the problem is that once you're a hero, you have to stay a hero."

"I'm not a fucking hero, I threw a drunk out into the street. He died. He was going to die anyway."

"What was it you said to me about that line in Aliens?"

"Eh?"

"Ever since then, half of you has been living in some fucked up film world where you are always the fucking hero."

"Aw fur fucks sake Charlie, what have you been snorting?"

"Look Danny, I'm only trying to help but you're gonna end up in big fucking trouble unless you cut this shit out. You're a trainee lawyer; you don't have a bat cave. Who did you think you were when you decided to get the Finches? Eh? Who was it this time? Al Pacino? Were you bringing justice for all?"

"Fuck off, Charlie, lets cut the crap, what happens now? Do I get turned in?"

"No."

"Cheers."

"On one condition."

"Who's living in films now?"

"No, this is no film, this is life."

"OK, what's the condition, do I have to pay for the poor boys treatment in hospital?"

"No, you have to stay away from Kelly."

"What? You can't be…"

"I am, I mean it."

"Saw your opportunity then, lover boy?"

"Danny, do you really think you have any future with Kelly after what you did to her brothers?"

"What does it matter, it looks like it has been decided for me. See ya Charlie."

Danny wandered off back in the direction of town. Charlie stood still and watched him go. He felt a bit guilty. Maybe he'd gone too heavy on the stuff about his Dad, but he was right, he was becoming a danger to himself. He looked at his watch and started walking towards to the bridge to cross to the court. On the way over he phoned the office and got them to taxi over his notes.

At the corner Danny stopped and looked back at Charlie crossing the river.

"On ye go, you smart-arse, shows what you know, I was Yul Brynner this time."

Fourteen

The view from the top flat afforded a wide and clear view of the surrounding streets. Especially the one that leads down from the postal depot. Every morning, sitting at the table, eating a paradoxically child-like cereal, they watched the postman descend the hill. As the road is being crossed, so is their doorway and they run to the ground floor to lie in wait.

All postmen had long since given up on anything like delivery to the inhabitants in these flats. The door is opened and the letters are thrown in. The hand is swiftly withdrawn and away.

They descend on the mail like animals being fed in the zoo. They know what they are looking for. One letter, one handwriting. Identified, torn up, binned. The one letter that every week could change the life of its recipient.

*

"Faucet! That's another fucking one, faucet? What's all that about?"

"Good one, yeah, faucet, doesn't make any sense at all really. What about diaper! Now that one really is mental."

"Aye, aye, diaper, full of shit, ha! Full of shit!"

"You know which one really annoys me? Lawyer."

"Lawyer? What's wrong with that?"

"Exactly, everyone is so used to it now. We're solicitors for Christ's sakes. Fucking dumb American bastards."

"Do you come from England in London?"

"Exactly, they may have a lot of bombs and have put a man on the moon but they sure as hell can't teach geography."

*

Down by the river he had seen his new dreams disappear and his old nightmares resurface. It seemed entirely appropriate that Danny retire briefly to

96

the pub. And, on finding Arthur there bedding in for the afternoon, it seemed even more appropriate to join him for as long as his Platinum Visa could carry them. Probably a few miles short of casualty or oblivion, whichever came first.

The conversation had meandered freely from the initial questioning with regard to Danny's apparent ill humour. Answers to the questions had been fairly sketchy but enough for Arthur to decide that Danny should stay with him for the afternoon. This led to a brief call to the office to say that Danny was helping him with some work and wouldn't be back. This, of course, had nothing to do with any sympathy on Arthur's part but if you were going to hold court it was usually a requirement to have some courtiers.

Any questioning about Arthur's presence in the pub was met with an impenetrable barrier of non-answer that even Paxman couldn't break down. All he would say was that even things that happen a long time ago could still return and bring problems. This is not entirely what Danny needed to hear at this time but he understood enough to stop asking.

Their conversation had been interrupted by an American tourist who had strolled to the bar. Despite having very little history, the Americans have developed enough of a National Dress to make them instantly recognisable. In the same way that a man in a kilt walking into a Chicago bar would be instantly recognised as being "Scotch", the gawdy waterproof, floppy hat, loose fitting pants and a camera round the neck quite clearly pointed to a Chuck or maybe a Hank. He approached the bar surveying the array of whiskies displayed on the shelf.

"Hi, I'm Hank." he addressed the barman like he had swallowed a loudhailer.

"You don't look too hungry big yin."

"Excuse me?"

"Never mind."

On hearing this opening exchange, Danny was reduced to uncontrollable giggling. Interrupted but undeterred, Hank carried on.

"My name is Campbell, Hank Campbell, I'm over here looking into my clan."

"Aye." The barman wasn't used to this, the look on his face said "if I'd wanted this kind of shit I'd work in Edinburgh".

"Do you have any Scotch from the lands of Clan Campbell?"

"Ye mean Whisky?"

"Yes sir. Whisky."

As the barman turned to face the array of Malts behind him, he winked at Danny and Arthur.

"The Clan Campbell ye say?"

"Yessir."

"Well, they were a Clan of expensive tastes. I've only got this but it's a wee bit dear."

"Deer? I didn't know they used deer to make whisky."

"It's ex-pen-sive, a nip of this will cost ye £40."

"Make it a double!"

And with a flourish he opened his waterproof to expose a large money-belt straining under the pressure for his extensive gut and the wad that lurked within.

"Hey, and give me a Coke."

The barman poured the drink and put the Coke on the bar next to it. Hank picked up the whisky and sniffed it.

"Mmmm...now that's more like it. I was beginning to wonder about these Campbell fellas, what with the massacre of the McDonalds and all, I was beginning to think I should change my name to Lipschitz."

Polite laughter turned to abject horror when the bottle of Coke went straight into the whisky and the whole thing downed it one.

"Well, here's to ya, fellas." And with that Hank left. Arthur was unable to speak. Danny asked for him.

"What did he just waste with that Coke?"

"Don't worry, I charged him for the Bowmore, I poured him a Grouse."

And so the American baiting began.

*

They were sitting on the step just below their barricade. One stood up and let a long thread of spit drip from his lips and then detach falling silently down into the stairwell. It joined previous attempts on the ground in a glistening circle like the aftermath of a snail race. Some had deviated from their intended path and landed on the banisters below, slowly sliding down the varnished wood on landing.

One of these was only narrowly avoided by the Beatle Man as he came out of his flat for one of his very few forays outside his normal routine. He lifted his hands just before its path down the banister was unpleasantly lubricated. He gave it a disgusted look and, taking a cloth hanky from his pocket, wiped both his hands.

He straightened the now obligatory baseball cap and, with a silent nod, summoned the other over to look down the stairwell. It was now dark and the stair lights lit the white suit brightly as it made it to the bottom and disappeared out of view.

They looked at each other and, without a word being exchanged, the plan was in place. He went through the barricade door and into the storm door behind. Moments later he appeared with a screwdriver and they ghosted their way down to the door of the Beatle Man's flat.

The storm door took a while but they had experience of Mrs. Moyes' door so they were getting faster. The other one kept watch as he took the locks out one at a time. With the storm door open, they both entered the small vestibule and made short work of the internal door.

As with all the mayhem that they brought upon the world, little was pre-meditated beyond a few minutes and so, on entering the flat, it wasn't immediately clear what to do next. They were immediately struck with the tidiness of it all. This was in sharp contrast to the shithole that they lived in only a few yards above. They lived in the flat that seldom got tidied or even visited by anyone who had ever had a thought of tidying.

They walked with a strange stepping gate over the immaculate carpet as if expecting to be stepping over debris. The tidiness also gave them the problem that there was nothing obvious to ransack or destroy. Every wall was white and free from any pictures or any other covering. The living room had a wooden floor, varnished and then painted white. Even at night the streetlight streaming in through the vertical white blinds reflected brightly from its surface. The room contained a single white sofa opposite an ageing turntable. Two black speakers stood out sharply on either side like two pieces of snowflake obsidian dropped in the snow. Leaning against the right hand speaker were a dozen or so vinyl albums. He picked them up and looked at them. Some had pictures on them; some were double albums that opened like books. One of these was white; others were red and blue. They looked dull and the stereo was too crap to steal and too boring to smash.

They went back into the hall and across into the bedroom. Again, everything was white. A bed lay on the floor, only a mattress; its immaculate white surface barely visible against another white wooden floor. This time, four dark rectangles faced them from the wall opposite. In the gloom of a room away from the street they looked like four blackened windows. Ready to play, what's the day? They turn on a light and see that each of the four shapes was the picture of a man. They had stupid long hair and a couple of them had moustaches. The one top left wore glasses.

This at least gave a chink of something to ransack and they jumped over the bed and went to rip the pictures down. They were thwarted by a layer of varnish securing them tightly to the wall.

"Fuckin' nutjob man."

They went back into the hall and, sensing that the time limit for a safe break-in was approaching, had to think of something to do before leaving. Like graffiti artist and a newly painted wall, they realised that the whole flat was an unspoiled canvas. He went back into the bedroom and, with some balancing difficulty, did a shite on the bed. The lack of decent nourishment in the diet made in quite loose and it landed with a splatter and immediately started soaking in to the perfect white cotton. The other one came from the kitchen with a white towel and rubbed in the still warm puddle. Walking to the wall, he coloured in the four faces and finished it off with the word "Shite" in large brown letters.

In the living room, the records were being taking out of their sleeves. They made perfect Frisbees and flew well across the room and ended with a satisfying shatter against the wall. The remaining vinyl was thrown on the floor and, with a run up, was used as surfboards across the polished floor. They left dark scratches in the wood like some giant hand had scratched its nails across the surface.

The turntable was turned onto the floor and the speakers kicked in. He stood on the sofa and started to piss the word "weirdo" onto the white throw.

It ran out before he got to the "i" but it remained somehow appropriate. The criminal internal clock finally struck done and they turned and left as silently as they had entered.

Back at the top of the stair another long greasy spit was already dangling its way down to the ground. Fuckhole's pendulum.

"Fuckin nutjob man."

*

"So they gets on the boat and says 'shall we take a dictionary?' nah, we'll make up our own words"

"Ah, but, but, what if they did take a dictionary?"

"Eh?"

"Well, they might have taken a donkeys old dictionary that had lots of old shite words in it and they just kept using them!"

"Arthur, my man, you just might be on to something."

"And, maybe we used to send them dictionary updates but then we had that big war thing so we said "fuck off, you're not getting your dictionary this year!""

"Just like Oor Wullie"

"What?"

"If I was bad, ma Ma would say, you're not getting yer Oor Wullie this year."

"Bad boy."

"And then I would say, but it's the Broons this year!"

"Oh no, not good. What would Grandpa say?"

"No, so she would say, we'll you'll not get that either."

"Serves you right."

"Aye, but I still got it anyway."

"Jings!"

*

Danny and Arthur were most of the way through the second bottle of whisky. It showed. Like all drunken conversations, words got italicised for no apparent reason. They laughed for a while and the conversation rambled on in random directions.

"So, these things that happened a long time ago, why are they coming back now?"

"Wit?"

"You said, earlier on, about stuff that happened a long time ago?"

"Did I? Well, aye, everyone's got bad memories Danny."

"But they're in the past, what's the problem now?"

"Look, don't you worry about Arthur."

"I'm not worried, I'm just nosy!"

"You're a good lad Danny, aye, just you concentrate on that lassie of yours."

"But how do you..."

"Arthur has his sources, just you look after her OK."

100

"Well, that might not…well, I'm not sure how much longer…look, sorry Arthur, I'm a bit pissed. I think I'll head."

Danny didn't give Arthur time to persuade him to stay. He picked up his jacket and was out the door before the conversation could go any further down a road he wanted to avoid. Bemused at first, Arthur sat back and watched him leave; he shouted goodbye and Danny held up a hand as he disappeared through the door.

"Young love, eh? How about a wee brandy for the road?"

*

Darkness had long since descended by the time Danny emerged shakily from the taxi. The street was far quieter than normal. The usual wheezing thunder of bus or truck had been replaced by the occasional hissing of car sliding past on the rain soaked road. The muffled beeps of the pedestrian crossing could be heard at the top of the street where the road disappeared over the brow of the long shallow slope of the drumlin hill. A single car sat at a flashing amber light waiting for no one to cross, cursing the passer-by who had pressed the button to annoy the traffic rather than stop it.

Danny paid the taxi driver through the side window of the taxi, giving the driver a moment of panic as it looked like Danny was on his way, wallet unmolested. The huffing and puffing of the diesel engine faded of into the distance and, with the distant beeping now stopped, the street was quiet.

Danny turned towards the door and stopped abruptly as he began to hear an eerie noise emerge from the background of silence. It was very faint and it took a few moments of concentrated, drunken listening for Danny to pinpoint its origin and sound type. It was singing coming from within the close. Only the echoes of the slow, regular voice could be heard through the solid wood door.

Stepping forward uneasily, the door opened like a large volume control, the sound increasing and becoming clearer as it swung across.

"…And in the end…"

It was a man's voice, strong but singing gently.

"…the love you take…"

The voice was beginning to break up and carried sadness with the almost religious echoing from the stone walls.

"…is equal to the love…you…make…"

It seemed a struggle to get the last two words out. There was a pause and the same phrase started up again.

"…and in the end…"

It was interrupted by Danny turning the corner of the stair and finding the Beatle Man sitting ashen faced on the step just below his front door. It was clear that there was something wrong but Danny asked the question anyway, as rhetorical as it was stupid.

"You alright mate?"

The Beatle Man looked up and shrunk away from Danny, back against the step he was sitting on. Unable to pass him and seeing that he was causing a bit of upset Danny decided to stand and stare for a while longer until something happened to break the deadlock or he passed out, whichever came first. He wasn't too bothered which. The silence lasted a good few hours in drunk time. The kind of hours that pass that make you need a sausage supper only a short while after a three course meal or make you think that the girl that knocked you back had had more than enough time to reconsider.

Danny huffed a bit to try and produce some kind of reaction. The Beatle Man's head was now in his hands. Danny looked to the skies a bit lost of inspiration and quite a lot in need of a piss. He noticed the door was slightly open and the newly bright wood of a jemmied door. The cause of the situation was more apparent but the desire for pointless rhetoric had not diminished.

"Someone break in mate?"

There was no response so Danny stepped round the Beatle Man to investigate the door. As he did so the Beatle Man stood up. Danny reached to push open the door but was restrained by a firm hand on his forearm.

"No! No! No!"

"Awright mate, calm down."

Danny reached for the door again but the grip on his arm got tighter.

"Look, why don't you just go back inside and do your singing there, eh?"

The grip on Danny's arm was relaxed and The Beatle Man started to cry. Through the tears that now ran down his ghostly face he started to sing again.

"...is equal to the love you make."

Danny took advantage of the musical interlude to push open the door. Looking inside he saw very little. It looked like the place had been cleaned out.

"You want to be phoning…"

As he stuck his head inside the storm door, the Beatle Man pulled him back. His arm was forced up his back and he was ushered quickly away from the door.

"No!"

"Right, right, fucksake, my fuckin' arm, I was only…"

The grip was released, the Beatle Man darted into the storm door and in an instant it was slammed behind him.

"Fuckin nutjob man."

Fifteen

Eyes like slits, head forced downward by the torrent from the sky, Danny stepped out of the close and headed for the underground station without noticing the fire damage and boarded windows of Laxmi's shop. The headache was not as bad as it had been with the Hungarian beer but it was that particular type of whisky headache that is accompanied by the Chinese men's Gymnastics team going through their drills in your stomach. The soothing effect of the cold rain on his head was in a nullifying balance with the pain caused by the drumming sound of the large drops rattling onto his skull.

He was thankful for having been drunk the night before. Sleep came quickly and was not hindered by thinking about what to do about Kelly or the fact that the only friend he had in Glasgow was the only thing between him and the jail. And even now, in the dreich light of morning, it was struggle to think about anything more than getting through work and getting back to bed as soon as possible.

He bought a return ticket for the underground and tried, for the umpteenth time, to make a mental note to get a Transcard. The money he got from Arthur was about to run out and with it the ability to Hackney about the city. The ticket flew through the machine and he pushed the barrier back to avoid any collision with his tender gut. Similarly, the escalator seemed too much of a cerebral balance challenge, so he clumped his way down the brown tile steps towards the platform.

All the familiar sensations of the underground returned. The strange smell, the unsettled air, like standing in a pig farm watching a tornado approach. He battled his way through the throng of bodies collected on the land bridge between the valleys on each side. Everyone stood staring at the curved wall in front of them. Posters advertised shops, events and pantomimes. Danny turned to face the wall.

Nearly a felon, losing his girlfriend, with a hangover, in the rain, on the way to work to face an evil woman who's work he had not done, about to barf onto an electrified rail and there it was in front of him, Gerard Kelly's face on a poster. It was just his face, disembodied and sitting in the middle of a large yellow star. He looked like a dog with one of those cones that stop them biting their stitches. There were some other minor Scottish celebrities all equally badly presented. What did they all do for the rest of the year?

A low rumble could now be heard and Danny's ears strained to work out which direction it was coming from. Then the rush of foul smelling air told him that it was going to appear on his side. The tunnel wheezed and groaned; a subterranean mirror of the symptoms that affected so many on the surface. People shifted in their shoes and jostled to get the places they knew would line up with the soon to be opening doors.

The orange worm burst from the tunnel like a low budget version of Dune. Using the crazy human logic that causes traffic to go slower and horrible crushing accidents, as the train slowed to a stop, everyone inched forward to gain those vital extra few seconds. This, of course, made it impossible for anyone to get off and therefore made it take far longer for the train to get boarded and get on its way. This happened at every stop and every station all through the day. Occasionally there was some guy in a uniform shouting at people to get back or a tannoy announcement doing the same. All to no effect. There was something in the ether triggering an automaton hormone to compel the motion forward. It was nothing to do with social status or intellect. It was worse at Hillhead where all the lecturers brushed everyone else aside with folio cases filled with notes on queuing theory.

A door opened in front of Danny and he tried to step back to let people off. Public opinion was to the contrary and he was thrust forward by its weight. Grumblings, excuse me's and pardons and the train was loaded. Being thrown on first, Danny got a seat and so managed to avoid the balancing act in the middle of the carriage that formed part of the entrance exam for the Moscow State Circus.

Dozens of rain-soaked bodies filled the warm, cramped carriage. Those who could hang on did so by thrusting their armpits forward, broadcasting the strain of their walk to the station in a hermetically sealed anorak. A noxious steam of acid rain and human sweat permeated all available space and clung to the perspex windows obscuring the darkness beyond. The carriages lurched round invisible corners. The people standing, hanging by one hand, swung about like carcasses on hooks.

The brakes squealed and the carriage burst into the false light of the next station. No one could see outside but everyone knew the station. It was a simple matter of counting. The familiar scrum occurred at the doors and then the train was off again. A few more cycles of descent into darkness then rebirth and it was time for Danny to fight his way to, and out of, the door.

A river of bodies flowed along the platform and up the flights of stairs before finally emerging into the darker light of day. It was still raining. The cold water and fresh air was a relief after the oppressing warm and smell of below. Danny pointed his head to the sky and cooled his face. The quiet sunlight, dispersed through the clouds soothed the eyes after the harshness of the bright underground. He headed off towards the office. First the first time since he had arrived back in Glasgow, there was little trace of a spring in his step. This was his first day of real life. He was going to work.

*

"Look, Arthur, I'm not saying it was him for sure. I'm just asking if you think it was possible."

"Anything is possible, it just sounds a wee bit unlikely to me."

"So, your saying that he's not capable?"

"No, he might be capable. He bloody better be, I gave him a job, I'm just saying that I've got a bastard behind the eyes and I've got to be in court in 30 minutes."

"So, what should I do?"

"Do what you want."

"Pull him?"

"If you must, I can't stop you. I'm just a lawyer, not the law."

*

Charlie arrived at work and suffered the now familiar agony of waiting for Kelly to arrive. It was almost as if she knew this when she herself arrived early and instantly calmed the insects swarming around inside him. Doubtless she was making up for her very early departure the day before, but Charlie was thankful, whatever the reason. He gave her a moment to get settled at her desk and headed for the toilet via her desk.

"Eh...hiya, how...how are you?"

"Fine thanks and...thanks for, well, yesterday, y'know?"

"It's...well, not a problem, I'm sorry it happened."

"Yeah, well, it's maybe not a surprise, they're not the...mmm...best behaved."

"Still, don't think they deserve...well anyway, how about I...well, what are you doing for lunch today?"

"I've got sandwiches with me."

"OK, well fine, maybe another...must go to the loo, I'll see you...eh...later."

Kelly smiled and Charlie walked off towards the loo. He could feel her looking at his back and had to talk his legs through each step to get them to the toilet door without tripping. This caused an awkward straight-legged gate that suggested he had already been. Kelly smiled. She knew that he liked her. And she liked that.

Charlie sat in the toilet and berated himself for his ham-fisted attempt to ask Kelly out for lunch. As far as he was supposed to know, she and Danny were still an item and Danny was still his best mate. Appearing to be the kind of guy that would ask out his best mate's girlfriend was not the image he was going for. But, on the plus side, he'd found some balls.

"How are you doing today Danny?"

"You got any Irn Bru handy?"

"Ah, I see, well, I feel responsible for your condition today, so take it easy. And, don't worry, Wendy's out all day."

"Cheers, I'll get this stuff done anyway, it'll be easier to keep my mind occupied, stop it thinking about how much it hurts."

"Aye, fair enough, look I'll see you later, I'm off to court."

"Cheers Arthur."

"And, eh, Danny, how is it going back at the flat?"

"Oh, eh...fine, why?"

"Eh...nothing, I'll see you later."

Arthur left and Danny returned to typing various emails to Charlie. Some that capitulated and some that told him to fuck off. Others that were friendly and others that were hostile. All were deleted before being sent. He shutdown his email and got on with the search he should have done the day before. The rest of the day he remained functional with a closely controlled diet. A couple of cans of Irn Bru got him to lunchtime and the replenishing Big Mac meal. It was a coffee filled afternoon until, at 4:30, he got an email from Charlie.

Danny,

I meant what I said. This is serious, I'm not f**king about. You and Kelly are finished. Do it kindly and do it now.

Charlie

"Oooh, asterisk, asterisk, what a ponce."

Danny looked at the clock and decided that he'd suffered enough for one day. He'd allow himself to leave early and get the chance to avoid the battle with humanity on the tube back west.

Despite the usual assurances, it took until late in the afternoon before the glazier finally arrived to repair the damage to the front of Laxmi's shop. He had hardly exchanged a civil word with Shazia all day and the delay in the repair was becoming an increasing source of tension.

Like all good tradesman, the glazier got out of the van with a healthily list of excuses. In third place on the list were "those idiots in the office". A close runner up was "the nightmare traffic today, is there something on?" The winner was the inevitable "non-standard size of glass". They all passed clean over Laxmi's head. He had turned off his ears a long time ago to protect himself from Shazia and her incessant desire to uproot his life to place unspecified. He only had to shut off for a few more hours; she was going away for the night.

Shazia had gone upstairs before the glazier arrived so he was able to sit in the shop in peace as his window on the world was restored to its former mesh covered glory. The work completed, Laxmi silently signed the work order and the glazier was on his way. He took the invoice and shook his head at the number at bottom. He just got back to his seat at the till when the bell above the door signified a new arrival.

"Hi Laxmi, just saw the glazier, what happened?"

It was Danny and he'd arrived at a bad time.

"You."

"Me? What do you mean?"

"You happened. We lived OK here until you turned up and started interfering."

"What? Was this…"

"Yeah, the Finches, the ones who would 'never know that you're involved, Laxmi, don't worry'"

"I left those bottles miles…"

"Really? Well, how do you explain a smashed window and a fire in the front of the shop?"

"How do you explain anything they do? You don't. They didn't know it was you. It's just their usual shite. You are just nearby."

"Yeah, maybe, but it still took someone to make them angry, didn't it, you can't deny that."

"So, they've never done anything to the shop before? You put all the mesh on the windows for fun? All these locks are just door jewellery?"

"Look, this is different. Now I'm going to lose the shop."

"How?"

"Shazia, she's had enough and I can't say I blame her."

Danny's heart sunk lower than its already subterranean position. He already had a deep sense of loss hanging over him. He was going to lose Kelly and now Laxmi was going to lose his shop. Was it because of him? Would Kelly have got tired with him anyway? Would the Finches have pulled Shazia's final straw before long? This was all the comfort he had.

"Maybe it was inevitable, eh? Did you think they would ever actually stop?"

"I dunno Danny man, all I know is that I've no idea what to do now. Shazia's Dad is involved now and he's not happy. He's been on the phone to my Dad already. It's a bloody nightmare."

"I don't get it. What's it got to do with them?"

"You don't understand, I have to listen to them, respect what they say."

This was so far removed from Danny's interaction with his Dad that there was nothing he could understand. He was so tired that even basic language was at the edges of his comprehension.

"Look mate, I'm sorry. I didn't…well, you know…"

"Aye, well, it's too late now eh?"

"How about I buy you a beer?"

"How about I force you to drink some of mine that I can't sell?"

"Sounds like a plan."

"I'll shut the shop at 6, you come to the flat?"

"Can you make it 7? I could do with a bath and a snooze."

"Fair enough."

"What about Shazia?"

"She will be away at her parents, scheming probably."

*

After spending a lifetime of shy reticence Charlie was emerging from his shell. In a twisted interpretation of knowledge being power, the hold he now had over Danny was the fuel that powered a voice for his long-standing desire. This voice first had to silence all the other ones that complained about exploitation of the situation and the demeaning of his feelings. He found this surprisingly easy as he reasoned that these were necessary evils to achieve a situation that would be better for Kelly and him. The inherent arrogance of the reasoning got lost somewhere in the mix. It's a lawyer thing.

To make best use of this newfound confidence Charlie took the unusual step of leaving at a reasonable time to enable him to walk past the reception desk on his way out. He was aware that he had perhaps jumped the gun a bit earlier on.

"Hi, I'm just off home."

"Ok then, I'll see you tomorrow."

"OK then, see ya."

The longest journey starts with the smallest of steps.

Sixteen

Danny lay in the bath and stared fixedly at the newly repaired hole in the ceiling. The shape of the new plaster outlined the hole through which his new life had fallen. The hot tap still thundering a torrent into the bath, Danny slid down under the water stopping only when his toes burned. Sitting up again slowly, he stopped the tap, pushed the door closed and returned back under the hot, soothing water. The heat rushed into his body and, with his ears under the water, he could hear his heart beating loudly. With the door closed there was little light in the bathroom and the warm, throbbing darkness was just like a womb.

For the first time that day, the pounding in Danny's head stopped and he slipped off to the welcome arms of the sleep he had been gagging for all day.

*

The light was on. The line round the hole in the ceiling was more prominent than before. With a crunch, a small saw poked its nose out through the filled-in crack. Slowly at first, and then with increasing speed, the saw moved round the line of the repaired hole, hacking through the plaster with a wheeze that turned into a chilling whine. A flurry of chalky dust obscured the final few strokes as the circle was completed and it fell cartoon-like into the empty bath. A face appeared eerily in the cloudy chasm that remained. A hand wafted the dust away and gradually the word "dumber" appeared on the forehead of the head that was now descending through the ceiling. It was a Finch, the young thug. The one that had greeted Danny's arrival with a head butt. He was now marked for life. As was his brother. They were now lashing out and bringing even more misery to their already worn out victims. The wiry body descended through the hole, dangled for a moment, then jumped onto the floor. The face looked drawn in, weary and streaked with dried in tears. With head lowered, he trudged off into the hall. Just as another face appeared in the

109

hole. Wrinkled and covered in what appeared to be cream, Mrs. Moyes peered uneasily downward. As she looked around the room below, it was possible to see a green tea cosy on her head. She descended carefully, hanging by both hands, letting go and slowly falling down onto her feet. In one hand she held a scrunched up newspaper page. As with the previous visitor from above, her face was streaked with tears. She opened up the newspaper and scoured the words for signs of her son. With a final sniff, she stuffed the paper into her pocket and shuffled out the door. The next face shone bright blue. It was Laxmi; he descended quicker suspended on many arms each covered in gold and jewels. He landed without a sound. This time there were no tears but his eyes glowed red with anger. Danny got back into the empty bath and lay among the dust and debris. He lay back and stared directly up into the hole. From the darkness another face loomed. Drops of blood fell from the hole and landed on the white of the bath. The face came closer and bloody wounds could be made out. It was Danny's Dad, the face that had lay on the step outside the house. Danny lay silently and stared fixedly upward. His Dad's mouth opened and was about to speak…

*

Danny sat up sharply in the bath. The water was now very cold. The dream, which seemed over as soon as it had started, must have been compressed into the last few moments of what must have been a long sleep. It was still dark and the dank cold of the water made the bath now seem more like a grave than a womb. Rising out of the bath, Danny joints struggled against the cold. Goosebumps stood out sharply on his skin and he shivered violently. Grabbing a towel he ran for the living room and stood in front of the fire, turning it up full. He dried quickly but before long his skin was burning even though his body still felt cold. He stepped away from the fire and the goose bumps quickly returned.

The doorbell rang. A quick glance at the clock confirmed that it had been a long sleep and that it was doubtless Laxmi at the door wondering what had happened to him. Shouting to the door, he threw on some clothes and greeted Laxmi still barefoot.

"What happened to you?"

"Sorry, I fell asleep in the bath."

"In the bath?"

"Yeah, I'm in agony and cold."

"Well, can I come in?"

"Yeah, sorry, just go through to the living room, I'll…eh…find some more clothes."

Laxmi walked through to the kitchen and put the beer on the table. Walking back into the living room he couldn't help notice the simplicity of the décor. It would appear that Danny had virtually nothing of his own. All the shelves were empty and the walls bare. He sat down on the settee. It was one of those settees that you only ever find in furnished flats. Like everything that "is not available in the shops", it was pretty awful. Laxmi stared out of the curtainless windows and was appalled by the thick layer of grime that covered all the glass. Many years of buses, lorries and taxis rattling by had left their mark. A light came on and Danny appeared in the room.

"Sorry mate, eh...can I get you...well, a beer?"

"Aye sure, go for it."

"Is it that Hungarian stuff again?"

"You say that as if you didn't like it the last time?"

"Well, it was fine, unlike my head the next day."

"Surely more a question of quantity rather than quality."

"I suppose."

"Don't worry, didn't think it was fair to make you suffer twice, I brought up some Budvar."

"Cheers, I'll go halfers..."

"No, it's no problem, it went past it sell by date last week."

"Ah, and I suppose..."

"Yeah, yeah, it's fine, honest!"

Danny smiled and walked into the kitchen, returning with two open, brown bottles. As always, the first drink gave Danny a jolt and the recent images in his dream made it stronger than normal. Maybe Charlie had been right. He tried to do some kind of mad hero thing and as a result had made things a lot worse for a lot of people, including himself. He still hadn't thought through what he was meant to or going to do with Kelly. It was still very clear what he wanted to do with Kelly but the fact that he hadn't yet also troubled him enough to avoid thinking about it. It all troubled him too much to think about for now. The immediate problem seemed to centre on coming up with a decent apology.

"Look, Laxmi, I honestly didn't think that this was going to happen".

"What?"

"Y'know, the damage to the shop, you having to move."

"Who says I'm moving?"

"Well, I thought..."

"You think a lot of things Danny, doesn't mean they are right now, does it?"

"I see your point."

"How's the beer?"

"It's, well, pretty damned fine actually."

"See, these sell by dates don't know what they are talking about."

"Whatever has happened or will happen, I'm still sorry that my stupidity has fucked everything up for you."

"Will you stop?"

"But, your shop was set on fire, your wife wants to move, all because I noised up the Finches."

"So, who noised them up the last time they set the front of the shop on fire?"

"Eh? But I thought..."

"See, there's that thinking thing again, you really should try to cut that out."

"I'll work on it."

"I really should be thanking you."

"What? Now who's the one who should try to cut it out?"

"No, seriously. I was just sitting back and letting all happen, avoiding it, hiding when I could, locking up, cleaning up. At least you tried to do something about it."

"For all the good it did."

"Maybe, but I felt ashamed that I forgotten so much."

"Forgotten what?"

"I was brought up as a Hindu. My family, especially my Grandad told me lots of great stories."

"I thought you were lapsed."

Laxmi lifted up his bottle to eye level.

"Perhaps more amended than lapsed."

"I see, but, no, to be honest, I don't see…"

"There are lots of things about Hinduism that don't make much sense but there are huge amounts of it that are really interesting and entertaining."

"Entertaining? I thought it was a religion?"

"It is a religion but a colourful one. And there is still a lot to be learnt from it."

"I don't get it."

"OK, are you a Christian?"

"No, agnostic at best."

"But, you'd never murder anyone would you?"

"No, I suppose not."

"But you'd probably have a go at coveting your neighbours wife?"

"Probably. But not yours obviously…not that I'm saying she's not worth…oh fuck…shut up Danny."

"Well said. So, you agree with one commandment but perhaps not another. See? Amended, not lapsed."

"So, what bits do you still like then? What made you feel ashamed?"

"The stuff in Hindu legends isn't like Christianity, it's not dull stuff like loaves, fishes and blokes with beds under their arms. It was far more exciting. Imagine the Bible rewritten by Tolkein with the film directed by John Woo. When you're young it's really interesting. Almost exciting. You probably dozed through most of your Bible lessons and then went home and watched Star Wars. Well I had all that wrapped up into one. I'm sure it wasn't deliberate but the Mahabharat and Bhagvad Gita were really good ways to get young people involved in their religion, it makes them more academic too."

"So you were really into it then?"

"Oh yeah, people getting their heads cut off and replaced with an elephant head, blokes turning blue, slaying evil creatures. It's great stuff."

"So, why the amending?"

"That stuff is all legend; it's fairy stories. Sure, there's morality and lesson in it but it's not exactly relevant. It's the modern face of a religion that you have to live with. There are lots of things I'm not too keen on. I hate the caste system and I love this…"

"Beer?"

"Yeah, do you know what would happen if my Dad saw me drinking this?"

"No."

"Neither do I, but I really don't want to find out."

"Really?"

"Fuckin' right. And that's another thing, swearing in front of him would be worse."

"Not exactly the same as me and my Dad."

"Not the same as many people."

"Well, maybe we were a wee bit different from that too."

"How?"

"He was an alcoholic, now he's dead."

"Sorry to hear that."

"I'm not, it was…well…never mind…sounds like maybe your family's way is better."

"It would be if it wasn't so hypocritical. Do you think my Dad disapproving of me drinking means that he doesn't do it? I know he does. Maybe that's what did it. I went along with it until I found his bottle of whisky. After that it didn't make sense."

"Alright, so you amended, seems reasonable, but what bit of this blue elephant head stuff makes it OK for me to nearly get your shop burnt down?"

"Revenge."

"Revenge?"

"There are so many tales of revenge. Although, it is meant to be a lesson towards peace and all that, in many ways revenge is seen as justice."

"And that's what…"

"…you tattooed on their head. That's what got me thinking. I remembered a story."

"From the Mahaby-wotsit?"

"Yeah, it was about the Naga. It was one of my Granddad's favourites."

"Let's hear it then."

"Eh? OK, but you'd better get another beer."

"Ah, the irony."

Danny wandered into the kitchen and got a couple of beers from the fridge. His head whirled with a weird kind of cultural confusion. A lame reference to a crap American film made him tattoo a couple of Scottish boys with the words "dumb" and "dumber". This seemed to have made some long distance connection and stirred the faded religion in lapsed Hindu. He walked back through with his Czech brewed beverage unable to suppress a smirk. It was just like in Jaws, unlikely drinking companions getting drunk over tales and songs.

"Farewell and ado…"

"What?"

Danny stopped singing and started to laugh.

"You go in the street, the Finches go in the street…"

"What?"

"Nothing, but we're going to have to work on your film knowledge. Just looking forward to the story."

"Don't get too excited, I'll be lucky to remember any of it."

"You can make it up if you like, it's not as if I can correct you or anything."

"Naga means snake. I think they were a tribe of people or something but in the legend they are actually snakes. There was another guy called Parikshita."

"Sheeta?"

"Yeah, lots of the names are entertaining. Anyway, he injured one of the Naga by mistake. And they meant him no harm."

"Just like you with the Finches."

"Exactly. Well this Naga guy is dying so he curses the dude and says he'll die of a snake bite within a week."

"I thought I was going to die from snakebite once. A big purple sick saved me."

"Mmmm…perhaps Western culture is colourful after all."

"It didn't seem so at the time, believe me. So, what did the Sheeta guy do?"

"He stayed at the top of a pole and was guarded all the time so snakes couldn't get him."

"Must have taken this curse seriously then?"

"It was best to in those days. Anyway, at the end of the seventh day he was feeling very happy with himself for having survived. He was about to climb the ladder up to the pole when he saw a beetle."

"Must have been George, he is into this kind of shit…eh…no offence."

"Don't worry, it makes me laugh now. So Parikshita says that he has nothing to fear from a beetle and, just then, it turns into the Naga prince, who bites him and kills him."

"Bummer."

"Yeah and thus the innocent Naga was revenged by his King. And that's what you tried to do, so don't worry about apologies."

"So, what the moral then?"

"Don't fuck with snakes?"

"Or beetles."

*

As was now becoming the norm, Danny and Laxmi drank until all the beer was gone. The strength of the beer or perhaps the stress of the day had taken a toll on Laxmi's legs and he seemed reluctant, if not actually unable, to walk. Danny, only marginally more capable, managed to get him on his feet and, in a reprise of his awkward walk with the drugged twins, hauled Laxmi out of the flat and to his front door.

A few shambolic moments passed as the now thoroughly amused Laxmi identified the location of his keys with random pointing motions. They were duly extracted from the pocket with further mirth and, after a few abortive attempts, Laxmi was returned to his flat safely, if not particularly soundly.

The noise in the stair must have disturbed an already anxious Mrs. Moyes. She poked her head out of the storm door as Danny passed on the way back to the glorious sanctuary of his bed. Danny calmed her and explained that it was "just a little high jinks". Her face softened immediately and the long waking of her loneliness now compelled her to chat.

"Isn't it terrible what happened to that poor man's flat. I just don't understand it. He's never said a word to anyone, never mind done anyone any harm."

Danny didn't want to talk. He only wanted to sleep. He certainly didn't want to linger further on what was now quite a painful subject.

"Aye, aye, terrible." This was not the time to reply with anything but closed statements.

"You know, I don't know who was responsible but I bet I could have a good guess. Mindless, just mindless."

Employing a tactic often used by people on the phone, he suggested to Mrs. Moyes that she might want to end the conversation.

"Well, I'm sure you don't want to be standing out here in the cold talking to me, so I'll bid you goodnight."

"Aye son, aye, goodnight son."

Danny knew who was responsible but he was no snake prince. His legs now felt much heavier climbing the remaining stairs back to the flat. He was pleased that Laxmi had forgiven him but was still, in some way, sorry for what he had done. And he still didn't know what to do about Kelly.

Seventeen

Danny had always imagined it like a knife hung on the end of a long rope. It must be hanging from a loop directly above his head like a long pendulum. He pushes it away but, after a while, it swings back, the knife slashing at him as it passes before disappearing in the other direction. At first he was weak and could only push so hard. This meant the knife came back quickly and the pain came too. As he got stronger, he could push harder and the pain would stay away for longer. Recently, he could go a long time without the pain, the pendulum staying out on a wide arc, sometimes like it was gone forever.

The image of his Dad in the dream was the first time the pain had returned since he came back to Glasgow. As always, it took a while to go away, the scar burning and then healing slowly.

The pain remained in the morning and was augmented by another in a now seemingly endless line of hangovers. The day passed quicker this time, the novelty of work already starting to be replaced by the realisation that the long sentence leading to retirement had started without hope of parole or reprieve. Being busy was now a relief and, luckily, a minor epidemic of stomach flu had decimated the workforce leaving Danny struggling to keep up with the work on one hand and keep his breakfast down with the other. The clock-watching was replaced with surprise at the hour and almost desperation for it to be earlier.

The work done, or as much of it as was feasible with his level of skill and authority, Danny rushed back to the flat, grabbing a pizza impatiently before diving nervously into the close. Once in the flat, he switched off his mobile, took the phone of the hook, made sure there was no booze in the flat and locked both the doors.

He had achieved most of his major objectives for the day. He hadn't thrown up on his desk, he hadn't spoken to Charlie and he'd managed to avoid Kelly both on the phone and in person. He still didn't know what he was going to do but he definitely didn't want to have to make it up as he went along. Just this once. Now all he had to do was not get pissed and avoid another hangover.

Unlike the day, the evening passed slowly. His now settled stomach urged his body to fill it quickly and so, with little chewing and even less skin remaining on the roof of his mouth, he wolfed the pizza in record time, returning his stomach to its accustomed aching.

Unable to move, he turned on the TV and spent the next couple of hours surfing between different ends of the spectrum of tripe on offer.

*

Charlie's pizza was eaten slowly. He used a knife and fork and chewed each piece before swallowing. The TV wasn't on, The Buzzocks Going Steady played in the background. Although not known particularly known for their poignancy, both 'Every Fallen In Love…' and 'What Do I Get?' had Charlie oscillating between making the call he wanted to make and just taking the CD off. He stared at the phone and urged himself to call her.

"You're shit, you're shit, you must admit you're shit."

He switched off the CD and turned on the TV, the Discovery Channel was showing a programme about the SR-71 Blackbird. He sat down and watched, even thought he'd seen it before. Maybe even twice.

*

Kelly sat in her room. She turned on the TV; Eastenders was just starting. Putting down her mug of tea, she slumped daintily onto her beanbag in front of the TV that sat on the shelf at one end of her large room. It was once the living room of the flat but it stopped being used so it was decided that she could make it into her own little studio. A quiet place away from the madness of her brothers and the sadness of her Mum. On the top floor, high above the noise of the buses and the bustle below, the wide bay window gave a view over much of the city beyond.

The insistent clatter of drums signalled the usual dramatic cliff-hanger and the end of Eastenders. Kelly looked up and realised that she had been daydreaming and had no idea how the tension was being held until the next episode. She had been thinking about Danny and trying to work out why he hadn't been in touch. Picking up her tea, she walked to the window and looked out. He was out there somewhere, not that pretty, but quite funny but it seemed, like so many boyfriends before, that he'd found out that she was from a family of nutters and had bottled it like all the rest. She took a sip of her tea. It had gone cold. It seemed appropriate.

*

Down below, another cup of tea was being gripped tightly looking forlornly out to the world. The end of Eastenders was as much the signal to put the kettle on as it was part of the constant reminder of Mrs. Moyes' son and how she hoped that somewhere out there he was alive and happy. She always held on to the almost delusional dream that one day he would turn up in Eastenders like he should have done. So she watched every episode. Even the

117

repeats, just in case she missed him the first time. The second time round she ignored the main characters and just watched the background.

*

Danny lay in bed and resolved to come up with some kind of plan before he went to sleep. He started by assimilating the facts. Kelly was a babe. No question. Top manto. Blonde, jugs, legs, sorted. She was also a member of what appeared to be Glasgow's premier nutter family; two of which he had scarred for life. He hadn't shagged her yet. This was the first point that needed further investigation. He hadn't shagged her. The longest he had gone before shagging any of his previous girlfriends could be measured in hours. Why was Kelly different? She seemed special, there was no urge to get the job done and move on. A feeling he wasn't used to. But was it love?

Of course, another problem was that if he stayed with Kelly his so-called friend would probably grass him up. Or would he? Maybe not. Either way, if he loved Kelly and thought there was a chance of it being worth it then why not risk the chance of jail or death by psycho-brother.

Still, it would be high risk. If he was going to even consider it he would have to be very, very sure. In Danny's mind, there was only one-way to be sure. It had to be tested empirically.

*

The bra came off like a dream. Like all bra removing dreams, it came off first time, quickly and unleashed a pair of quite remarkable breasts. She was kneeling on the bed and the bra dropped across her thighs, the skin tightened by the legs tucked beneath her. The breasts didn't move, magically hanging in the air before finally succumbing to an almost imperceptible sag. But still the puppies sat up excitedly, their little wet noses begging to be kissed. So he did.

It was a pleasant sensation, the softness of the skin against the lips, the feel of her hair on his face as she leant forward. Delicate kissing turned to urgently pressed mouths. Tongues flicked in and out. The kissing stopped and was replaced by two heads desperately trying to get inside the other. Head still craned forward, mouth still locked by an airtight seal of saliva; he reached back and started to haul off his jeans. A tricky task with two hands was now made much harder by using only one hand. And the fact that it was much harder. Button flies are not for the passionate, disengaging briefly, he sat back and opened the jeans and forced them down over the now highly attentive obstruction. She lay back, head on the pillow, her legs only slightly open. He leaned forward and the gates parted. They paused briefly, looking each other in the face. A wry, almost dirty smile was on her face. And then she was on his. Plunging his head down, she opened her legs eagerly and with the very first touch her body arched with a pleasing groan.

Like a cup of tea on a cold day her moist warmth was as refreshing as it was pleasing. His tongue toyed with her eagerly as her body writhed beneath him. Reaching down, she grabbed his elbow and started to pull him up the bed.

"Fuck me" she said simply. It was the kind of clear, unambiguous command that men long for. With the kind of ease NASA can only dream of,

118

he rose up and slipped inside her in a single, sweeping motion. A short gasp was followed by a long supplicating groan. Slowly at first, and then with more urgency he started to ride her. Long strokes, then some sort ones, the occasional deep push. Her nails sank into his arse and she let out her first word.

"Oh" she said.

Now was the time. This was when he would know. It was the time for concentration, for other thoughts. It was usually the time for a weird sort of clarity, when thoughts are at their purest, not altered by circumstance or desire, when the mind is open only to the truth. It was now he expected to think of her, to see her face, to know that he loved her. But instead the pendulum swung back.

The bloodied face of his Dad, his Mum being thrown against the wall. Danny fought to get it out of his head He fought to get his Dad out the door. In a waking dream he battled with the pictures in his head and the memories that went with him. Beneath him she bucked and writhed, revelling in the force of Danny's attentions. The thoughts wouldn't go until, at the moment of orgasm she dug her nails deep into Danny's back and the pain woke him from his nightmare. He finished himself off as quickly as he could; she was still clearly pleased at this extension to her pleasure. Rolling off to the side, he moved her long, jet-black hair off the pillow and he lay down. Moments of silent panting passed. Danny stared fixedly at the ceiling.

"I suppose I can allow you a few minutes of silence."

"Eh?"

"Woah…that was. Eh…pretty spectacular."

"What was?"

"Very funny, the fireworks display, what do you think?"

"Oh aye, yeah, eh…thanks."

"I should be thanking you."

"No."

"You were like an animal, a wild fucking animal."

And he was. He had thrown him out the door, protected his territory, and defended what he had to defend. Slowly, the pendulum started to swing away again, the sudden realisation that he had just administered a monster shag helping its progress back into the distance recesses.

"You sound surprised?"

"Yeah, I am a bit, I'd heard you were shite."

"Well, it takes two to tango, you weren't so bad yourself."

It was a shameful lie but the shameful truth would have been worse.

"I shagged you to find out if I loved someone else. I expected her to be in my thoughts when I was in you. It didn't happen. Instead I was possessed by an image of my now dead father and the fight I had with him that ultimately led to his death. My sexual performance was in no small part related to the distraction caused by these thoughts and the aggression that accompanied them. I have no idea if you were any good or not. In fact, for most of the time, I didn't even know you were there. The good news for you is that it turns out I don't love her, the bad news is that I'm not entirely sure I can remember your name."

Not even Danny could have got away with that and anyway, why spoil it? Word would get round. Glasgow's nurses were now his. So Kelly didn't need to be.

Eighteen

The plane waited on the apron for another plane to land. The kids heard the engines whizz by and thought that they were off. Peering out the window into the dark Dad could tell that they weren't on the runway yet. As the landing plane taxied off at one end of the runway, the plane pulled slowly forward. It seemed to drive straight across to the other side of the runway before swinging in a wide arc and pointing finally down the middle.

It lurched again to a stop. People moved uneasily in their seats as the engines gave out a slow hum. The plane held for only a minute but to the waiting family it seemed like forever.

"Is everything OK?"

"Aye, aye, they'll just be finishing off their pint." The joke was weak, the accompanying smile weaker. Dad squeezed Mum's hand. The kids bounced excitedly.

The engines began to spin faster. The noise grew but still nothing moved. A second increase in noise and the plane started to move forward. Slowly at first and then with a final thrust began to pick up speed. They were forced back in their chairs. The kids smiled broadly as the older, wiser knuckles whitened. The plane went straight down the middle banging loudly on the runway lights. With each bump everything in the overhead lockers rattled.

The plane got up speed and stayed on the ground. They looked at each other, sharing the same fear of running off the end of the runway and then, just as their eyes looked away, the nose lifted, the bumping stopped and the plane eased into the sky.

Their heads were pressed firmly back into the headrest; the hydraulic whirr and bump of the gear coming up whitened the knuckles further.

The engines throttled back and the plane seemed to sink in the sky. Fingernails dug into Dad's hand and drew blood. He didn't flinch. The plane started to turn, the wing appearing in the window. The flaps came up and it levelled out. Everything seemed to settle down.

Blood came back to the knuckles. They looked at each other and smiled. The kids look up, still grinning. Dad winked "we're on our way now".

"Tower, tower, fire in engine 1, losing power in engine 2, we're…shit, oh shit…"

*

"Bet you didn't expect to be seeing me?"

"No one expects the Maryhill Inquisition."

"Yeah, very funny, get in the car."

The car was unmarked but, on getting in, Danny could see all the usual trappings of a police car. That, and the policeman sitting in the driving seat.

"So, you've finally decided to follow up on my complaint then."

"No."

"No?"

"No."

"So why I am being treated to a ride in a police car?"

"Look, I don't have time to fuck about OK, so, just for once will you leave the smart-arse on the pavement."

"Now, now, language…"

"I fucking mean it Danny!"

It was clear that Sergeant Murdoch really wasn't in the mood so Danny decided to go along with it.

"OK. What?"

"Keep away from the Finches."

"What do you mean? They attacked me remember?"

"Just keep the fuck away from them, OK?"

"I live in the same building."

"I don't mean that, I mean stop fucking with them."

"Eh?"

"Don't play the daft laddie with me, I know about the tattoos, I know what you did."

"Woah, woah, I have no idea what your…"

"Danny, for fucks sake, don't fuck with me, I know you did it but they don't, lets leave it that way and you stop fucking with them, OK?"

"But…"

"No buts, just get that flat sold and get the fuck out of there OK?"

"OK."

A call came through on the radio and the sergeant responded. As he did so, he motioned for Danny to get out of the car. Somewhat taken aback, Danny got out of the car and watched it drive away, his brain as yet unable to come up with the questions that would normally pop straight into his head. The blur in his head continued all the way to work. He walked awkwardly having wounded his knob beyond all recognition the night before, each brush off his leg breaking even more of the glass in his boxers. He arrived at work with embryonic questions forming in his head. They were quickly aborted. The phone rang. It was Charlie. This was to be a day of retribution.

"What the fuck did I tell you?"

"I've not been near her."

"I told you to let her down gently."

"I will, don't worry, I agree with you, I'm not going anywhere near her any more, I'll talk to her and…"

"…explain why she saw you at a club last night leaving with some girl with dark hair?"

"Aw shit…"

"Aw shit indeed, she's just arrived upset at the office…"

"Look Charlie, I was…"

"You were what? Don't give me it Danny, I know exactly what you were…"

"But nothing…look, don't even bother breaking up with Kelly, just don't speak to her, OK?"

"OK."

First the police and now a lawyer. Someone somewhere seemed to be trying to tell him something.

"Danny, can I have a word?"

"Eh…yeah, sure boss, what is it?"

"In my office."

Still in a daze, Danny trudged behind Arthur, walking with his head bowed like he had so many times on the way to the Headmaster's office.

"Jeez Danny, you look like shit."

"Look like, feel like, the entire set."

"Yeah well, this'll help…"

Reaching under his desk, Arthur pulled out a whisky bottle and two glasses in what appeared to be a well-rehearsed manoeuvre.

"No, it's a bit early…"

"It's never too early, here, stick some water in it if you're squeamish."

Danny took the glass and looked through it and out into the many golden images of the morning glinting through the crystal facets. He rotated it slowly in his hand. The Victorian skyline of Glasgow spun like a dreary kaleidoscope. He'd only been back for a matter of weeks and already the joy of his arrival had all but gone. This morning hadn't gone well and he had a feeling that it could soon get a bit worse. Declining the water, he necked the whisky in one.

"So, I here there was a wee bit of trouble round at the flat?"

"Trouble? No, not really…"

"The man below you? His house got trashed?"

"Oh yeah, yeah, I saw him as I came up the stairs. He seemed upset, I tried to help him."

"Yes. Upset, yes. Do you know what happened?"

"It was nothing to do with me."

"Did I say it was?"

"No. Why so jumpy?"

"Early morning whisky."

"Look Danny, you've not off to the best of starts and I think that I'm to blame for putting you in that flat."

"No, the flat is fine, I'm happy there…"

"Danny, I put you there hoping that your presence would help sell it. Since you arrived it has been a war zone."

"That's nothing to do…"

"…with you, yes, OK, whatever. Let's just say that you have helped me realise that having someone in that flat makes little or no difference to it getting sold."

"Well, I'll need to time to find somewhere…"

"No, no, you won't, you can have my flat in town for a while."

"But won't you…"

"No, I, well, my wife and I are, what is it they call it 'trying again'? I'm moving back to Drymen."

"Should I be offering congratulations?"

"It's 9:30 in the morning and I'm drinking whisky, you decide."

"OK."

"Get Malky and he'll help you get your stuff moved. Not today though, desks are looking quite empty out there today, take a day off later in the week and get yourself sorted."

"Look Arthur, thanks, y'know. It'll be…I'll be…well…"

"I know, I know, now fuck off and do some work, I need to phone my wife and…"

"…here."

Danny handed Arthur the whisky and, with a cheeky wink, left the room.

*

Charlie had thought about it a long time. He was now bored of masturbation and was still too reticent to get porn of any kind to make it any more interesting. He couldn't take any more Discovery Channel. There were too many animals that were getting more than him. There had been girls before he'd liked but he'd done nothing, they might have liked him, he didn't know but what he did know was that none of them were Kelly. This time it had to be different. He had to do something this time. It wasn't desperation for sex, it wasn't even desperation for Kelly, it was solely because he couldn't forgive himself for not finding out, for not asking. He expected to get nowhere but he still had to know.

He'd already warned Danny off and had almost admitted that he had done it selfishly. Now that Danny had done it again, he wasn't going to hesitate to exploit it. He phoned Danny with a barely suppressed glee. Having already made the decision this was too much of a gift. He would forget about whatever misgivings and guilt he may have and just do it for a change. Kelly would be feeling rejected. She'd be wondering why Danny did what he did, why he ignored her in favour of someone else. She'd be vulnerable and Charlie had to use this to his advantage. It might be the best chance he will ever get. You can't be a Minister's son forever.

"Look, Kelly, this might not be a good time but I was wondering if you fancy popping out for lunch today…eh…together I mean."

*

Sitting at the table it got dark without her noticing. The late afternoon sun giving way to a darker sodium glow. Her eyes moved between looking blindly out of the window and to the cup of tea as she brought it to her lips. Outside a bus was having trouble with its clutch and the energetic free-spin of the diesel made her sit up. She turned to look at the clock on the shelf but couldn't see it in the now dim light. She stood up, pressing her hands into the table to help free her joints and raise herself up. With the lamp turned out she could see that it was nearly 8. Tea or TV. Both. She walked to where she had left the remote. It lay on top of a pile of newspapers, not yet piled. Reprimanding herself, she picked them up and folded them neatly before placing on top of the appropriate pile. The papers were lying on top of a copy of the script her son had been reading. She kept it and read it occasionally. Going back for the remote, she noticed it and started to read. It was only a few pages before the end when she stopped, hearing a voice in the close.

*

Danny left work late. He didn't want to get back to the flat early and the only other alternative was going to the pub first, which he wasn't in the mood for. The most important thing was to get into the flat and back out again in the morning without bumping into Kelly and without there being any more aggro. He got the impression that a good number of people were encouraging him to avoid that. On the way home he was torn between looking forward to going back to Arthur's flat and the Jacuzzi and feeling guilty about leaving the old flat and the people that lived there. He wasn't even sure if he'd say goodbye. Whatever pathetic attempts he had made to help had come to nothing or perhaps less. Perhaps it was time to disappear quietly. He phoned Malky to arranged to get his stuff moved in the morning.

"Malky?"

"Eh?"

There was a lot of noise in the background. Danny craned his ear into the mobile. It was the late night dogs. Someone appeared to have a lot riding on the riderless greyhounds.

"Malky?"

"What?"

Unsurprisingly, Malky was struggling to hear. Somewhere behind him someone seemed to be inventing a new, if not commercially viable, form of Scottish porn.

"Come on ya fucker! Come on ya fucker! Come on! Come on! Yes! Yes! Yeeeeessssssssssss!"

125

It was the money shot. It sounded like the end of a long accumulator. The screaming continued for a while and then receded. Malky stepped outside into the relative calm of the busy street outside.

"Malky, it's Danny…"

"Aye."

"Someone seemed happy…"

"Aye, wee Maurice got a yankee up."

"He'll be celebrating later then?"

"No chance. He's just won his giro money back. He's just avoided a doin' of his wife."

"Good for him. Did Arthur speak to you?"

"Aye, yer on yer toes across to Arthur's place."

"What time then?"

"Ten Tattoo?"

"What?"

"About 10ish?"

"What did you say about tattoos?"

"Nowt, just a shite joke."

"A what?"

"Y'know, like Chinese dentists?"

"Eh?"

"Two Thirty."

"Aw, fuck off Malky, see you at 10."

Danny hung up; he was nearly at the door of the flat. He was about to wonder why Malky had mentioned a tattoo when Mrs. Moyes' door opened.

"Hiya son."

"Oh, hullo!"

Oh shit. Should he tell her he is going?

"I heard you in the close. Just thought I'd say hello."

"Oh, thanks. What that's you've got there?"

"Oh, it's just my boy's script, y'know for the play he was doing?"

"Aye, aye, I remember you said."

This was too long to be standing in the close. Danny started to get that nervous feeling in his arse.

"He is about the same age as you?"

"Who? Oh, your son?"

"Aye, aye."

"Oh. Look I…"

"Do you want to come in for a cup of tea?"

"No, no, I need to…"

"Aye, aye, I know, you must be busy…"

On top of whatever guilt he already had this was not the conversation or situation of choice. Given that he only had a few hours left in the building, now was not the time to start acting as a surrogate son. Still he felt he owed her something.

"I'd love the read the play through, can I borrow it?"

"Aye son, aye, please, here…"

Danny took the loose pages and put them into the outside pocket of briefcase. As he did this he moved for the next step up.

"Goodnight then."

"Aye, goodnight…son."

Nineteen

It was the middle of a long hot summer that seemed to be lasting forever. Endless days of sunshine, exploration and games of football that continued long beyond the daylight. For three boys it was the best of times, every day starting with a discussion, on the wall outside the corner shop.

"Fitba?"

"Nah, not today day, Malky's ball's burst and I'm not playing with one of those fly-away jobs."

"But, we have to…"

"Don't worry, wee Barry's back from his holidays tomorrow, he's got a brand new ball. Full size."

"His Mum says we can't play with it."

"It's a ball! What else is he going to do with it?"

"So, what today then?"

Lugs was the natural leader of the three, slightly brighter than the other two, he always seemed to take control, even when it didn't really matter much.

"How about going up the field along the canal?"

"What for?"

"Climb trees."

"Climb trees?"

"Aye."

"What for?"

"No, to get high, get it?"

They didn't. Sometimes Lugs was a real pain. But they liked him, somehow him being brainy made them feel more secure. He always knew what to do.

"Where are these trees then?"

"Along the canal, then up into that farm place."

"Alright then, better get a bottle of juice though, that's a long way."

"Is that all you think about Johnny? Eh?"

"Aye, Deeko, aye."

They got a bottle of juice and headed off down through the hole in the fence and down the path created by hundreds of short-cutters to the towpath of the canal. It was a good couple of miles walk along the canal before they could cut off across the field. They stopped to look at everything interesting thrown in the canal and every plant that could be used to stick to or harm each other. A couple of times they had to stand to the side as a cyclist went by. Then a couple of girls, slightly older than them, walked passed the other way. All three fell unusually silent. Only Lugs looked up.

"Nice day."

"What?"

"Nothing."

"You're Arthur aren't you?"

"Aye, and you're Mary."

The girls turned and walked away giggling. The boys did the same. Once they were far enough away.

"How do you know her?"

"She lives above my Nan."

"She was lovely."

"What would you know Deeko, eh?"

"Well, I…"

"Bet you've never even had a wank yet?"

"I have!"

"Have you! Deeko's a wanker! Deeko's a wanker!"

"Shut it Lugs, alright?"

"Aye, whatever, you're not saying much Johnny?"

He stayed silent, he was generally quieter than the other two but this time seemed different. Leaving the towpath they cut up through the flimsy wire fence and into the hedgerow that surrounded the wide expanse of wheat. It was getting even hotter as the sun swung round directly above and all the juice was long since gone. They trudged with some difficulty across the rutted field, the long stems up to their shoulders. At the other side of the field stood a long line of rough, overgrown trees in the middle of which was the tallest, a gnarly old oak. Leaving a long narrow channel of flattened stems behind them, they walked on towards the shade of the big tree. Arriving at the base, they collapsed on the small root buttresses, enjoying the relative cool.

"So are we going to climb?"

"In a minute, jeez, I'm knackered."

"Come on Deeko, ya fat wanker."

"I'm not fat, bet I can get higher than you."

"Yeah?"

"Yeah."

"Guys, guys, what's that?"

"Where?"

"Over there. Smoke."

"Oh yeah. Come on then fatty, lets go up and have a look."

All three climbed. Johnny was quickest as usual. Lugs and Deeko both struggled in their own way, Deeko because he was slightly overweight, Lugs because he wasn't really the outdoor type. Johnny paused on the lowest prominent branch, a long, strong platform pointing out towards the southern horizon. After a few moments, the others joined.

"Come on Johnny, that's not high enough, come on!"

"Guys, you can see the fire from here, the field is on fire, over in that corner, I don't think we should…"

Before he was finished, the two had passed him, their usual awkwardness temporarily overcome by the inspiration of competition. At another large branch, about 25ft up, they stopped again and sat in a row on the bough, legs dangling down above the edge of the field. Smoke from the corner of the field rose in wisps, mostly white with the occasional puff of black.

"Do you think we should go and call the fire brigade?"

"Is that all you think about Deeko? Bloody fire brigade."

"Well, it's a fire, isn't it?"

"Yeah, it's a fire in the middle of nowhere. It's just 'cause you want to see your mates in the brigade."

"They're not my mates; I just want to be a fireman, right, what's wrong with that? What do you want to be?"

"Dunno, a Doctor maybe."

From anyone else this would seem a ridiculous idea but it seemed right for Arthur.

"What about you Johnny?"

"A policeman."

"Polis? You're going to be a polis?"

"Yes."

"You seem sure."

"I am."

"Wow, you've got it all planned then."

"Not it all."

"I suppose you know who you're going to marry too."

"I think I do."

The other two laughed out loud at such a bizarre idea.

"Go on then, who is it?"

"Mary."

"Mary? The girl we met at the canal?"

"Yes."

The others laughed even louder; John didn't even break into a smile. He meant it. He didn't know how, he didn't know why, but it was all he could think about from the moment he saw her walking along the towpath. Lugs and Deeko laughed, John sat silently, his face remaining unchanged. The wind was now blowing across the field into their faces, the smell of the fire, a familiar smell of summer now strong in their nostrils. While they were talking the fire had spread half way across the field. John finally broke his silence.

"Guys, I think we should get down out of the tree, now!"

"I can't do it."

"What do you mean? You got up there, you can get down!"

"Johnny, I can't, I…"

Already on the lower branch, John looked up to see Lugs frozen on the branch above.

"Deeko, get him down will you?"

"How? He's in the way."

"Get past him then!"

"I can't!"

"Stand up and walk past him."

"Stand up! Are you…what the…"

"Some fuckin' fireman you are Deek. Come on Arthur; get your arse down here. The fire is getting closer."

"I can't, I fuckin' can't, it's too high."

Looking behind him, John could see that the fire was only a couple of hundred yards away. Above him, his two useless mates sat frozen on the branch. It was about 15 minutes flat out running to anything like civilisation. He climbed up higher, above the two statues, and combed the horizon for anything or anyone that could help.

*

"Pigeons Malky? I'm not putting my stuff in with a van with pigeons."

"They're in a cage fur fucks sake."

"They smell."

"No they don't."

"Malky put your head in the back of the van."

He lumbered out of the cab and came round to the back. The pigeons were in a small hutch sitting in the bit above the cab of the Luton Transit. Even though they were fifteen feet from the metal rolling door the smell was quite powerful.

"Ah cannae smell them."

"Malky, your eyes are watering."

"Hay fever. Get your stuff in and lets get out of here before I get a ticket."

"Why do you have pigeons in the back of the van?"

"I can't tell you."

"Malky…"

"Oh, fuck it, they're Arthur's."

"Arthur's! Fuck off…"

"They are. Do you not know why him and his wife split up?"

"I assumed it was because he was a bit of a shagger?"

"No, no, she didn't seem to mind that. She hated his pigeons."

"I'd never had Arthur down as the pigeon type."

"He's always had them, ever since he…shit, here's a warden, let's shift."

They loaded quickly; Danny didn't have a lot. As they drove away, Laxmi came out of the shop and looked bemusedly at Danny. Danny responded with an "I'll call you" hand signal. Malky crunched his way up to top gear eventually drowning out the frenzied cooing from about their heads.

Danny hoped that he could have whole the day off but a call from Arthur took him into the office after unloading at the other end. He arrived at his desk and was immediately put to some frenzied work with a guy called Robert who he had only ever exchanged a nod with while taking a slash.

"Morning off?"

"Something like that. Did you know Arthur has pigeons?"

"Fuck off."

"It's true."

"Yeah, yeah, look, we've got work to do."

"I know no one would believe me, that's why I took measures, well, feathers."

"What?"

"Look in my case?"

"What for?"

"Feathers!"

"Can we get on with some work?"

"You don't believe me? Look…"

"And then we can do some work?"

"Yes, absolutely."

"OK."

Robert went into Danny's case and brought out the feathers and script that Mrs. Moyes had given him the night before.

"OK, so there are pigeon feathers."

"It's from a horseman apparently."

"A what? Aw fuck it, can we get on with some work, hang on, what's this? This is a shock, you're an actor!"

"No, no, it's a long story."

"Most plays are."

"Catcher in the Rye, eh?"

"What? Yeah, whatever, can we do some work now?"

"OK, just don't go walking past the Dakota Building."

"Eh? The what?"

"The Dakota building. It's where John Lennon lived."

"So."

"And he was shot outside it by a guy carrying Catcher In The Rye."

"Really?"

"Really."

"So, can we…"

"…do some work? Certainly."

*

132

The road arched over the hill towards the forest. The sun had not yet risen but a glow was illuminating the horizon. The Forestry Commission signs indicated that the turning off the main road into the forest was in a couple of miles. The Police Panda had headed out towards the forest in response to calls about a noise and another about a fire. None of the calls was conclusive so the call went out on the radio for someone to go take a look.

With a sigh that knew that this would mean working beyond the end of the shift, he had turned the car round and headed off in the direction of the forest. The hill steepened, he dropped a gear in the Mk I Escort and hurried towards the summit. The next call that came on the radio made him hurry more.

The calls from the public had been correlated with reports of a plane being in difficulty and finally disappearing off the radar. His heart quickened as he realised that it was very likely that he was headed for the scene of a plane crash and, given the remoteness of location, he was going to be the first person there. The forest was ablaze.

A low glow came from a wide area of trees. A pall of thick black smoke rose from the treetops backlit by the newly rising sun. The size and intensity of the fire could only mean that the plane had been carrying a lot of fuel when it crashed soon after take-off. He knew right away that no one was going to survive.

Before getting to the bottom of the hill, he radioed back confirming the reports and requesting as many fire engines and ambulances that could be made available.

He parked the car and quickly realised there was nothing much he could do. There was nothing discernible in the forest and the crash area seemed widespread. The fire was concentrated in one area but it looked like the debris was scattered much further. He called again on the radio and was instructed to secure the area to prevent onlookers or any other unauthorised people getting near. He told the radio room to call his wife and tell her that he was going to be late.

Twenty

Walking along the street from the car park, Charlie felt a foot taller than normal. At his side was Kelly, the girl he loved and the girl that every man looked at as she walked past. And she was with him. Charlie the scholar, Charlie the plain, Charlie the dull, Charlie on the arm of a beauty. To everyone passing by it appeared that Charlie must have money. In Charlie's mind, he'd just got lucky and was in no mood to worry about what other people thought and in even less of a mind to let Kelly go now that he had her. Although, he hadn't yet had her, that was for another day. Tonight he was going to enjoy his first night with her. Every time he looked at her, his stomach sank, every thing about her affecting him physically and not just in the usual way. Her smell was intoxicating, her laugh uplifting, the touch of her hand soothing. This was as happy as Charlie had ever been.

Entering the restaurant, the smile on Charlie's face broadened. The flowers were on the table; the champagne was in a bucket at the side, just as he had asked for. The final part of his transformation was freeing himself to spend the money that his natural conservatism made him horde, he religious upbringing made him feel guilty of having, never mind spending. Everything he had worked for, his degree, his career, it all made sense now. The best restaurant in town with the best girl. Every minute, every second he repeated in his head.

"This is what it was for. This is what it is about. No one will take this away from me."

Kelly seemed happy and a little overwhelmed. First dates to her were not usually like this and it was all a little confusing. This confusion continued with the menu that made little or no sense. Even the things that were in English were unrecognisable. Charlie helped her order politely and with great care. Kelly saw something in him that she had never seen before. He was genuine.

134

After dinner they chatted easily about nothing in particular until it went in a direction familiar to Kelly.

"I don't understand why you haven't been snapped up a long time ago?"

"What do you mean?"

"You are so beautiful."

On this occasion, the wine was letting Charlie's tongue say the words that had been in his head for so long.

"No, no…"

"Oh, Kelly, you are so very beautiful. You're funny, you're gentle, you're kind…"

"Oh stop it."

"Only if you agree with me."

"Will it shut you up?"

"Yes."

"OK, I agree, I'm beautiful."

"So, why no long term boyfriends? Why no ring on finger?"

"Oh, I dunno, things just never seem to work out."

It never did work out for Kelly. Somehow her family spooked them all. Her brothers always got in the way. But they always would be in the way. If she was going to be happy, she needed someone who could cope with that. She usually hid her family as long as she could but maybe Charlie was different. Maybe she should get it over and done with. If it was going to work, it would have to work now.

"It's my brothers."

"I know."

"Then why did you ask?"

"I wanted you to say it so that I could tell you that it doesn't matter. It won't make any difference."

"You don't know that."

"Oh, I do, I do, I promise you, they won't be a problem."

*

This time there was no intrusion from the pendulum. His performance was not as extended or as powerful but at least Danny actually took part and was able to enjoy it. Especially as she was much hotter than even his wildest dreams had suggested. She was perhaps disappointed but she knew what Danny was capable of and maybe she couldn't expect that every time. Anyway, the Jacuzzi makes up for that.

They had been out for a long night and the beer and Aftershock were starting to take effect. Danny drifted off into a very, deep sleep.

*

The buildings reached up high, their points meeting above the street completely obscuring a sky that would surely have been a blackened and angry. Rain fell from the hidden clouds, odd spots illuminated by the searchlight glow of the street lamps as they fell. Walking along the street, Danny clutched the papers to his chest to keep him dry, ducking past the dark figures that poured

135

down the pavement towards him. Far in the distance, light glowed from the sanctuary of the doorway. Jogging now, he bumped into more people as ran, barking complaints in return.

As he approached the door, the pavement emptied until there was no one else around and the street fell silent. A white figure emerged from the building, standing out brightly against the dark surroundings. It was his Dad. Danny clutched the papers tighter and, avoiding eye contact, headed for the door. He turned as Danny passed him and pulled a gun from inside his jacket. Seeing this, Danny turned as the full force of the bullet sent him reeling back against the steps. As he fell, the papers flew up in the air. Danny fell onto his back and the papers floating down above him, slowly drifting down so that the title on the front page could be easily read. "Catcher…"

Danny woke up with a jump. Looking around it took him a while to remember where he was. Gradually getting his bearings he realised that someone was missing and then, as more blood filled his head, he remembered that nurses always left early. A shower, a wank and a coffee and everything was back in order and he headed for work. Shoes, keys, bag. Sticking out of the bag was the piece of paper that had floated down onto his head as he died in his dream. The dream flashed back into his head. His father in a white suit, in a big city, maybe New York, shooting him outside a building. He had seen that white suit somewhere before. It was the Beatle Man, his suit. His revenge.

Things started to join up in Danny's head. He had to check it out. He went to work and did very little, spending most of the time completing the mental jigsaw. Mrs. Moyes' son was gone, no one knew where. The Beatle Man was a huge Beatles fan and was clearly a bit mad. So, there is Mrs. Moyes' son, holding the script for Catcher in The Rye and he bumps into the Beatle Man in the close. He thinks that he's the guy that did John Lennon and takes his revenge. It was the Beatle Man. Shit, it has to be. The jigsaw was finished. Well, the edges at least. But God, the police weren't going to believe him. He was already a marked man with them. He'd need real evidence and the only place to get that was in the Beatle Man's flat.

He left quickly from work and only stopped briefly at the flat to get a screwdriver. Raking through Arthur's utility drawers he laughed at the fact that every house seemed to have a drawer that contained everything without a natural home and the fact that he found a pigeon fanciers book, well thumbed and not without odour. Right at the back, behind the outsize utensils, candles and a half-empty box of matches, he found a screwdriver.

"Screwdriver", he said out loud to no one in particular.

Chuckling, he went to the phone and arranged another shag as soon as possible. Changing quickly into vaguely dark clothes and, at the same time mourning the passing of his Killing Joke phase, he jumped back in the car and headed back west, parking within sight of the close but back from the door of Laxmi's shop. A half-hour of buses, cars and street crime passed without any sign. It struck Danny that waiting on a virtual recluse to leave his house perhaps wasn't the most productive use of his time. He decided to give it ten minutes more, as much to cover his own stupidity as anything else. It was only during the brief period of admonishment that he noticed that there was no lights on in the Beatle Man's flat. In his head he had a picture of the tenement at night and there was always a light on. Or maybe not, maybe his mind was playing a trick on him. It did that a lot. Like when he had lost something, he could always imagine the thing lying somewhere as if he had seen it there, but never had.

It would be a big risk to take. Working from a mental image of place he had only ever really seen at night when he was drunk and very rarely from this side of the street? Maybe not. He at least had to check the back for lights too. At least he knew that the back door of the close was always open. The Finches had kicked it in so many times no one bothered fixing it any more. He drove the car to the other side of the close, away from the shop on the other side. He jumped out the car not allowing whatever remained of his common sense to talk him out of it. For extra cover he crossed the street in front of a bus and then, sticking close to the wall, headed for the close. At the door he listened into the dark space for any sign of people or of doors opening or closing. Nothing but the echoes of the passing traffic. He ducked through to the back and out the damaged door. Lights from the surrounding houses lit up the collection of drying greens and bins, the clothes lines criss-crossing the space like a giant cat's cradle. The grass was long and wet and concealed a junkyard of discarded, rusting metal and slug-sodden cardboard.

There were no lights on this side of the close either. Creeping back inside, Danny listened again for the faintest echo of any life from within but there was no sound. He took off his shoes and left them behind the door in the dark. The stone floor was cold against his sweat-dampened socks. The banister was cold against his sweat-dampened hands. Similarly, air against forehead. At the door, the doorbell and knocker stared at him, tempting him into making a final check that the flat was empty. But how much noise would they make? Enough for someone else to hear? Presumably not as much noise as would be made if he broke in with the crazy fucker still in the house. He had to try it. Pressing the doorbell he heard no sound. Was it working or just ringing so far inside it couldn't be heard? Fuck, fuck. This was taking too long; someone would be in the close soon. Indecision filled his head. To knock, to break in or to fuck off and forget it.

"What the fuck am I doing? What the fuck am I doing? What the fuck..."

With a slight click and then a shove, he was inside the storm door, his insistent breath filling the cold air. Closing it quickly behind him, he listened for a reaction from inside. The noise of his own breathing filled his ears as he strained towards the glass. Nothing. Praising himself for what turned out to be the best choice (if there had been a noise he could still have escaped behind the anonymity of the interior door) he failed to notice the luck that had come with his panic. In Danny's world you post-justify everything according to its merits.

The interior door was a bit more of a problem but a firm push with the base of the hand onto the screwdriver and lock gave way. He always assumed that qualifying as a lawyer had in some ways defied his upbringing. Sometimes it is handy to know that some things never leave you.

The grooves of the polished floorboards dug into the soles of his feet. Unable to turn on a light, they acted like tramlines keeping him on a safe road away from walls and things that could be knocked over. A few yards down the hall it was the end of the line at rug junction. This, at least, afforded quieter steps and by then there was enough of a dim orange glow coming in from the rooms surrounding the hall to make crashing into something less likely. Danny peered into each door in turn to rid himself of the final worries that there could still be a sleeping man lurking somewhere inside. It was only when faced with the impenetrable gloom within that it finally dawned on Danny that searching a flat in the dark without a torch where the only sources of light would get you caught was really fucking stupid.

"This is really fucking stupid. Jesus fuck. Danny."

Another pendulum, this time swinging between sense and delusion, hit Danny. Only this time it was almost more of shock. Most of the swing was spent in delusion and only as its further extent did sense ever enter the equation.

Danny decided to leave before it went mammaries vertical. He headed for the door and the pendulum swung back again. One last look in the only room with enough light to see.

An almost empty room, lit from outside by the lack of curtains and the reflection of the plain white walls. At one end a desk across the bay window. On it a book lay open. Crawling on all fours to avoid the gaze of anyone higher up across the street, Danny approached the desk and poked his nose above the lip. It was a bible, opened wide because of a spine broken in the middle. It was open at the Gospel of John. Danny scanned the page for anything that might give him a clue. On the right hand page the words "The Gospel Of John" had been added to with the neatly written word "Lennon".

"Mad fuck."

Getting back on his knees Danny crawled back out and retraced his glide along the wooden tramlines to the door. He closed the interior door and then reprised the anxious listener role of a few minutes ago. Again, his increasingly loud breathing got no reply and he was able to scuff his way silently back to the back door and the sanctuary of the dark. And his shoes.

There is something that should always be remembered about the back green of a tenement. Cats tend to hang about there at night. One thing that should be remembered about cats is that for some probably explicable reason they tend to like to crap in things or on things. The most crucial thing to remember, especially in deserts, jungles and back greens, is always look in your shoes before putting them on. The left foot went in without an issue but the right foot encountered a still warm cat shit.

"Fuck." Too loud. "Fuuuucccckkkkkk". Quieter, in a drawn out whisper.

The shoe was thrown off quickly somewhere into the deep grass. One shoe, at this stage of the proceedings, was less then useless, so the other quickly followed. As did the realisation that he had just broken into a flat and then left evidence at the scene.

"Jesussss." Still the talking breath.

Shoes were one thing but actually being caught was another, he'd have to leave them.

Ducking back through the close he made it to the door. He reached out for the handle as it open magically before him.

"Hi, Danny, you come back to get some more stuff?"

"Oh, eh, Hi, Laksh. Yeah, I was just ... y'know."

"Can you smell something?"

"Smell...eh...no?"

"Those bloody cats again, I bet you."

"Aye, eh, look, I need to, eh…"

"Aye, aye, on your way, I'll see you…"

"Yeah, phone you later."

"Sure, sure…"

Danny rushed out before his heart got tired of the abuse and tried to leave his body. Crossing the road he tried to walked normally with the wet of the street and the sharp jabbing of the pavement and road making hot coals seem attractive.

Laxmi heading through the door of the close, stepping from side to side to avoid the line of cat-shit sock prints that came from the back door.

*

Heavy rain rattled what remained of the corrugated iron roof like marbles falling from the sky. The roof slumped in towards a large hole in the centre and the water from the sky ran like a torrent down the rotting, metal channels and fell like a circular waterfall into a puddle on the overgrown concrete floor. The deafening rattle amplified off the brick walls and only the loudest of the screams could be heard above it.

Hands tied behind the back, thrown down onto the floor. The head cracked off the floor. Blood started to run off into the base off the waterfall. The head was grabbed by the hair and pulled back. With a single stroke, a knife was pulled swiftly across the neck and all life was gone.

The blood flowed thicker and faster now in all directions. It ran along a rough edge in the concrete and left the building under the metal door hanging at an angle from only its top hinge. A pool of blood began to collect just outside the building.

The flow of blood slowed. A saw was taken out of a battered old cloth bag and starting through the back of the neck, the head was removed. The body was dragged to the side and left against the wall, the blood continuing to flow from the neck stump, further tributaries joining up with the main flow out of the building.

The head was placed in the centre of the circular wall of water, directly under the hole in the roof. The very pale face staring directly upwards, lifeless eyes reflecting the grey of the sky.

The blood outside encouraged some crows to brave the rain and they pecked at the bloody pool before being encouraged to enter by the ever-strengthening smell of exposed flesh and the promise of an even better meal. Then they scattered as the commotion continued inside.

Twenty One

Below him the other two clung tightly onto the branch in fear. The scan of the horizon revealed nothing and no one. John knew he'd have to do something. The wind seemed to have increased and the fire approached with increasing speed and ferocity. There were maybe only a few minutes before the flames reached the base of the tree. The trampled ground between the field and the tree line could provide a little more time.

Climbing down, he passed the two frozen statues and their muffled complaints.

"Where are you…?"

"No, you can't…"

John climbed down to the ground and looked around again. Nothing. From the ground he looked up. It was definitely too far too jump, the flames would definitely get anyone lying on the ground with a broken leg.

"You are going to have to climb down!"

"No, we can't…"

"Climb the fuck down, hurry up!"

"NO!"

There was only one thing to do. Climbing back up, John held onto the branch just under Lugs.

"Get on my back."

"What?"

"Get on my back!"

"No!"

It was the last straw.

"Get on my FUCKING BACK NOW!"

His voice held an authoritative, adult tone. Lugs reacted immediately and edged over until John could firmly grasp his body flopping, lifeless with fear, over his shoulders. With his one remaining hand, John carried Lugs down to the ground. With just a few feet to go, his grip weakened and Lugs fell into the thick grass under the tree facing the oncoming flames.

"Get out the way!"

Time really was running out now. Pushing Lugs aside John headed back up the tree for Deeko. Lugs ran behind the tree away from the flames and kept on running. Deeko had got the idea and when John arrived back up the tree he didn't need to be encouraged. A bit heavier than Lugs, Deeko was difficult to get into a good position. His arms already filled with lactic acid, John struggled to get Deeko down the tree.

"You're going to have to help."

"I..."

About 8 feet above the ground, John's arms finally gave in and the two boys fell to the ground. John first, Deeko on top. Falling at a angle, Deeko snapped John's left arm as he landed. John, winded, screamed silently, his mouth open but unable to make a noise. Deeko, forgetting his fear, was apologetic and, back on the ground, seemed more able to handle the situation. The flames were now a few feet away. Deeko helped John up, his screams now audible, as he supported his broken arm. They struggled their way to 50 yards behind the tree and both boys threw-up. John from pain and shock. Deeko from shame and the sight of John's bizarrely angled arm. Lugs was nowhere to be seen.

Holding the thick bushes aside, Deeko got John through the hedgerow and down onto the single-track road that led back home. Now safe from the flames, Deeko told John to sit and wait. The walk would be too long and he was in too much pain. Making sure that he would be OK, Deeko set off at a frightening speed that he sustained the two miles back to the houses. When he arrived there was already a commotion, the arrival of Lugs sometime before had already had all emergency services alerted, the fire brigade for the fire, the ambulance to rescue the presumably charred bodies from the field. Lugs embarrassment increased as it was realised that his supposed heroics were merely an over-dramatisation of his somewhat cowardly escape. Deeko told the police where the ambulance would find John and, despite a searing pain in his lungs, insisted on going with them to make sure they found him.

That night in the hospital, John's arm already well on the way to recovery, Deeko and Lugs came to visit. Or rather, at their parent's insistence, to thank John for saving them now that Lugs' version of the story had been replaced by the truth from Deeko. The parents went outside for a fag and left the three boys together for the first time since they been up the tree.

"Johnny, I'm sorry, I..."

"No, no, Luggsy, no bother..."

"You did great, Johnny, y'know?"

"Aye, cheers Deeko."

"So, Johnny, everybody's saying you'll be a fireman now."

"How?"

"Cos you're not scared of fire and you carried us down from that tree."

"No I never, I dropped that fat lump."

"Aye, well. So you don't fancy the fire brigade then Lugs."

"No, no, I think I'll give that a miss."

"I quite fancy it." Deeko seemed very serious.

"Really?"

"Aye, I'm just imagining how you feel after saving us, must be great. I could cope with that."

"With what?"

"Being a hero."

"A hero? Me?"

"Aye."

"No, no, I'm just too brainless to get scared."

John and Deeko knew what he meant. Lugs was the brainy one and he bottled it. Lugs knew it too but couldn't say anything. He enjoyed being the brainy one but he wished he was more like John, stronger, faster, and braver. But he knew he never could be. From that day on his bond with them stayed he same but only because he wanted to be forgiven, not because they were the same. John and Deeko never did join the fire brigade but, when they time came, they both joined the police on the same day, trained together and graduated together. In most people's eyes, Lugs' brains took him further but in Lugs' eyes it was a poor second choice, all a coward could do. It just so happened you got paid more money for being a coward.

Charlie opened his eyes to the dark room. Gradually the familiar shapes of wardrobe, drawers and TV started to form and confirmed his surprise that he was in his room after all. It had obviously been quite a absorbing dream. His eyes flicked around looking for any more light but found very little. Gradually, he became aware of his body lying out in front off him, exposed to the cool air by the absent duvet now piled at the side of the bed. It still didn't feel right. There was a strange sensation in his head that he couldn't quite understand. He felt like he had awoken in someone else's body. He knew the torso and limbs below him were his but they didn't feel like his. Fearing that any movement would spoil the sensation he kept perfectly still. He remembered a film where a guy ended up inside another guy's head. It was a bit like that.

"Being Charlie." he said out loud to the surrounding gloom.

"Eh?" came the unexpected response.

Whoever it was inside Charlie's head banged on everything he could find to make him turn round. "It's Kelly you fool." he shouted, "she's next to you, remember? Last night?"

It all came back and he allowed his body to move again. First a broad smile lit up the gloom and then some blood redistributed itself about his body and threatened to block out his view of the foot of the bed. Suddenly aware and suddenly embarrassed by the emergent erection, he reached for the covers. As he sat up, delicate lips kissed his back and his embarrassment was gone. She had seen quite a bit of that already.

This was all a bit new for Charlie, waking up next to a girl and not just any girl, the girl. It was all quite new for Kelly too. She had never done this on a first date before but, then again, no one had asked.

Charlie struggled with his first words. He was desperate to ask if she had enjoyed it but too terrified that she might say no and that she'd like to get going and, no, maybe not again thanks. He remembered just in time that only by overcoming his insecurity had he got here in the first place. Now was not the time to let the side down. Stopping shy of going for the early morning sex option that currently suggested itself under the duvet, he kept it simple.

"Coffee then shower or shower then coffee?"

"How about we have a shower and then we have coffee?"

On his way out of Charlie's head now, the little voice added "We? Whay-hay!"

*

Ma' Finch woke to an unusually quiet house. Normally by this time she'd be hearing the shower of Kelly drying her hair. Her mobile was at the side of the bed and she glanced at the small screen, it read, "1 message received". Grasping it in her claw-like hand, her chubby fingers dabbed at the buttons until she read "Staying with a friend, C U amorra Kx". She relaxed back into the numerous pillows that covered most of her bed. Still perfect silence around the house. She didn't like it. Looking at the picture on the wall she said, "The boys will be waking up soon, eh?"

Twenty Two

Charlie left first for a client meeting. He did actually have a meeting but would have invented one even if he hadn't. Turning up at the office with the receptionist wasn't really his style. It's not that it was necessarily wrong or particularly frowned on. It had been done before, although not with Kelly. No one had really made too much noise. Young lawyers full of hormones and money, young girls with a fondness for at least one of them. It happened all the time. To Charlie that was the problem. He had always been the one to frown and now it was him. Except that this was different. This wasn't about BMW's and quasi-prostitution, he was in love and he hoped she was too. But that's not how it would seem, that's not what they would say. Hypocrite. That's what they would say. And Kelly would hear them. But then again, she would see him avoid her in the office; she would start to feel rejected. He'd have to talk to her; he had to make sure she understood. He had come too far to make a twat of it now.

*

It was an unusual place for Danny to be. In all his years at University he only ever ended up in the library if he was following a girl or finding someone to copy their notes. It wasn't clear to him what he was following now but here he was in a library sitting at a PC on the Internet. All around him was silence punctuated only by the occasional stamp of a date on the inside cover of a book. Danny brought up the web browser and typed "lennon" and "assassination" into the search box. Many hits appeared on the screen. Over the course of many clicks and even more reading, Danny absorbed all the information he could find relating to the shooting of John Lennon by Mark Chapman. It was true, Chapman was carrying Catcher In The Rye, in fact, he got Lennon to autograph it not long before he shot him.

Kelly arrived at work worried. Worried that she had left Charlie's flat unlocked. Worried that she had slept with him too soon. Worried that word had already got round the office. Worried that...a note was on her desk. It said "worried that the boys are away". It was from her Mum. She had turned her mobile off the night before and forgot to turn it back on. This she now did, hurriedly fumbling for the button ergonomically hidden from anyone with fingernails. It finally beeped to life and took an age to find the network. After another 30 seconds, it beeped again and the voicemail symbol appeared. The mail arrived with a thump on the desk in front of her. She jumped, looked sheepish and then smiled.

"Everything okay Kelly?"

"Eh? Eh...yeah, sorry, no, I'm fine."

Finally getting her shit together Kelly sorted out the mail and then headed for the loo to listen to the voicemail. She was greeted by the face of someone else. This was not how she usually looked at work. Getting ready in someone else's house was just not the same. Ignoring that for now, she pressed the button and listened to the English woman tell her she had two messages.

Message one.

"Kelly love, sorry to bother you hen it's just that I've not seen the boys, no sign of them this morning, just thought you might know where they said they were going, eh, anyway, hope you're OK, I'll eh...aye, OK then."

Message Two.

"Hi, its Charlie, just wanted to, eh..." Click. That one can wait. She phoned her Mum. The boys still weren't back. Not particularly unusual but her Mum sounded more worried than usual. Her Mum told her not to worry, they would turn up, and they always did. Kelly didn't like how her Mum sounded. Just in case, she phoned her Uncle Derek.

"I'm sorry I gave you guys all this trouble". Danny let out an audible guffaw and caused a few people to turn round disapprovingly. All this trouble. It's what Chapman said by way of some sort of apology. It was all madness, none of this was making much sense and Danny was about to give up whatever it was he thought he was trying to do. He clicked on one last link and details of the police report came up on the screen. They had searched Chapman's flat. They had found a bible. Hang on. Open at the gospel of St. John. Wooahhh. With the word "Lennon" written in. It was the same as in the Beatle Man's flat. Danny sat back flabbergasted. It was true, he had been right all along. This was it; he'd done it. The pendulum was far, far away. His mobile rang. The tutting nearly drowned it out.

The day started like most others for Sergeant Derek Murdoch. Woke up, fell out of bed, dragged a comb across his head. And these days it was his head, there wasn't much else to comb. One of the positive points about wearing a hat

146

to work. Unless you believed the gang of eternally complaining ex-coppers who blamed the hat itself or the stress of the job for their hair-loss. To them he would always say "take a look at your Dad and if a lollipop wouldn't look out of place in his mouth then don't expect to look like Tony Curtis when your 60." Very few people understood what he was on about. But that was normal too. It was a painful experience to suddenly discover that you are a comparative intellectual surrounded by people you thought you were like. You're a working class boy; you do working class things and follow working class rules. Being clever is dangerous, being ambitious is worse. Even joining the police was enough of a rise above station to cause comment. And then, 10 years into a career, you discover the mind you never thought you had, the crosswords you can finish, the new interests, the books you read, the art you like, the life you wished you had, the wife you wish you didn't. But now it's too late to turn the ship round. Sometimes people call it mid-life crisis. But it's not really like that. The crisis happened much earlier, the moment when he forgot to realise, forgot to reach. The moment when he choose a path before he chose himself. And now it was the same path every day, to the same car, to the same desk, to the same old shit. Arseholes and potholes, speeders, zoomers, incidents and accidents, hints and allegations. Call me Sergeant. For that is what I am now, that is my identity. I'm a police officer, not an art lover. The old master will stay covered up by the uniform and standard issue moustache. If only he'd been brave, like Arthur, and made the right choices at the right time. If only he'd been like Johnny and actually wanted to do it, felt a calling. No instead, he had been a follower, all because he looked at everyone except himself. And now this shit again.

"Aye, OK love, I've have a wee look but don't you worry, y'know what the lads are like."

He waited until she had hung up and threw the receiver down angrily. This is exactly what he meant. Bloody good for nothing lawyers rubbing the supposed quest for justice in his face. There was only one thing they were after. And yet they said they were all on the same side. Bollocks. Arthur was an old friend but he was only ever on Arthur's side OK, so maybe it was jealousy or frustration from choices long ago but there was Arthur proclaiming to be a man of the people for the people with his multiple houses, multiple women and now multiple pain in the arse employee. Back in the car and out into the street to see what the hell was going on. He drove round to the flat slowed by the regulations he had a duty to follow and by the drivers around him being frightened to a snails pace by the presence of the blue light. Pulling up outside the shop he gave a wave to Laxmi who was outside the shop washing the windows. Like anyone who hasn't called them the arrival of the police is never a good sign. Hesitantly, Laxmi returned the welcome.

"Oh, morning Sergeant. Eh…everything OK?"

"Och aye, although you have missed a bit."

"Missed a…oh aye, the windows, well, aye."

"Have you seen the Finch boys around lately?"

"No, not for a few days, that's why I'm washing the windows, don't normally get enough peace, it's been nearly 6 months since it was last done and, y'know, with the buses and that, I could hardly see out."

The relief of not being in any trouble had loosened Laxmi into a ramble of words.

"So, generally quiet, nothing else funny you've noticed?"

"Eh...no, just enjoying the peace, you know how it is."

"I wish I did. Aye well, better be off...oh, one thing, you seen that young Danny round much lately?"

From his initial rambling relief, Laxmi was now in silent hesitation. Murdoch knew it and Laxmi knew Murdoch knew it. He liked Danny but he liked being out of trouble more. It had occurred to him that Danny seemed to have been up to something the other night. He had no idea why he would have been out the back of the close as the footprints suggested. All he knew was that he had done nothing wrong and hadn't seen anything that he necessarily should have reported. That would have to do. Getting his shit together, he told it straight.

"Aye, he was round the other night. I met him in the close. I thought it was a bit weird because I know he moved out."

"Weird? Maybe he was just picking up some stuff?"

"Aye, mebbe, but he didn't have any shoes on."

"No shoes?"

"Aye."

"Did you ask him what he was up to?"

"No, no I never. Look, I'm not trying to say anything here like, but he was in a bit of a hurry to get out I thought."

"No, no, I see, I understand."

Murdoch knew there was more to come. He wouldn't even have to ask.

"And, well, look, he's not in any trouble is he?"

"Why do you ask that?"

"I dunno."

"You were saying, and...?"

"It's probably nothing but I think he might have been out in the back green too."

"That's not weird is it?"

"It is in your bare feet. Have you been out there? There's shite everywhere."

"Well, that's true in so many ways."

"Aye."

"Top left corner."

"Eh?"

"You missed the top left corner."

"Aye cheers."

"You mind if I take a look through the back?"

148

Surprised to have been asked, Laxmi stepped aside and ushered Murdoch through. Before he had crossed the step, Laxmi was already back to busily scrubbing the glass. Walking through the stretched S of the close, Murdoch again wondered why the boys in CID considered questioning such an art. It was easy; you just didn't ask many questions. And as for the SOC boys, that was also a skoosh. Quick look outside, no obvious signs of entry on the windows, the long grass hadn't been moved much so no one had walked across it in a while apart from a flattened patch a few yards in. In the patch lay two shoes. Without touching them, he looked around. One of the shoes appeared to smell of and, on closer inspection, be full of, cat shit. That told him all he needed to know. Cats can't shit in shoes with feet in them and cat shit doesn't get flat unless you stand on it. He left them untouched and re-entered the close. Keeping close to the wall, he examined the floor. If it had been stood in, it had been carried. There wasn't much but the signs were clear. Cat shit on the stone, spaced like footprints. He stood up and paused for a second positive that he has heard the line "cat shit on the stone" before. Bob Dylan?

He walked up the stairs but there was no sign of the shit. The shoes had been taken off downstairs and the person had come up the stairs in their socks to be quiet. The cat left a present when they went to go back for them. He climbed to the top floor and checked all the doors on the way down. There was only one door that looked tampered with but it was hard to tell, it had been done in before. He knocked on the door but there was no answer. Which was strange. This was all a bit odd. He headed back to the station.

"Arthur, it's Derek."

"How the hell are you big yin?"

"Aye, lets leave that one until later."

"Like that is it? Fair enough. What can I do for you today?"

"It's that bloody laddie of yours, he's at it again."

"Who Danny?"

"Aye, Danny, that right pain in the arse."

"What's he been up to?"

"I dunno, he been nosing about back at the flat, I think he might have been into the flat for a nose about."

"The flat he was staying in?"

"No, the flat."

"Oh."

"...and the boys are off somewhere again."

"Nothing new there."

"No, but there's something a bit odd. It's time to make it clear to that boy of yours to stay well away."

"Aye."

"I mean well away."

Twenty Three

Danny dug the vigorously noisy and vibrating mobile out of his pocket to turn it off. He hit the button just as he saw that it was Arthur phoning. Eyes bore into him from above books and notepads. He collected his papers and sprinted out through the large glass doors into the bright Charing Cross sun. The noise from the motorway made it impossible to call so he ran round the seemingly endless walls to the back of the Mitchell and turned the phone back on. One voicemail. Click, listen.

"Danny, I don't know what the fuck you've been doing but stay away from that fucking flat or, God help me, you'll be out a job and you'll be asking people for burger orders for the rest of your life. Don't bother phoning me back, just cut out whatever shit you are pulling and get your arse back in here and work for a fucking living."

It was one of those messages that forced the phone further away from your ear as you listened. When it finished Danny declined the offer to delete it and hung up. Confused, he decided to listen to it again but with a whisky this time, for clarity and strength. The pub was full of the usual morning weirdos, night-shift nobodies, giro-spenders, laying down a solid foundation of life avoidance for the rest of the day. He ordered a whisky and headed for a seat as the thunder of a hundred tokens rained from the puggy. Like the rain, they would soon rejoin the cycle, fed back round the endless loop of hope and false triumph. He listened to the message again, downed the whisky in one and stepped back outside. It was raining. The sound of the cars passing under the bridge had changed, the rumble softened with the slow breath of the rain on the tarmac.

This was not making any sense. He had never heard Arthur like that. How had he found out so quickly? How did he know at all? Did he know at all? What was he so spooked about? This was not the same Arthur he knew. He was together, he was smart, and he handled things. He didn't rant down a phone making ridiculous threats. This wasn't making any sense at all. Why did he want him to stay away? What did he think he might find out? What did he think he might have already found out? Jesus! Did he know about Mrs Moyes' son?

He'd have to go back into work. Anything else what be too suspicious. With any luck Arthur would be in court. He probably was; he called from his mobile. Yeah, of course, he'd have phoned from the office if he had been there. One bus and one packet of chewing gum later he was at the door. One deep breath and he was at his desk and working. Arthur was nowhere to be seen. He kept his head down and his ears sharp. Arthur defied the laws of physics, sound travelled faster than light, you always heard him before you saw him.

Danny decided at first that working late and looking about was a good idea but, on reflection during a thoughtful and relieving dump, he reasoned that this might be a little suspicious. He left at a normal time and set himself up in the coffee place across the street with a grande latte and a broadsheet to hide behind if necessary. One by one the lights in the office went off. One by one the staff approached him and asked him if he like anything else. After a couple of hours he relented and shelled out for another stupidly named, overpriced hot flavoured water. By 8 o'clock, all the lights were out, a couple of grande latte's had gone and an unknown number of grande pish had been recycled back into the water system for resale. His exit was accompanied by barely concealed scorn from the various antipodean staff and he crossed back across the now dark street and into the foyer of the office. The security guard was off "doing his rounds" of the various places you could get comfortable enough to get a snooze. The lift took forever to descend the few floors to street level. Like a boiled kettle, it defied all known proverbs and arrived with a loud bing. On the third floor Danny left the lift and punched in the code that let him into the main part of the office.

He sat at his desk and unlocked the screen. He had left himself logged in so that his login time couldn't be traced. He hadn't seen evidence of anyone who would know how to trace a login time, he had been worshipped as a deity when he had re-installed a printer driver, but it seemed a sensible precaution. Like all the best searches, Danny wasn't all that sure what he was looking for. He knew Mrs Moyes' son was gone; he had been carrying Catcher In The Rye. The Beatle Man was a Beatles nutter and had stuff that connected him to Mark Chapman. He knew that someone somehow wasn't happy with him sniffing about. The obvious thing to do was to find anything relating to the Beatle Man. But how? He didn't even know his name. But he did know his address. And he knew the address of the flat above him that this firm was trying to sell.

He went over to the current property files and pulled out the folder for the flat he had lived in. There was nothing much in it of any interest. A long record of people who had been interested in buying it but hadn't, presumably because of the Finches. Letters from solicitors withdrawing offers quoting "extraordinary circumstances". There was nothing. A dead end.

Danny was convinced there had to be something and if there was, it wouldn't be lying wide open for all to see. Perhaps he should try the computers.

*

Kelly had phoned home throughout the day and the boys still hadn't made an appearance. Her Mum didn't sound too worried but it was hard to tell, she had a way of hiding things, of not reacting to circumstances. She went straight home miming a brief "I'll call you" to Charlie as she left. Back at the flat everything was still very quiet. Her Mum was sitting in the corner with the remote control on one chair arm and a full ashtray on the other. The smoke hung low in the room.

"Hi Mum. No sign of the boys?"

"No, no, they'll turn up, they'll turn up."

Like anyone convincing themselves as well as others she was forced to repeat the hopeful statement. It was not lost on Kelly. Even through the haze of smoke she could see the worry in her Mum's face.

"How about we just get a chippy for tea tonight, eh?"

"What's that hen?"

"A chippy?"

"Naw, naw, I'm OK, I'm OK, you get one though, my purse is on the mantle."

Kelly ignored the purse and headed out. She didn't want a chippy either but she wanted to phone Charlie. She was worried and her Mum wouldn't like it if she was sharing the worries outside the family.

"Hi Charlie, its me."

"Oh, hiya, hang on, I'll just…"

She knew. He was still in the office. He was finding somewhere he could talk.

"Hi, its me again, I'm back. How are you doing?"

"Oh, I'm, well, it's the boys…"

"They're still not back?"

"No."

"Oh Jesus."

"What?"

Charlie seemed more agitated than she was expecting. He was meant to be calm and convince her why she shouldn't worry.

"Well, eh, you know, I'm sure they'll turn up. They always do, don't they?"

"Maybe, but you sound funny. What's wrong?"

"Me, eh, nothing. I'm fine, just a bit distracted, you know, this case going to court soon and…"

"Yeah, of course, I'm sorry, I'm just a bit worried, y'know?"

Charlie knew. He knew too much. He knew who had tattooed the boys and who might have now taken it all a bit too far. Now was not the time to share that with Kelly. He had only just got this far with her, to tell her anything now would mean revealing that he always knew who had tattooed them and, in the current circumstances, saying anything would be fatal to his future plans.

"Look Charlie, I probably should stay with my Mum tonight, is that OK?"

"Sure, yeah, of course, I'll see you tomorrow and we can maybe go out when the boys get back, OK?"

"Yeah, thanks."

"See ya."

The relief in Charlie's voice was perhaps too evident. He'd have time to try and find out what was going on.

*

The best thing you can say about lawyers is that they are clever but they are not smart. It took Danny about 10 minutes to guess Arthur's password. He was lucky that at some point of his time at University he'd done a side course on IT and he actually attended and listened to the lecture on social engineering and password hacking. Of all the things he was supposed to have learned at University, this one thing now seemed somehow the most useful. It was simple really. Assume that people are fundamentally stupid and you won't go far wrong. So there it was, staring him in the face and then running down his throat "laphroaig".

"Cheers Arthur!" he said to no one in particular.

Arthur's desktop was almost empty. It was obvious he hardly ever used the machine himself. His recent documents list contained more images than documents. The network looked a little more promising. Arthur's folders looked well organised, split into various job functions and case types. It was mostly dull administrative stuff and was clearly organised by Jenny, not Arthur. In the conveyancing area he found a directory list of properties including the flat he had stayed in. In that folder he found nothing new, just the electronic versions of things he had seen before. He was getting nowhere. Coming back up a level he put his head in his hands and started almost blindly at the screen. Then he saw it, half way down the list, a property that shouldn't have been there. Penny Lane. It was too much of a coincidence. He stared at it a while longer as his breathing got more urgent until he frantically double-clicked and looked inside.

There were many, many files. Before he started to read, Danny scanned the office and outside. Everything seemed clear. He started to read. It took him an hour to read it all. By the end he was sure he knew where he would find Mrs. Moyes' son. He logged out. Carefully replaced the badly encrypted whisky and, pausing only to send a quick email, left the office and all remaining semblance of sense behind him.

Twenty Four

Charlie had always been a hot property. Even before he had left University word had got round about him. It was a bit like US College sports, he was the prize draft pick and everyone wanted to secure his signature. If the Scottish law community had had the equivalent of the Heisman trophy he would have won it. Arthur had been tipped off very early on and made sure he was best placed to grab him when the time was right. Charlie strolled to his expected 1st and swept all the associated prizes. Soon after he got a message from Arthur that was immediately followed by a meal, a night out and an invitation back to Arthur's penthouse flat.

Charlie loved the law. To him, becoming a lawyer was not a route to wealth or fame; it was a chance to do what he had always wanted to do, practice law. So, when Arthur told him about the rewards that were available for his employees and ultimately partners, Charlie asked questions about the kind of work Arthur's firm practiced, what kind of cases could he expect to be working on. To Arthur this was somewhat odd but he had seen this kind of academic legal virgin before. He knew how to pop them. The "one day all of this could be yours" speech usually did it. Wide eyes became high expectations. Arthur always got his man; he very rarely tried to get a woman. His recruitment policy was only legal in that it involved a law firm. This was not necessarily a reflection on his opinion of female lawyers, it was more an admission that if he hired it, he probably try to shag it and that just wouldn't do.

So there he was, the prize catch, a young brilliant talent ready to be moulded into Arthur's image. Except that he wasn't ready. He wasn't even impressed. Charlie wanted the work, not the rewards. What Arthur was offering was high value but low interest work. Despite all of Arthur's efforts Charlie came to see him at his office and sitting opposite him, politely turned down the

154

offer. Arthur couldn't speak; he was almost at the point of standing up and welcoming him onboard before the words started to make some sense.

Everyone knew Arthur was after Charlie and everyone expecting him to get him. But it didn't happen. Arthur had lost his touch, lost his appeal, rumour had it he had lost his wife too, and he had lost it. It was a low point for Arthur and he blamed a large part of it on Charlie. Arthur saw it as a crime and, through a pretence of a polite demeanour; he saw Charlie from time to time and smiled the smile of the insincere and aggrieved.

They both knew that Charlie would one day return to the scene of that crime. Arthur hoped it would be to beg for the job he had offered. Charlie assumed that Arthur was too omnipresent to be avoided forever. Neither of them expected it to be like this.

"Charles."

Arthur spoke slowly and quietly as he motioned Charlie into his office and towards the large leather chair in front of his desk.

"Mr. McWilliams."

Charlie didn't really know the depth of Arthur's feeling towards him but even if he had he would have been the same. This was a law office with another lawyer. This was his world.

"Arthur, please, call me Arthur."

"Arthur."

It was like a mini-roundabout in a town full of old people. Two cars, waiting at their white lines, seeing who can be the most polite, beckoning the other forward for what can seem like days.

"So, what brings you back here? Finally seen the error of your ways?"

Arthur's clutch slipped and he lurched beyond the white line and rudely took off round the roundabout leaving Charlie sitting politely by.

"No, no, everything is great, should make partner pretty soon."

Revving his engine violently, Charlie raced off in pursuit.

"Good for you, good for you."

Feathers spat from Arthur's exhaust.

"You'll know that we have a friend of yours working here, Danny McColl?"

"Oh yes, yes indeed. I was actually here to see him."

"Well, don't let me hold you back, on you go."

"He's not there. That's why I'm in here."

"He's not there?"

The surprise in Arthur's voice was more than his usual demeanour normally gave away. Danny should be there. He should be sitting outside working, keeping his head down and his nose out of the way. Back in control now.

"He must be out at a client."

Charlie didn't know where to take this. He had come to see Danny, make sure his suspicions weren't true and get back to work. He hadn't expected not to see Danny and he certainly hadn't expected to be making small talk with big mouth. But where was Danny? Arthur's evidence had to be considered questionable at best.

"Really?"

"What do you mean, really?"

"I mean, are you sure that's where he is?"

"What?"

Danny was a friend and a lawyer. It would normally be wrong to potentially wreck his career before it had started but something wasn't right and Arthur's level of irritation wasn't making seem any less wrong. Charlie looked around, stood up, pushed the door fully closed and sat back down.

"Right Arthur. The bullshit stops here. Either you know where Danny is, or you don't. If you don't, say you don't and I'll be on my way."

"Look wonder boy, maybe you can talk to people like that in the excuse for a law practice you work for but you don't do it to me and not in my office."

"The Finch boys are missing."

"Who?"

"Don't give me that, you know who they are. The psychos that stop you selling that flat that you inflicted on Danny in a half-arsed attempt to get it sold? The ones that broke his nose?"

"Those little scrotes? Missing? Bombed out their heads in an alley more like it. Take your crusade elsewhere. Ah, no, wait a minute, don't tell me, you're banging the sister aren't you?"

"Her name is Kelly and any relationship I have with her is a private matter and nothing to do with this."

"Well, thanks for the lesson in etiquette. At least I know now you are banging her. Good effort, she's a good piece of tail, great baps."

Charlie stood up in the fury that Arthur was hoping for. This was getting way out of hand. Danny and now Charlie. Danny was OK, he was gallous but dumb. Charlie was a whole different barrel of fannies. He knew the score. Charlie saw the intentional misdirection. He sat down chastising himself and brought the debate back on subject. He ignored the validation that a reputable swordsman like Arthur recognising the quality of the catch would usually bring.

"The Finch boys are missing. I think Danny has something to do with it. Either you know something and can help or you don't."

"Why Danny? So they butted him, he got over it."

Charlie looked Arthur directly in the eye.

"He tattooed them."

The eyes have it. Arthur paused. Not long but long enough.

"You knew?"

"Knew what?"

"That he had them tattooed. On the forehead? You knew. Jesus. I don't believe it. You knew and you did nothing."

"I think this conversation is over."

"What?"

"Take your fairy stories elsewhere."

"Is that it?"

"That's it. You had your chance to learn from me. You refused. Go out and learn it for yourself."

Charlie stood up and extended a hand.

"Arthur."

Surprised, but programmed to reciprocate, Arthur grasped the hand. Charlie leant in and squeezed tighter.

"I know you know about the tattoos. You probably know more. You also know that whatever it is that I'll find it out. It's the talent you tried to buy, isn't it? Have a good day."

Charlie released the hand and swung round swiftly out the door before Arthur had a chance to respond. Sinking back in his chair Arthur waited until he saw Charlie turn the corner at reception and then turned the knob to close the blinds embedded in the glass walls of his office. His programmed hand, slid open the desk drawer to his right and reached out for the Laphroaig that sat exactly at arms length. It wasn't there. Looking down he saw it was a few inches over and out of reach. He thought nothing of it, reached a little further and poured himself a large glass. Holding the glass in one hand, he flicked through his Rolodex with the other. He stopped at J. Downed the whisky in one and picked up the phone.

"Professor Johnson."

"Professor McMillan would always have sounded better."

"Arthur, this better be quick, I'm about to head to a lecture."

"Well, just as long as you don't give me one."

"That'll be the day sunshine."

"Now now Professor, was that innuendo?"

"Arthur, I need to go?"

"Right, right, OK, I need to see you."

"Look Arthur, we agreed, if this was happening at all then it was happening slowly."

"Its not about that, it's a, well, professional matter."

"You need a consult?"

"No, not me."

"I need to go."

"Can I come round to the house?"

"Yes, yes, 8 o'clock."

"Wine?"

"Arthur…"

"OK, see you then."

*

Back out in the street, Charlie contained his fury at the pompous twat and congratulated himself for not being foolish enough to work for him in the first place.

His surprise, however, was far from contained. He had stood up to Arthur; he had seen him and threatened him. This was not Charlie he knew. It was the

Charlie he had always wanted to be. Bravery to go with the brains. Strength with the studiousness. Now he seemed to have it and he knew why. It was her. And now it was for her. He didn't care about the Finches. He didn't care what that arsehole Danny might have got involved in. But there was not much he could do. He could track down Danny and see what, if anything, he had to do with it. But if it its nothing? He could only support and encourage the police to do more. So, for now, he had to concentrate on finding Danny and hope that he had nothing to do with it.

There was no answer from his mobile. Charlie had tried the night before too with the same result. He tracked down the number of Arthur's penthouse where he knew Danny had been staying. Nothing. He tried the obvious pubs; few were open and those that were, were either empty or highly suspicious of someone sticking their head in the door wearing a suit. They were certainly empty enough to be sure that Danny was nowhere to be seen. Most of the things running through Charlie's head told him to give up and leave well alone. The things that were left were more than a little concerned about the confluence of events unfolding. But, as it stood, there really wasn't much to do. Danny was nowhere to be found and it wasn't really possible to search any further than the obvious places.

He headed back to the office. Kelly's gazed was fixed on the door waiting on him. She stood up sharply with wide eyes as he came in, expecting answers and hoping for the worry to be over. A slight shake of the head took the brightness from her expectant eyes. He stopped briefly at the reception desk pretending to check for mail.

"Are they back yet?"

"No, I just spoke to my Mum. Did you find anything out?"

"No, I...well, nothing, but...I'll keep trying."

He felt he had disappointed her but he had done everything he could. It was difficult to leave her with nothing.

"I'll make a few calls and see what else I can find out, OK? Let me know if you hear anything."

"OK."

Charlie took the few letters that were for him and walked slowly back to his desk. Someone stopped him and asked him a question. He wasn't listening. They had to repeat the whole question before he realised they weren't even talking about one of his cases. Back at his desk, he logged in and a cascade of overdue appointments flooded onto the screen. As he snoozed them all, they revealed the unread emails beneath. Daily news, stock updates, some client stuff, Danny.

The first of the unread messages, sent at 10:30 the night before was from Danny. No subject. He paused, the mouse point wavering over it waiting on the double click. It was a moment of nervous hesitation. It was as if he was at a crossroads and the content of the message was the decision. It reminded him of the moment of opening his exam results only this time he was much less sure of the outcome.

He checked around him and then double-clicked almost frantically, slamming the door to get the tooth out as quickly as possible. It appeared on the screen.

Peachy,
I'm on to something. If you don't hear from me I'm going here.
D

Beneath the text was a hyperlink to a map site. Charlie clicked on it. It took a while to appear. A map appeared in the centre of the screen but it was nowhere Charlie recognised. A red circle indicated the place Danny was talking about. It appeared to be in the middle of a forest. Charlie hit print and then zoomed out to get more of an idea of where it was and printed again. Locking the screen quickly, he almost sprinted to the printer to make sure he got there first. The printer took and age to warm up and take the two solitary pages before eventually feeding them out.

Charlie snapped them up quickly and headed for the door and, in his rush, forgot that he had to pass Kelly to get there.

"Charlie! Where are you going?"

"Eh...nowhere...just...out, y'know...nothing."

"Charlie?"

"Kelly, it's nothing."

"I don't believe you Charlie. Tell me now or I'll scream."

"Right, get your coat. I'll tell you on the way."

Twenty Five

He had left the office and trudged through the rain to the underground and caught one of the last trains round the circle and back to the flat. He changed into jeans and his Stenhousemuir top, stuck on a jumper and headed out to the car. It wouldn't start. Rain rattled off the thin metal roof and bonnet. The engine, coughed, spluttered and died. If he carried on, he was going to flood it. Had it been that Danny actually hadn't wanted to go anywhere, this would have been a sign and he would already be in the pub. Probably after changing out of the Stenhousemuir top. But he had somewhere he wanted to go, needed to go and the sign, like all the undesirable coincidences that go unnoticed, was invisible to the unwilling eye.

He waited a few minutes to let the engine settle. Opening the glove compartment, he raked in the miscellany for the battered old atlas he hoped was still there. It was and after some random flicking and the addition of the internal light, he found his destination and the rough route he had to take. The heavy rain ran down the road next to him like a glass sheet sliding downhill. Downhill. Looking round the deserted road behind and ahead, he let off the handbrake and the car lurched silently forward. With a shove of the gears and a twist of the key, the engine barked into life.

At the bottom of the hill, Danny turned left and headed out of the city. The internal light was still on and in the darkness he could see his face reflected in the windscreen.

*

In the darkness he could still see faces. People shuffled uncomfortably in their seats. It was a warm morning and the heavy rain hung in the air smelling of people and their clothes. With every passing minute it seemed to get warmer. The coughing started as more moisture caught in the back of people's throats.

No one spoke. This was beginning to take the shine off what was, on the face of it, going to be pretty good day.

The day before had been a day of achievement. Of finally getting there. But above all, it seemed like a day of freedom. To most people, realising a life dream was a joyous moment. Yesterday, he only felt relief and acceptance. Sitting silently in the dark, he felt it was time to go home. For a little while at least.

*

It was nearly midnight before Danny turned off the brightness of the last A road and into the almost total darkness of the thin dark line of the single-track road. He slowed nervously as his eyes adjusted to the gloom and he remembered how to turn on full beam. An animal bolted off the road in a streak of reflected light from its eyes. Danny slowed further as the road turned sharply into the dark avenue of a forest. The car crashed through a deep puddle in the heavily rutted road. With an apologetic wheeze, the engine died.

Without the boost of the alternator, the battery struggled to illuminate the dark of the trees. Danny paused for a second as the dark closed in. Grabbing at the keys, he tried to twist the car back to life. It struggled to turnover before finally dying again. This time the fear of the dark masked the fear of the flooding and Danny tried again, pumping at accelerator, pulling the choke out full. The flooded car sat on the flooded road, dead and going nowhere for quite some time.

"Fuck."

Danny slammed his hands into the steering wheel. Realising that the headlights were too much of a luxury he turned them off. The dark closed in further. With the rain now stopped, Danny stepped outside for some air. The moisture hung invisibly in the dark air. Danny walked in the direction he knew the road took for the next 100 yards. After his third step into a puddle, Danny decided to give up the pointless meander and head back to the car. The rain started again, heavier than before. The heavy drops crashing into the surrounded trees made the forest come to life with a thousand snakes all hissing at the side of the road. A walk became a jog became a sprint until Danny crashed into the still warm body of the dead car carcass. He opened the door and dived inside, the bites of the hissing reptiles invisibly snapping at his ankles.

This was all another sign. It should have been the end of the dark road. Either way Danny could go nowhere so could do nothing but get ready for a night in the car. He pushed the front seats all the way back and, pulling the old blanket from the backseat, lay down as best he could. The extreme dark was strange at first, no streetlights; no passing flash of headlights; just dark. Even with his eyes shut, Danny knew it was very dark beyond. After a while the rhythmic clatter of the rain started to have a hypnotic effect and Danny slipped from the dark into the darkness of sleep.

*

He only knew he had fallen asleep when the lights came back on as the train lurched back into motion. Eyes blinked frantically like startled onlookers at

Bikini Atoll. Only these onlookers wore suits, clutched newspapers, carried brollies and furrowed brows, resentful at the delay to the start of their next unremarkable day.

A loud and pointless apology barked over the tinny intercom. Faces grimaced, eyes reached to the sky still far above ground. He had been down here too long with these people. As the train emerged into the light of the next station, he decided to get off, not really caring where it was. On the white tiled wall, a large sign announced "Westminster".

"As good as any." He got up and the joined the flow of bodies rushing for the door. Like air flying out of a punctured space station, pulled from the outside.

*

And then the darkness of dreams. It was a whistle-stop tour of everything. His Dad, bloodstained and dying, his Mum sitting sad and alone. This was not a dream of stories and imagination. This was an inventory. A long corridor in a dark museum displaying the painful memories of life in each of its dusty cabinets. As he walked along the corridor, so the memories continued. His budgie as it flew out of the window, as vivid as it was when he was 12. A fragment of an image left over from his Granddad's funeral. And at the end, a door. At the door stood a man in a white suit. The Beatle Man. He was about to open the door. Danny walked right up to him. In the last cabinet was a pile of newspapers. They were from Mrs Moyes flat. Danny looked up as the door was opened before him, the door that he knew would lead him to the answer. The door he knew would lead him to Gary Moyes. He emerged into the light.

*

He emerged into the light. Climbing the final few stairs, he reached pavement level below the monumental height of Big Ben. In all his time in London, he had never been here before, making the familiarity of what he saw all the more strange. The rain had stopped and a bright, sunny day had broken out making the pavement glisten and steam. Up on the bridge, more familiarity. A scene he had seen in so many films, a star in its own right. Familiar and somehow appropriate. He stood on it feeling like an equal. Soon he'd be a star. Westminster Bridge. Gary Moyes. Two stars. Joined at the feet.

Standing on the tallest point of the bridge, he leant on the wall and did his best film star pose. In his mind a tracking shot came down from the top of the London Eye, swooped round the Houses Of Parliament and finished with a tight shot of him looking sincere but sensitive dropping a rose into the river from the bridge.

The image made him laugh. Not least because it wasn't the kind of shot that most soap operas had the budget for. He'd mention it in his next and last letter to his Mum. He laughed because he was happy and because he had made it. He laughed because the sun was shining after the rain. Light had come from dark. And it was a dark night that had propelled him to London in the first place. It was that messy, painful night that had forced his hand, the pain that he had undoubtedly caused him Mum. It was the dark that had created the light. And somehow that just seemed funny.

*

It had been a good night. Too good maybe. He'd met a guy in a club and after several drinks too many, they had hurried back along the emptying streets towards his house stopping at every lane entrance for a snog and a grope. They made it back to the close and entered.

"Come on."

"No, no, wait."

"What is it?"

"My mum...she doesn't..."

"Know? Jesus, oh well, about time she found out then."

"No, I can't, really...it's not that..."

The sentence was ended by an urgent kiss. Drunken faces pressed together, almost coalescing in their desire to get nearer to each other. And then one face was gone, down and the mouth was put to a different purpose.

The noise, even this late at night, had not gone unnoticed. Emerging from their flat above, a couple of the Finch brothers heard voices and groans coming from the close below. They crept silently down the stairs and appeared at the top of the final flight just as he erupted into the back of the genuflecting mouth before him. He let out a loud groan as the Finches crashed down the stairs.

He withdrew just as a boot crashed into the side of the cum-filled head. He fell to the floor, the white liquid dripping from his mouth and running into the blood coming from the side of his face. Gary tried to fight back but they overpowered him and, with both hands up against his back they jammed him firmly against the wall. Seeing his chance, the head-giver seized his chance, got up and sprinted for the door, leaving Gary to face the rest of the beating.

"Faggot, fucking, faggot."

With each word they punched and kicked as if setting a violent metre for their abusive poem.

" Do. That. Shit. In. Our. Close. Would Ye?"

After a few minutes Gary was unconscious and lay bleeding and bruised on the floor of the close. Minutes passed. The younger Finch brothers withdrew and their older brothers appeared. A bucket of water was thrown over Gary and he woke up, spitting blood from his mouth as he sat up.

"You listen here."

"Eh..."

"I said listen here and listen good. In the morning, you leave. Don't care where. Just go and don't look back. You're kind aren't welcome round here. I don't want to see you in this street again. If we do, you'll get a worse beating and your poor Mother will hear about what a sick wee pervert you are. Don't speak, just nod."

Gary nodded.

"Good. Now fuck off."

With a final kick in the groin, all the Finches withdrew upstairs leaving Gary to gradually get to his feet and wobble slowly up into the flat. He didn't sleep that night at all. As soon as the sun came up, he got up, packed a bag and got ready to leave. He wrote a note and left quietly out the front door. Outside, he collected up his bags and put the note through the door. Without a single glance back, he pointed his bruised and bloated face at the sun and headed for London. Something he had always wanted to do. Now seemed like a good time.

As Gary left, he was being watched from the floors above. Seeing the note going into the door, the Finches waiting until Gary had left the close, sneaked down, jammed open the storm door and took the note, unread. Ripping it up, the headed out into the street just as a taxi pulled through the lights and headed for the train station. Every week he wrote her a letter, every week they intercepted it and ripped it up. Naturals.

*

"Hi Mum, it's Gary. Sorry, I got the number of the shop from directory inquiries."

"…"

"Mum?"

A large crashing sound.

"MUM?"

After a few moments, there was the sound of the receiver being picked up again.

"Gary? Son?"

"Mum! Hiya. Aye, it's me. How are you doing?"

"Eh…aye…fine, son, fine, Gary, I…"

"Look Mum, my money's running out, I'll be home tonight, OK?"

"Aye, son, aye."

The money ran out. Mrs. Moyes put the receiver down and sat down next to the teapot. That night, tears welled up in her eyes as she surveyed the hundreds of neatly folded newspapers now scattered all over the floor in front of her.

*

Danny walked through the door and into the light. The bright light of morning streaming in through the trees and warming the inside of the car. After the cold of the night it was very welcome and Danny tried hard to use the new warmth to recover the sleep he had lost during the dark, cold night. But it was too bright. It was 6am. Danny tried to move but his contorted skeleton scraped and groaned in its not-so-orthopaedic folding bed. With a stretch, he managed to get a door open and legs swung out into the sudden cold of the morning. He got up quickly, jumping up and down outside to restore his skeleton to its correct shape and get the blood flowing to the parts that had been cut off during the night.

In the light of the new day the forest looked far less foreboding. The car still sat in the puddle that had drowned it. Danny left it for now and walked off down the rutted road in the direction he had been heading. The air was cool and fresh and, despite the early hour, Danny's head felt clearer than it had for quite a while. He thought again about why he was now walking through this forest this early in the morning and, although it began to feel like a long shot, he still felt convinced that what he had seen and read had brought him to the right place. The problem was, he didn't know what he would find and so he didn't really know what he was looking for.

A crossroad in the forest forced him to make a choice. The gradually thinning tarmac was intersected by a dirt road, two deep tyre grooves separated by a grassy hump down the middle. Looking each way, Danny tried to see the building that he believed would at least be the beginning of whatever it was he was here to find. It wasn't clear but there seemed to be a building through the trees to the left so he headed that way.

As the road curved to the right, the corner and then the sidewall of an almost derelict building appeared from behind the trees. The roof seemed to be partially collapsed and, in the centre of the long wall, metal doors hung loosely at an angle, held only by the top hinge. Crows hopped about in front and flew off as Danny approached.

A wrecked building in the middle of nowhere. He'd got it wrong. There couldn't be anything here. The rusted door pushed easily aside, the building looked gloomy inside, the sun still too low to get in through the hole in the roof. Danny stepped inside. A large piece of wood crashed down on the back of Danny's head. Suddenly it was dark again.

Twenty Six

Moira sat in her favourite place in the kitchen, looking out over the garden and to the wider expanse of the fields beyond. The red wine made a satisfying glugging sound as it pulsed into the glass. Like so many times before, she saw the dark form of Arthur's car brow the hill and start the descent towards the house. This time it was different. She wasn't wondering where he had been, what perfume would he smell of, who he had been with, how much over the limit he would be. She was wondering if she really wanted him to come back and how much she was going to make him beg. He was going to come back. That much was certain.

She took a long sip from the glass. The smooth, full-bodied liquid warmed her. The crunch of tyres announced the arrival of the A8 in the drive. She sat waiting for the sound of the door and the meeting of Italian leather with Italian ceramic. Then she remembered the poor bastard didn't have a key and was now standing outside the house that he designed, built and paid for like a tradesman hoping for some work.

The door swung open as Arthur raised his fist to knock.

"Punch me and you're out."

"Hey, dollface."

"Hey, fuckface."

"Now, now, no need to be like that."

"Really?"

"Well, OK, I'll give you that one. Is that wine I smell on the go?"

"Nothing gets passed you."

"It's what my clients pay for."

"Yeah, you're ability to sniff out alcohol at a distance."

It was always like that in the beginning. Quick fire verbals, followed by flirting, drink, bed, sex. Moira never thought she was the type to be swept off her feet but back in those days at University, Arthur had been such a firecracker, energy, bravado, and intelligence, someone who was going somewhere. It was only when he started going places with whisky and other women that it changed. But whatever it was about him, he still had it. And she still wanted it. He was still a bastard though.

"So, what brings you here? We agreed to a couple of weeks from now, didn't we?"

"Yes, yes, no, its more a professional visit I suppose."

"Professional? You want to enrol for a course?"

"No, it's about John."

She stopped dishing out the pasta halfway through the plate.

*

Moira Johnson had been the star student in the Medical Faculty. It came as a disappointment to many in the surgical and other seemingly more "worthy" areas when she chose to specialise in clinical psychology and psychotherapy. It made no sense to many, so much talent apparently being wasted. Everyone blamed the influence of the equivalent star from the legal faculty, leading her away from surgery and into the world of the mind.

In her chosen field she remained at the top and the forefront. Consultancy came quickly and her further specialism into criminal psychology and involvement in a few high profile cases had made her a bit of a minor celebrity for a while. And then came John and the continuing bad influence of that damned lawyer. From then on, the high-flying career was eased into the background. She told herself it was the kids, it was the desire to spend time as they grew up. It made sense to go back to the faculty, to teach, become a Professor, to slow down. In the back of her mind, she always doubted that she had done the right thing and, with that, the acuteness of her judgement seemed somehow impaired. But maybe her judgement had been right anyway. After all, nothing had gone wrong.

*

"What about him?"

"Well, its probably nothing but…"

"But what?"

"Do you think he could be violent?"

"Violent? What kind of violent? What has he done?"

"I dunno, maybe nothing, probably nothing."

"Arthur?"

"Well, could he be violent?"

"There were no obvious signs of a violent tendency at the time."

"Oh come on, don't give me the NHS hedging, I may be a lawyer but I'm not feeling litigious right now."

"Just as well for you."

"What?"

"Look, I told you at the time, didn't I? I couldn't be sure of his mental state. He was trained. There had to be aggression in him. Just because there were no signs doesn't mean it wasn't possible."

"But there were no signs?"

"Lets not go over this again. You got what you wanted, didn't you? He's out. And now you come to me after all these years asking if he could be violent. I told you then and I'll tell you now. I don't know. He needed to be observed in a controlled context, but no, that wasn't good enough was it?"

"OK, OK, I know what you said but lets just set that aside for now. What could be the most obvious things that might make him violent?"

"What kind of violent?"

"I don't know, angry, aggressive, you know, violent?"

"Oh come on, I need more than that, is this how you prosecute a case? Can you decide if someone is guilty without knowing what they have done?"

"Work with me here."

"OK, OK, I'd say that he wanted to protect. He was trained to protect. The most likely thing to wind him up would be if something happened to something he wanted to protect."

"So, if someone threatened him or his possessions, things that he loved and treasured?"

"In theory, yes, he could get a bit pissed off."

"Is that a technical term?"

"It's as good as you're going to get with the case history you're giving me."

"OK, thanks."

"What? Is that it? OK, thanks? Come on Arthur. What's going on? What has happened?"

"Nothing, nothing has happened. I was just thinking that maybe I should have listened to you before and that we've only been lucky up to now. Come on now, pasta."

The rest of the night passed amicably with the desire to avoid the subject further and a fair amount of wine keeping things friendly. The latter almost certainly being responsible for an earlier return to sexual relations than Moira had planned.

Arthur would have been happy that perhaps he was putting his life back together again quicker than expected but the worry was the stronger of the emotions. He tried to not say too much, she was too sharp for that but he had got enough. It wasn't looking good and despite an empty scrotum and the bucket of red wine slowly becoming blood and piss in his body, he slept fitfully.

In the morning the wine again had its effect on the conversation. Pounding heads made mouse eyes in the bright light of the sun emerging over the hill. Grunts and groans, coffees and scones. It suited Arthur. There was only one conversation he needed to have that morning.

*

"Deek, its Arthur."

"Hello there."

"Look, I think we might have a problem."

"A problem."

"Look, there might not be much time, meet me there."

"Where?"

"You know where."

"Has he gone back again? What's up?"

"Don't know yet, but I have a very bad feeling."

"Should I bring her?"

"God, I dunno, I dunno…"

"Well, should I?"

"Yeah, you better had. I'm going straight there, I'll see you there."

"OK."

Arthur waited until he knew he was out of sight of the house and, flooring the accelerator, kicked down the automatic gearbox. With the blood still pounding in his head, sped off into the unknown morning.

*

It was difficult for Charlie to avoid Kelly's questions. It was a long drive at that time of the morning. Out of the city and towards the red circle on the map that seemed to be in the middle of nowhere.

"Where are we going?"

Charlie handed Kelly the printer-friendly print out from the web site.

"Here."

"Where's that?"

"No idea. Seems to be in the middle of a forest."

"Eh?"

"I know, I know, why are we going there? That's where Danny said he was going."

"Danny? What's he got to do with this?"

"I don't know."

"Charlie, you're not making much sense."

"None of this makes sense. Danny sent me an email; he said he was going to the place marked on the map. That's all I know."

"I don't get it, why are we wasting time chasing Danny into the countryside when my brothers are missing."

"Look, I told you to stay didn't I? You're the one that wanted to come."

It wasn't a tone Kelly had heard from Charlie before. She sulked back into her chair, arms folded.

"If you don't want to come I can drop you off here."

"Has this got anything to do with my brothers?"

"I dunno, it might."

"It might?"

"Yes, it might. Don't ask me anything else because I don't know. We'll go. It could be nothing. If it's nothing, we'll come straight back and look elsewhere, OK?"

"OK."

"…and you're going to stop it with the body language?"

On another day, in different circumstances driving out into the country with Kelly would have been ideal for Charlie. The sun was trying it best to shine and with the traffic thinning and eventually left behind it was a scene he had often dreamt about. Unfortunately the mood in the car was not as dreamt. Kelly wasn't looking lovingly into his eyes, the stereo wasn't playing Sparky's Dream by Teenage Fanclub and there was no picnic in the boot to eat in a field when they arrived. This was no picnic. It was, at best, a wild goose chase. Charlie didn't want to think about the worst.

It took a couple of wrong turns and the associated 3-point versions before Charlie finally turned down the rutted road through the forest. The map was next to useless at this point, the Ordnance Survey clearly getting bored this far up the arse end of nowhere.

"Where now?"

"Deer with no eyes."

"What?"

"No idea."

They passed the crossing in the road.

"Look!"

It was Danny's car, sitting just off the track a couple of hundred yards away. Charlie reversed back a bit and turned towards the car. He pulled in behind, shut down the engine and cranked on the handbrake.

"Wait here."

"Like hell."

Charlie tried his best to make it look like he wasn't creeping up behind the car. It seemed fairly clear no one was in it but you never knew what could hide low in the seats.

"He's not here."

"Well, where is he? This is the bloody middle of nowhere!"

There was no one in the car. A blanket lay thrown over the passenger seat. Charlie tried the driver's door. It was open. He climbed in to have a look around. The air was sweaty and farty. Danny had spent the night here. He pulled back the blanket. There was a map, much like his, and a cardboard folder, full of assorted papers. Charlie started to read. It was a set of photocopies of a whole range of documents, mainly legal and one medical report. He read the medical report first. A few paragraphs in, he stopped in shock. He looked up. Kelly was nowhere to be seen.

Twenty Seven

As the plane engines lost power, the tip of the left wing clipped a tree and threw it into a cartwheel. The nose pitched into the ground killing the helpless pilots instantly. The remainder of the front-end of the fuselage followed it in, the heavily fuel laden wings bursting into flame and engulfing the entire area in a massive fireball. The enormous force of the cartwheel broke the back of the plane and the tail section flew on and out above the rapidly building flames. Leaving the inferno behind in came down in a clearing, sprinkling seats, luggage and people like salt from a cellar. Some of the debris crashed down on a small farm outbuilding, smashing a hole in the rusting iron roof.

*

The three of them never really spoke about it and perhaps never realised it but everything between them changed after that day up the tree. Somehow the balance had been upset. The ever confident Lugs had been shown to be inferior to John, at least when it came to bravery and resourcefulness. This made Lugs remove himself a bit from their group so he could concentrate on being superior to those that weren't as aware of his failings. He still hung about with John and Deeko from time to time but as they got older and they started thinking about exams and qualifications, Lugs went his own way.

Deeko dreamt of music, of being in a band. He wanted to be famous, a great guitarist and could be regularly heard beating the hell out of a battered old acoustic. The strings were old and dull as were his tunes and ideas. But he kept going, kept up the dream.

John didn't have a dream. He had a calling. And it was as simple as it was achievable. He did what he needed to at school, learned enough, stayed fit and walked straight into the police as soon as he was able. It was pretty much all he had ever wanted to do. He played along with everyone saying that he'd be a

171

fireman after the day at the tree. There was no point in telling them otherwise. It wasn't up to them what he would do.

When the time came, Deeko's dreams weren't coming true and, rather than make a reasoned choice of his own, he followed John into the police. He was bright enough but had to work hard at dropping enough weight and getting fit enough. This he did with considerable effort. But it was still less effort than trying to think about what he actually wanted to do. He never did give up his dream. The police was just something to do until he could get he music together. Before he knew it, he was married, he had a kid and a career and a life had formed around him, almost without him noticing. One that was now almost impossible to shake off.

Lugs, like John, was just as single minded. For him it was also to be the law. Although it was to be prosecuting not enforcing that was to be his calling. He was so high in his class at school, that they got special lessons from the University for him in advance of him ever seeing the gates, never mind entering them. When he did see the gates, he walked in tall and proud and straight to the top of that class too. The years passed as quickly and as well as he did. Until, at the end of the course, a sheet of paper went up on the notice board with his name at the top. 1st Class Honours. Arthur McMillan. Known to his school friends as Lugs.

John was a model officer. A real star, a real believer in the principles and the laws he was upholding. He took a fair amount of ribbing from the more seasoned operators that just saw him as raw. He would come round eventually and join in the institutional cynicism.

Occasionally they would bump into each other. John was at a different station from Deeko but they sometimes worked together when a big operation was put together, usually football related. Sometimes they would go for a pint but probably more out of feeling that they should than wanting to. John believed in the police, believed in doing police work. It just paid Deeko's bills. In the end, Deeko's longevity got him somewhere. He bumbled along, annoyed no one, impressed even less but, after so many years and with many others leaving the force, he was eventually made Sergeant. But it was only fake pride that made him smile the day he became Sergeant Derek Murdoch. He would still rather have been Captain Sensible.

John married very young. He always knew he would marry Mary. The girl he adored from an early age and whom he told he would marry before either of them had left school. They had a family planned and underway soon after. As sure as A follows B, John set about his life in the order and manner he had decided. The only thing he couldn't decide was the sex of his children. It was with huge delight that he received the news of his first daughter, something he had be longing for after the first two sons. After that, he was less concerned about the sex of his next child when the pregnancy was announced. It was even less of a concern they day he found out it was to be twins. The day he set out into the forest to investigate a call about a loud noise and maybe a fire.

*

172

He drove the panda as far as he could before the road was blocked by the intense red flame being blown across the break in the trees by an ever-strengthening wind. The trees on the other side were already well ablaze. To his right, there was only trees engulfed by fire, their blackened trunks standing out against the intense red and orange. The air crackled and roared around him. Ash and debris blew out from the trees and he had to shield his eyes. The wall of heat was now very strong. There was no point going any further. Nothing and nobody was alive. It was a job for the fire brigade and then the investigators. With the fire spreading quickly, all he could do was to find anything that could lie in its path and get them out of the way. Moving back up the road, he found a crossroads that had a rougher track that took him in the direction the fire was travelling. The rutted road showed signs of the deep tracks made by tractors. If there was a farm nearby he hoped they had heard the noise and got out of the way already.

The dirt track was very rough and he could only manage a jog at best. He tracked the fire as it moved through the trees parallel to him. Its path has slowed and he was now ahead of it and, with no sign of a farm or any other life, he slowed to a walk. The road curved slowly round to the right. He walked down the left hand side, giving him the maximum view into the distance. At the apex of the long curve, he could see the end of a squat white building in a clearing immediately in the path of the flames.

Picking up the pace again, he headed for the building. Beyond the edge of the trees he could see into the clearing, a small dirt courtyard in front of the building. The ground was littered with debris. He could make out the shapes luggage and seats and, as he got nearer, bodies. None of them were moving. He ran over. Those that were in one piece were all dead. He tried to avoid the decapitated body parts that lay strewn all around.

With the centre of the fire almost half a mile away, it wasn't clear where all this had come from. A rusting old tractor sat next to the door. Climbing up onto it seat, he looked around the area. There was no obvious scar in the trees from the direction of the main fire. It was like they had just fallen from the sky. He jumped down and ran round the back of the building. Standing leaning against the tree line of the forest beyond, the monolithic tail section of the plane stood dwarfing the conifers below. Its jagged metal edge had dug deep into the earth and it stood, like an eerie statue, a totem to modern transport, its windows now empty. There were no bodies and no sign of life on this side of the building.

Back on the other side, the door of the building was heavy and stiff. His first attempt failed. Looking about he found a rake and, with a heavy downpour starting, forced open the door. Happy that the rain would stop the fire approaching any nearer, he could wait in the building until the rain eased off.

Inside it was surprisingly light. Something had landed on the roof and a large hole now let in the light that would otherwise have been absent. In the circle of light created by the hole, he could see more debris from the plane. What looked like a seat and maybe some luggage. The rain clattered off the roughly arranged plastic and fabric. He approached it cautiously, steeled by the horrific sights he had already witnessed.

Part of a seat lay face down to the floor. He thought he could see some hair sticking out from beneath it. The seat lifted easily. A child. Lying under clothes and some smaller bags. Pulling this away, he saw it was not a child. It was only a head. He struggled for breath and covered his mouth in shock and to suppress the gagging. As the final bag was moved aside. He found another head. The movement caused it to roll until it bumped against the first head. Its final roll revealed the face. A face identical to the first. Tiny little heads from tiny little bodies ripped off by the sharp metal of the roof.

He reeled back. His chest bursting, unable to breathe. The rain continued to clatter down through the hole and on to the upturned faces of the twins. A section of the weakened roof above twisted under the relentless pressure of the rain until finally it detached.

The edge caught him on the back of the head as it fell. He collapsed to the ground shielding the four eyes staring up from the floor from the sky from which they had come.

Twenty Eight

The sun had long since dropped below the remaining roof. The eerie atrium of the gaping hole now only provided meagre illumination. As the sun dropped further still, occasional shafts of light aligned with the gaps in the hinges of the door and beamed across the room, the dust in the air dancing in the glare of the newly formed limelight. There was very little noise, only the background provided by the leaves in the trees and the birds on the breeze. They flew by occasionally, flapping and calling out. As the darkness set in, they started to talk to each other more regularly, sharing the stories of their day. Then the sun was gone below the horizon, clouds rolled in and darkness came. With the clouds came an ever-strengthening wind. The loosely hanging door caught the wind life a windsurf sail. Swinging about its loose mast, it's clanging caused an irregular beat than made an uneasy rhythm for the night.

The wind blew stronger and the door banged faster and more insistently. Then the rain came, faster and more rhythmic rattling off the metal roof. The door banged, the roof rattled and the night time cacophony was completed by the background hiss of the rain on the leaves all around.

Later that morning the rain poured in again through the hole in the roof. In the dark corner of the room, Danny lay, still knocked out from the blow to the back of his head. Neatly placed in the recovery position, he faced the door, a thin line of dried blood across his face. Puddles formed again and then ran off in small rivulets to all corners of the room. One ran to Danny, the cold water immediately bringing life to his face. His eyes opened to a blur. Open or closed, his eyes saw the same thing. Then the pain. The back of his head throbbed. He tried to bring his hands up but they were both tight behind his back, his shoulders locked from the prolonged time on the floor. Everything hurt and he couldn't move. His breath quickened in panic. He didn't even know where he was. As his eyeballs bulged out searching for focus, the vague reflected gloom

175

started to reveal shapes. The brightest of which Danny began to recognise as the door through which he had entered. The door was all he knew about this place. That, and the fact that he was here. He must have hit him; he must have tied him up. Is he still here? Danny closed his eyes again to listen for another presence but could only hear the syncopated sound of the weather. And then it stopped and the sudden silence revealed the birds again, happy that the rain had stopped and the clouds had started to move away.

The early morning sun crept higher in the sky, its light creeping across the floor as it entered through the hole in the roof. Danny could watch the hours pass as it transited without ever moving from the opposite corner of the room towards the centre. At about, what Danny estimated to be, 9am, he started to see shapes in the middle of the room. It looked like other people, like him, held captive on the floor. He shouted out to them but got no answer.

"Gary. Gary Moyes? Is that you?"

Nothing.

He could now see enough to know that he wasn't there. And still the light moved across the room. Slowly it began to reveal more. There were people there. He could see heads. Maybe bodies. They must be unconscious like he was. Nothing seemed to be moving. More light. More detail. Two bodies, curled up with their back to him. Maybe another two, their heads facing him from the centre of the room. A cloud moved away and the brightness was turned up on the whole scene. There were faces pointed at him from the centre of the room and...Danny gulped at what he saw and couldn't believe. Words, writing, apparently on the faces.

The pain dug deeper into Danny's head as he struggled to turn away from the scene that faced him. Now, as clear as the new day that shone down through the roof, two lifeless faces stared at Danny across the floor. On the forehead of each was a single word. Dumb.

The horrors and the realisations all hit Danny at once. His body convulsed and threw up. Acrid bile was all that remained and he wretched violently as he struggled to spit it from his mouth. He turned his face to the ground as he continued to convulse violently, his body thrusting against the restrictions of his bindings. His mind shifted quickly between two sets of images. The one in front of him now and the one he had already pictured from the details he had read.

Then a noise, footsteps. Before he knew much more Danny was standing on uneasy legs.

The first punch broke Danny's barely repaired nose. It snapped easily at the bridge leaving his face Picasso red. The blood poured from what looked like a wide-open hole in his face. The punches continued to rain down. The floor and walls were turning red. Cheekbone cracked, jaw broken. The pleading words turned to groans, the groans to grunt. And then nothing but the incessant thump of fist into an ever-softening face.

Then it stopped. No more blows. But the pain didn't decrease. Danny couldn't see much through swollen eyes. A dark shape moved into front of him and then away. Footsteps moved around behind him. A foot pressed him in the back and, with hands tied behind the back; he crashed his already mangled face into the rough concrete floor. He lay, unable to move, blood and teeth flowing from his mouth.

"What are you doing here?"

It was a voice he recognised but it sounded different. Maybe it was his shattered face; maybe it was the strange echo of the broken building. He couldn't see to be sure who it was but he couldn't answer.

"What are you doing here?"

It sounded like him. But...

"Who sent you here? Why are you here?"

But if it was him, surely...

A hand grabbed his hair and pulled his face up from the ground.

"Answer me or it gets worse."

It was him. Danny tried to answer.

"No one sent me here."

The words were as mangled as his face.

"What?"

"Nothing!"

His hair was pulled back further and Danny let out a scream.

"Aaaargh! I don't know anything, fuckin' nothing, fuck..."

"What are you saying boy?"

"Fuck off."

He let the hair go and Danny's head crashed back down with a sickening thump. Then the back of his hair was grabbed and he was hauled up and sat against a wall. Upright again, he had to spit the blood out of his mouth to breathe, his nose no longer an airway. Blinking, he could finally start to see a little, although it was still blurred.

"You did it didn't you?"

The tone seemed different.

"No."

"Admit it."

"Admit what?"

Danny struggled to speak or to think. And then the pendulum returned. This is what it must have been like. This is what he did to his Dad. Hit him, bloodied him. Destroyed him. A sudden and unexpected grief. Maybe for the first time, an admission.

"Just admit it and we can get this over with."

Danny knew he had done it. One last kick in the ribs and he had to confess.

"I did it."

"What? Louder!"

"I DID IT, OK? I killed him; I killed the drunken old bastard. Happy now? Are you fucking happy now?"

He walked away and Danny breathed deeply, unable to think but desperate to stay alive. Tears ran down Danny's face burning the wounds on his face.

With the admission of perhaps inflicting a more rapid end to the life of his father came the more immediate yet still clouded signs of guilt for the scene before him. In one way he had been right. There was a victim and the assailant was as he expected. Only the victim was wrong. This wasn't the lifeless face of Gary Moyes facing him across the floor. It was clear from what he had read that this was always a disaster waiting to happen. The hunter always lurked in the woods. But he had been the beater. He had invited the prey to run before the gun. And with that came the new guilt. The one that arrived only because he had denied the previous one. Yet perhaps it was still an odd justice. If this was to have happened, then why not to them. Nothings. Nobodies with no bodies. Justice? No. But perhaps the guns would now fall silent and everyone else would be safer. Or would they? The moments of guilt were now replaced with terror. Surely he would be next. He'd crossed too near to the line of fire. All that remained was one final plea for mercy. If not justice for all, at least for him. The selfishness of survival.

"Please don't kill me…please…"

He was gone for now. No one responded. Was he gone? Running from his crime. Or was he waiting, reloading for the next sweep across the moor. Whatever happened, Danny had to stay awake. He fought back the sleep that would lead to the inevitable unconsciousness. To keep his mind active he started to sing.

"Please don't spoil my day, I'm miles away and after all…"

"I'm only sleeping."

The reply came from the corner opposite Danny. A softer quieter voice than before. Footsteps approached. Danny braced himself for the inevitable attack. It didn't come. The rope binding his arms was cut and he was dragged to his feet. His legs struggled to support his weight.

"Hands up."

"What?"

"Hands above your head."

Danny couldn't comply. Nothing worked, everything hurt. His arms were grabbed and tied above his head and the rope was slung over a metal hook that projected from the wall.

*

Memo from Prof. Moira Johnson
Patient: John Finch

John Finch has suffered a severe psychological trauma resulting from his involvement in the air crash investigation. Exact details as to the cause of this are difficult to ascertain from Mr. Finch himself but those who worked with him on the search of the crash site seem fairly certain. It would appear that the details of the search work and, in particular, the discovery of the bodies in relation to his current family situation seem to have created a seemingly irreversible schism in his mind that has separated his own persona from his waking self.

Observations during sleep have recorded speech that seems to suggest that vestiges of his former self remain. These appear to be quite fragmented however and are not at all apparent during many hours of conversation I have had with Mr. Finch during treatment and counselling.

The trauma resulted from a confluence of various factors. The precise significance of each is difficult to determine. Clearly, the emotional trauma of the crash scene cannot be underestimated and the precedent for such occurrences is part of record. It has been noted that the decapitation resulting from the crash, although not untypical, was severe in this case. Particularly in the case of the young children that Mr. Finch discovered in the farm outhouse. This particular trauma must have had specific significance to Mr Finch as these were two twin boys. This incident was only weeks he had learnt of the imminent arrival of his own twins and this in itself must be considered a major traumatic factor.

It has been estimated that this trauma must have occurred only minutes or perhaps seconds from the physical trauma caused by the collapsing roof. This was clearly a major neurological event that resulted in a coma lasting over nearly a year. Although no obvious lasting brain injury was evident it could not be ruled out.

The initial trauma coincided with a lesser trauma in the life of Mr. Finch. At the time of the crash, the pop group, The Beatles, to whom Mr. Finch was extremely devoted, had just split up. This coming at the time of the trauma relating to the crash has left Mr. Finch attempting to repair the schism in his mind by healing the wound in relation to the demise of The Beatles. This has shrouded any of the pain relating to the crash and is clearly shielding and protecting him from this. As a result of, his obsession with the Beatles has increased to an extraordinary level.

All communication, verbal or written, is carried out only in the words of Beatles' songs. This is done with inexplicable speed and accuracy. A recorded 30-minute conversation has been analysed by music scholars and has been proved to be entirely accurate in relation to the works of Lennon and McCartney.

At this time, I can see Mr. Finch presenting no danger to either society or himself and can see no reason why, with suitable supervision he cannot be released immediately into the care of his family assuming suitable arrangements can be made.

However, due to the extremely unusual nature of this case, I would recommend that Mr. Finch is continually assessed on a weekly basis, to ensure that he continues to present no danger and that all attempts can be made to restore his former personality.

*

Even as she typed it Moira wasn't sure. Sure, Arthur and Derek would watch him but she needed to be more certain. But, as ever, she had let Arthur persuade her. He shouldn't have been able to, just as he shouldn't have been able to stop her taking the case in the first place. She should have stepped aside.

She knew this man. This is why there were rules. This is why emotional attachment could lead to mistakes. All she could do was hope that it didn't go wrong.

Charlie put down the medical report and, leaving the car, set off to find Kelly. Unable to make sense of what he had read he headed off to the crossroads and, with increasing panic, turned right. He walked for a few hundred yards and started to get a bad feeling but still couldn't put together a coherent thought about why.

"Kelly. Kelly!"

His shouts got louder and more insistent. Running now, he arrived at a clearing. A rough patch of gravel marked where cars sometimes parked. Wooden posts marked the beginnings of pathways into the forest. All the grass looked intact. It was wet enough to reveal anything that had past through it. Kelly hadn't come his way. He ran back to the crossroads with increasing speed and concern. At the crossroads, he saw a police car and his concern turned to terror. Danny, the medical reports, the missing boys and now this; a police car in the middle of nowhere. Behind it was a large Audi. A portly man in a suit got out looking worried. Charlie watched as Arthur shook the hand of the sergeant and then they began to talk.

"Derek."

"Arthur."

"Well, is he here?"

"I don't know. I've not been round yet."

"Lets go."

"Arthur. What's going on here? Do you think…"

"Derek. I don't know, I really don't."

"What does Moira think?"

"Lets go."

"Arthur, do you think he could…"

"Lets just go for fucks sake…"

"Go where?"

Charlie had walked over to interrupt the conversation.

"What are you doing here?"

Derek look bemused.

"You know him Arthur?"

"Yes, I…Charlie, how?"

"I got a message from Danny."

"Danny? So that's his car there."

"Yes. And in it you'll find medical reports written by your wife about a certain John Finch? Is that who you are here to find?"

"Look Charlie, you just had back to town, there's nothing for you here, we'll deal with it now."

"No, no. I'm not leaving here without Kelly."

"Kelly? You didn't bring her here did you?"

180

"I couldn't stop her. Although I doubt she expected to meet her Dad today. Then again, if I'm not mistaken she probably already has, she just didn't know."

"Come on Arthur, for fucks sake, enough of this lawyer bullshit, lets go."

Derek headed off to the left towards the outhouse. Arthur struggled to run behind him like he had some many times when they were young.

In the corner of the room John Finch sat rocking on his haunches. Quietly at first and then getting louder, Danny began to hear him singing.

"And in the end...the love you take..."

He repeated the same line over and over until he broke down. Danny was beginning to get his pain under control and, with some strength returning to his legs; he tried to rock the metal that he hung on out of the crumbling wall. He was hoping to use the fact that his captor was in tears to try and get loose. Then his diversion was gone. The metal door swung upon and Finch stood up sharply.

At the door, hair fringed by golden sunlight, stood Kelly. She peered into the gloom. Before she could scream at the sight of Danny battered and hanging from the wall and her decapitated brothers on the floor, he had her hands round her mouth and a knife under her chin.

"Who are you why are you here?"

"Leave her alone."

Danny screamed with all he had.

"Why are you here?"

The knife dug into her throat.

"Leave her, for fucks sake, she's your daughter."

This only registered with Kelly but the confusion was not enough to overcome her terror. He threw her down and her head hit sharply on the wall knocking her out. Finch marched firmly over to Danny.

"What did you say?"

"I said that she was your daughter."

He slapped Danny across the face.

"Liar."

"You're John Finch aren't you? She's Kelly Finch. Your daughter."

"Liar!"

"And see those boys you killed?"

"They were your sons."

He stuck the knife deep into Danny's side. Blood started to pour steadily from the wound. Finch walked off towards Kelly. Before he got there, the door swung open again.

"Oh Jesus. No..."

Arthur entered first. Followed by Derek and Charlie. Finch turned to face them. From the corner Danny tried to explain.

"He's Finch, he's fucking Finch."

"Shut up Danny, we know."

Derek needed him to be quiet; he had to be able to talk to him.

181

"John, give me the knife."

Finch turned towards Kelly and picked her up.

"John, let her go and give me the knife."

Before he could get the knife back to her throat, Charlie ran at him, powered by something he didn't understand. With one swipe, Finch cut across Charlie's chest and he fell to the ground. He backed into the corner with Kelly.

"John, its me Arthur, come on mate, let the girl go and lets get out of here eh?"

From outside the door, some music started to filter through the scene of destruction and death.

"Nothing you can say, but you can learn how to play the game…"

Ma Finch came through the door holding a ghetto blaster. She had been told to stay in the car but, fearing the worst, had come to the building. Realising the scene that would face her, Arthur tried to shepherd her out.

"Mary, Mary, its OK, we'll get him."

She ignored him and started to sing herself.

"All you need is love, all you need is love, all you need is love, love. Love is all you need."

Finch dropped the knife and joined in the singing. Kelly fell to the ground and was swept up and away by Arthur. He walked towards the music. Derek stood aside and he walked forward and linked arms with his wife. She led him quietly out the door, the two of them singing. Derek followed staying a bit behind until he could safely grab and cuff him. He never noticed, he just kept singing all the way back to the panda car.

Back in the building, Arthur got Kelly settled safely outside and then did what he could for Charlie and Danny's wounds. Charlie's was superficial but he'd have to keep a lot of pressure on Danny's until an ambulance arrived.

"Jesus Christ Arthur, what a fucking mess."

Arthur wouldn't speak. He sat silently staring at the dead eyes that looked out from the middle of the room. Ambulances and more police appeared outside. Charlie was able to pick himself up and walk into an ambulance, making sure they took care with Kelly. Danny was put on a stretcher and carried outside. During everything and despite repeated questioning Arthur didn't speak.

The sun appeared from behind a cloud and thin lines of bright light shone through the vertical lines of the trees. Danny looked up into the new light and, perhaps for the first time he could remember, at least that didn't hurt too much. He had seen in Arthur's eyes the depth and totality of true guilt. Inside the ambulance, he asked the paramedic to wait. Arthur and Derek stood silently watching him being loaded.

"I'm sorry I gave you guys all this trouble."

They didn't understand.